Praise for

THE UNMAPPED CHRONICLES:

CASPER TOCK AND THE EVERDARK WINGS

"This whimsical, humorous, richly built world sets the stage for more courageous adventures. A delightful series opener." —*Kirkus Reviews*

"Perfect for fans of Narnia in search of more portals into new worlds." —*Booklist*

"Extremely satisfying." —*SLJ*

"A humorous adventure that resonates on multiple levels." —*Publishers Weekly*

"There is a rich tale to discover here. . . . This complex tale is anchored by familiar emotions while undertaking a thematic exploration of friendship and family ties." —*School Library Connection*

Also by
Abi Elphinstone

The Unmapped Chronicles Book Two:
The Bickery Twins and the Phoenix Tear

Sky Song

THE UNMAPPED CHRONICLES

– BOOK ONE –

Casper Tock and the Everdark Wings

ABI ELPHINSTONE

Aladdin
New York London Toronto Sydney New Delhi

ALADDIN
An imprint of Simon & Schuster Children's Publishing Division
1230 Avenue of the Americas, New York, New York 10020
First Aladdin paperback edition January 2021

Originally published in Great Britain in 2019 by Simon & Schuster UK as *Rumblestar*

Also available in an Aladdin hardcover edition.

Cover designed by Heather Palisi
Interior designed by Mike Rosamilia
The text of this book was set in Truesdell.
Manufactured in the United States of America 1120 OFF
2 4 6 8 10 9 7 5 3 1
The Library of Congress has cataloged the hardcover edition as follows:
Names: Elphinstone, Abi, author.
Title: Casper Tock and the Everdark wings / by Abi Elphinstone.
Description: First Aladdin hardcover edition. | New York : Aladdin, 2020. |
Series: The Unmapped chronicles | Summary: When Casper is transported to the strange world of Rumblestar, he must work with his first real friend, Utterly Thankless, to stop the monstrous creatures terrorizing the land.
Identifiers: LCCN 2019014488 (print) | LCCN 2019018186 (eBook) |
ISBN 9781534443099 (eBook) | ISBN 9781534443075 (hardcover)
Subjects: | CYAC: Fantasy. | Adventure and adventurers—Fiction. |
Magic—Fiction. | Dragons—Fiction. | Friendship—Fiction.
Classification: LCC PZ7.1.E465 (eBook) | LCC PZ7.1.E465 Cas 2020 (print) |
DDC [Fic]—dc23
LC record available at https://lccn.loc.gov/2019014488
ISBN 9781534443082 (pbk)

For Bertie, my godson

* * *

May your life be filled

with all sorts of wonderful adventures

(and may you remember to ask Godmother Abi to

come on a few of them from time to time)

Prologue

The trouble with grown-ups is that they always think they're right—about bedtimes and vegetables mostly, but also about beginnings. And, in particular, about the beginnings of our world. They have all sorts of ideas about big bangs and black holes, but if they had come across the Unmapped Kingdoms (which they wouldn't have because secret kingdoms are notoriously hard to find), they would have learned that at the very, very beginning there was just an egg. A rather large one. And out of this egg, a phoenix was born.

On finding itself alone, it wept seven tears, which, as they fell, became our continents and formed the Earth as you and I know it, although to the phoenix all this was simply known as the Faraway. But these lands were dark and empty, so, many years later, the phoenix scattered four of its golden feathers, and out of these grew secret—unmapped—kingdoms, invisible to the people who would go on to live in the Faraway but holding the magic needed to conjure sunlight, rain, and snow, and every untold wonder behind the weather, from the music of a sunrise to the stories of a snowstorm.

Now, the phoenix, being the wisest of all magical creatures, knew that magic grows strange and dark if used selfishly, but if it is used for the greater good, it can nourish an entire world and keep it turning. So the phoenix decreed that those who lived in the Unmapped Kingdoms could enjoy all the wonders that its magic brought, but only if they, in turn, worked to send some of this magic out into the Faraway so that the continents there might be filled with light and life. If the Unmappers ever stopped sharing their magic, the phoenix warned, both the Faraway and the Unmapped Kingdoms would crumble to nothing.

The phoenix placed the Lofty Husks—wizards born under the same eclipse and marked out from the other Unmappers on account of their wisdom, unusually long life expectancy and terrible jokes—in charge of each Unmapped Kingdom and, although the Lofty Husks in each kingdom took a different form, they ruled fairly, ensuring that every day the magic of the phoenix was passed on to the Faraway.

The four kingdoms all played different roles. Unmappers in Rumblestar collected marvels—droplets of sunlight, rain, and snow in their purest form—which dragons transported to the other kingdoms so the inhabitants there could mix them with magical ink to create weather scrolls for the Faraway: sun symphonies in Crackledawn, rain paintings in Jungledrop, and snow stories in Silvercrag. Little by little, the Faraway lands came alive: plants, flowers, and trees sprang up, and so strong was the magic that eventually animals appeared and, finally, people.

Years passed and the phoenix looked on from Everdark, a place so far away and out of reach that not even the Unmappers knew where it lay. But a phoenix cannot live forever. And so, after five hundred years, the first phoenix died and, as is the way with such birds, a new phoenix rose from its ashes to renew the magic in the Unmapped Kingdoms and ensure it was shared with those in the Faraway.

Time went by and the Unmappers grew to understand that every five hundred years another era would begin and, as long as the new phoenix showed itself to them on the night of its rising, the magic would be renewed and all would be well. Everyone believed things would continue this way forever. . . .

When you're dealing with magic, though, *forever* is rarely straightforward. There is always someone, somewhere, who becomes greedy. And when a heart is set on stealing magic for personal gain, suddenly ancient decrees and warnings slip quite out of mind. Such was the case with a harpy called Morg who grew jealous of the phoenix and its power.

Seeking to claim the magic of the Unmapped Kingdoms for herself, Morg breathed a curse over the nest of the last phoenix on the very night of the renewal of magic two thousand years ago. The old phoenix burst into flames, like the rest of its kind had done before it, but this time the flames burned black and no new phoenix appeared from the ashes. And so, Morg claimed the nest as her own.

But when things go wrong and magic goes awry, it makes room for stories with unexpected heroes and unlikely heroines. Which is exactly what happened next . . . That same night, Smudge, a young girl from the kingdom of Crackledawn, was somewhere she ought not to have been, and she saw Morg tear across the sky in the place of the phoenix. With the fate of the Unmapped Kingdoms and the Faraway in her hands,

Smudge, together with a monkey called Bartholomew, journeyed to Everdark, a place no Unmapper had been before. And it was there that Smudge tracked down Morg and locked the harpy's wings, the very things that held her power, inside an enchanted tree deep in the forest.

The Unmapped Kingdoms and the Faraway were saved, but without the magic of the phoenix, the Lofty Husks in each kingdom had to set about searching for a way to preserve what was left of the old magic until the harpy died, or was killed, and a new phoenix rose from Everdark. The answer, as it happened, lay with the dragons that roamed the skies and the seas. They could sense the threat to the Unmapped Kingdoms and the Faraway, so they promised to scatter their sacred moondust every night, and though it didn't grant as much magic as before, it was enough to keep things turning.

And that could well have been that until Morg died and a new phoenix rose. Except it wasn't. Because when a harpy is set on evil, she doesn't just slope away and give up. She plots and she plots and she plots until before you know it, she has hatched a new plan to steal the magic of the Unmapped Kingdoms. . . .

But I am getting ahead of myself, and a certain eleven-year-old boy from the Faraway wouldn't approve at all. At least, Casper Tock wouldn't have approved *before* the Extremely Unpredictable Event happened, because up until then he very much lived his life according to his to-do lists and timetables. Admittedly, the lists often only included one item—*grow up quickly*—but his timetables were much more detailed, from the five minutes he allowed himself before breakfast each morning to straighten the pictures on his bedroom walls to the half hour he spent before going to sleep every night refolding all of his clothes.

Casper liked to keep a tidy bedroom, an organized mind, and a tight schedule. That way, fewer things went wrong and there was less chance—or so he thought—of wandering into the clutches of school bullies Candida Cashmere-Jumps and Leopold Splattercash.

But no matter how many lists you write and no matter how many timetables you create, you cannot be responsible for your parents. They forget keys, lose handbags, misplace spectacles, and drop phones down the toilet. In fact, once you reach the grand old age of eleven, you can start to realize that your parents are hopelessly out of control.

Such was the case with Casper's parents, Ernie and Ariella Tock. They had been out of hand for quite some time and they were, in fact, largely to blame for everything that happened to Casper that dreary afternoon in March. Because if Ernie had come home on time that day and if Ariella had remembered her handbag, then perhaps the Extremely Unpredictable Event might never have happened at all.

But sometimes it is when people are late and handbags are forgotten that magic begins to unfold. . . .

Chapter 1

Casper crouched inside the lost and found basket in the corridor outside his classroom. The school timetable stated, very firmly, that he should be in Mr. Barge's geography lesson, but his own timetable, which was at this second folded neatly into his palm, stated that he should be exactly where he was—surrounded by dirty blazers and smelly sports uniforms.

Casper shifted his weight. Thirty minutes was a long time to be wedged inside a wicker basket, but it had become an important part of his Thursday afternoons. Because only by telling Mr. Barge that he had a piano lesson or a dentist appointment or an errand to run for the headmaster, and hiding in the lost and found instead, could Casper overhear the lesson *and* the homework instructions (thereby not falling behind in his studies or causing Mr. Barge to question his absences) while avoiding crossing paths with Candida and Leopold.

By and large, Little Wallops Boarding School was a friendly place—and with its wood-paneled dining room, enormous fireplaces, and stone gargoyles it was rather beautiful, too—but in every school there are rotten eggs, the sort of children who write complaint letters to Father Christmas and ask their parents for a pocket-money raise. Candida and Leopold were two such children, and while Casper had previously managed to avoid both of them because they were in different classes, this term Candida and Leopold's geography teacher had been out sick, so Casper's personal timetable had needed some considerable adjustments.

Casper risked a peep over the top of the basket. Mr. Barge always left his classroom door open (apparently it made hurling pupils out of lessons far more straightforward), and though from where he crouched Casper couldn't see Candida or Leopold, or any of his classmates for that matter, he had a clear view of his teacher, who was, at this moment, flinging exercise books toward his pupils.

"Down the center, Ben—quick, catch! On the wing, Ruby—look sharp!"

Mr. Barge, a middle-aged man the size and shape of a drawbridge, doubled up as a geography teacher *and* a rugby coach, and he often got the two confused.

Another exercise book shot, like a rugby ball, across the room, and Mr. Barge's voice boomed through the door and out into the corridor.

"Coming through, Oliver! You'll have to jump for this one!"

A short, sharp thump followed. Casper winced. He guessed Oliver had tried to jump for his book—and missed.

Mr. Barge performed several lunges, which made his suit squeak at the seams, then he threw his class a toothy grin. "Hustle in, Year Six. Hustle in."

There were a few nervous scrapes as the pupils pulled their chairs closer.

"We've all seen the newspaper headlines these past few weeks: What the nation thought was a one-off hurricane in England at the beginning of March has now escalated into a worldwide weather crisis. The hurricanes across Europe are becoming more frequent—the United Kingdom has been ravaged by gale-force winds four times in the last week alone—and"—he paused—"more deadly."

Casper shivered. He'd seen the news that morning. The

hurricane on Monday had been confirmed as the worst yet. Thousands of people had lost their homes where it struck in London and hundreds of casualties had been reported. And all that had happened *despite* the warning sirens recently wired up inside buildings across the country—because the hurricanes came fast, faster often than the time it took the weather service to trigger the sirens when the winds looked like they were picking up.

The hurricanes had been coming every few days for the last month, and they had flattened Little Wallops' cricket pavilion, ripped slates off the school roof, shattered windows, and left several high schoolers with broken limbs when the door to the sports hall had been wrenched off its hinges and launched across the gym. Corridors were lined with buckets catching leaks, and windows had been barred with planks of wood. But Little Wallops was still standing—just—and so far, there had been no fatalities. Everyone knew that could change, though; they were living each day on a knife-edge. An underground bunker was being dug to provide more shelter, but that would take time and even when it was ready, would the sirens give everyone enough warning to reach it?

"And that's not to mention what's happening further afield,"

Mr. Barge went on. "Multiple tornados are rampaging across America, whirlwinds are tearing up Africa, and typhoons are smashing through Asia and Australia. Meteorologists agree that climate change could be a key factor behind the recent weather disruption—we know global warming has hit critical levels in the past year—but that still wouldn't explain the haphazard pattern of these storms. Hurricanes normally come in from the oceans and hit coastal regions, but these ones are striking up left, right, and center, defying any recognizable weather behavior, which is why it's so hard to predict their nature. But our meteorologists are determined to get to the bottom of it all. And, as geographers, I feel that we should do the same, particularly since the school holidays this Easter have been postponed due to continued road and rail closures and we'll all be staying here until the lockdown is over and it's safe enough for your parents to collect you."

Casper could hear a few of the pupils nearest the door sniffing back tears. They knew that leaving Little Wallops before the all clear for resumed travel would be foolish, and that arguing with a man the size and shape of a drawbridge would be pointless, but that didn't stop them from missing their families. Casper felt suddenly relieved that he and his parents had been offered free accommodation in the school, as well as a scholarship place for Casper, because his parents both taught at Little Wallops—at least it meant they were all together now.

Mr. Barge pretended not to notice all the sniffing; he found crying children deeply unsettling. "Your extra homework task is to pick one of the disasters reported this week and produce a case file on it. Think what, where, when, who and—the biggest question—*why*? Climate change will come into it, of course, but are there other reasons for the strange behavior of these storms?" Mr. Barge rolled up his sleeves. "I'll expect your reports on Monday, and I want you to tackle this homework in the same way the mighty Shane Hogarth of the Wallop Wanderers tackled six of his opponents at once in the Rugby Sevens Finals last year." He paused. "Really look your homework in the eye and give it what for."

There was a confused sort of silence.

Casper craned his neck a little farther out of the basket and saw his classmate Sophie raise a timid hand. Sophie was the closest thing Casper had to a friend—they sat together at lunch and sometimes paired up for science projects—but Casper made sure conversations focused strictly on schoolwork. Because friendships, and all the complicated emotions and unpredictable feelings that came with them, had proved to be nothing other than disastrous for Casper in the past.

When he first started at Little Wallops, back in Year One, he had tried to make friends, but even then Candida and Leopold had singled him out as being different. They had teased and taunted Casper and every time he had tried to make a friend they'd somehow ruined things—until, finally, Casper decided that he'd had enough. Making friends was painful and messy and frightening, and despite his parents' best efforts to encourage him to try again, Casper decided it was just not worth the trouble. Life was a good deal simpler, and safer, without the trauma of tackling friendships. And so, little by little, Casper's world had shrunk until the very idea of taking risks, trying new things or even momentarily veering off timetable made him feel quite queasy.

Casper watched now as Sophie plucked up courage to ask her question. "S-sir, I'm holding a cake sale in the gym on Sunday to raise money for those who have lost their homes because of the hurricanes and I still have to make a few more flyers. Please can I have an extension on the homework?"

Mr. Barge flexed his biceps. 'Did the mighty Shane Hogarth ask for an extension when the Roaring Rovers were closing in at halftime?'

Sophie frowned. "Um, probably not, sir?"

"Then you have my answer." At that, Mr. Barge muttered something about a class scrum to finish the day off, but thankfully for his pupils, the bell rang instead. Casper's heart quickened. He had a matter of seconds to scramble out of the lost and found basket, blend into the stream of pupils pouring out of their classrooms and rushing along the corridor, then leg it across the library to the door that led up to the turret he and his parents lived in.

A tide of children advanced toward him and, clutching his timetable to his chest, Casper clambered out of the basket and joined the throng. He was small for his age, and slight, which helped with ducking, weaving, and scuttling by unnoticed. Down the corridor he sped, beneath the newly fitted sirens and past the buckets catching leaks—then, when everyone else peeled off toward their after-school clubs, Casper turned into the library.

If he had been a different sort of child, he might have paused to dilly-dally between the shelves and leaf through the books, but Casper wasn't one for detours. Especially when the librarian, Mrs. Whereabouts, was taking a coffee break in the staffroom, which meant there wouldn't be adult supervision in the library should Candida and Leopold appear. Casper nipped between the first few bookshelves, sidestepping the fallen plasterwork from a recent storm, then burst out into the aisle that ran the length of the library.

After a few strides he noticed the smell: the unmistakable tang of hairspray. Casper's chest thumped. Candida Cashmere-Jumps was in the library. There was a piggish snort from somewhere nearby and Casper's toes curled inside his shoes. Leopold Splattercash was in here too.

But that's impossible, Casper thought. *I followed my timetable exactly; Candida and Leopold couldn't possibly have made it to the library before me—I left the lost and found basket the moment the bell rang!* He gulped. *Unless they skived Mr. Barge's geography lesson too and got a head start on me. . . .*

Casper flung himself into a run, but as he did so, a girl and a boy slid out from a bookcase several meters in front.

Casper stopped in his tracks.

Candida was tall, thin, and terribly vain. She only ever smiled when looking at herself in the mirror and she only ever laughed when other people cried. Leopold, on the other hand, was small, round, and terribly stupid. If asked to recite the two times table, he broke out in a light sweat, and he still couldn't spell his own name. He and Candida had one thing in common though: money.

Candida's father had set up a luxury cashmere clothing range that was sold in every department store in the world, while Leopold's ancestors had done something very suspicious and *very* profitable with an ostrich egg and a diamond in the eighteenth century. But when money is the glue that holds a friendship together, the results are often deeply unpleasant.

Candida twisted her long blond hair around her finger. "You weren't the only one skiving geography, Casper."

"Yeah." Leopold sniggered, before stating something that was now blindingly obvious: "We skived too."

Casper eyed the oak door leading up to his flat at the far end of the library. If he made a dash for it now, he might just make it. But Candida had other ideas.

"Going somewhere?" she sneered, and then she closed five perfectly manicured nails around Casper's arm. "Because I was so looking forward to spending time with you this weekend now the holidays have been delayed."

"H-home," Casper stammered. "Just home."

Candida frowned. "But that turret's not really *home* now, is it, Casper?"

Leopold smirked and his double chin spread out like a greasy balloon.

"You don't belong here," Candida spat, plucking at Casper's secondhand blazer, then turning her lip up at his charity-shop rucksack. "The pupils at Little Wallops are from well-connected families. We're refined. Special. *Rich.*" She paused, and her next sentence dripped out like oil. "We have class."

"Yeah. Class." Leopold only knew about forty-five words, so more often than not he just repeated Candida's.

Casper thought of his mother, adopted into an English family from a Tanzanian orphanage, and his father, brought up on one of the roughest council estates in London. Together they had made their way in the world. Ariella was a PE teacher at Little Wallops and she also ran lunchtime yoga clubs (frequently attended by pupils who had geography with Mr. Barge) and Ernie taught design and technology (he could carve stools, build tables, make lamps, and fix almost anything that came his way).

But none of that mattered to Candida and Leopold. For them, growing up on an estate didn't mean high-rise flats and graffiti walls; it meant peacocks, walled gardens, and butlers called Cuthbert. And though Casper rarely yearned for friends, in situations like this he did. Badly. Because there was a tiny and very private corner of Casper's heart that was bruised and lonely.

"Trouble is, Casper, *you* don't fit in here. You're not the right color *or* class."

Casper felt his muscles stiffen at the unfairness of it all, but as Candida tightened her grip on his arm, he knew he didn't have the guts to stand up to her. Candida and Leopold were unpleasant to most people in Little Wallops, because nasty people just can't help themselves, but they were particularly dreadful to Casper because *everything* about him was different from them—and they didn't like it one bit. Candida narrowed her eyes at Casper's tight black curls and dark skin. "What do we do with misfits, Leopold?"

Leopold looked blank. It was the end of the day and he was running dangerously low on words. "Trash," he said after a while.

Casper glanced at the trash can in the corner of the room. It would hurt being dunked headfirst into it, but perhaps it wouldn't be as bad as when Leopold had sat on him during break, causing Casper to lose the feeling in his legs for a week, or the time Candida had burned his English homework and Casper had been put in detention on his birthday for failing to hand it in. But today, fate was on his side.

"Candida and Leopold!" came an old woman's voice from the doorway.

Casper looked up to see Mrs. Whereabouts walking into the room. She was a strange-looking librarian—she had spiky gray hair, a nose ring, and she *always* wore a turtleneck, even in the height of summer—but stranger than all of that was her accent. It was impossible to place it, and when anyone asked Mrs. Whereabouts where she was from, she simply waved her hand and said: "Here and there." But Casper had noticed that she often turned up at just the right time, and now was no exception.

"I hear from Mr. Barge that neither of you attended his lesson this afternoon," she said as she drew close to the group.

Candida dropped Casper's arm, then slowly, disdainfully, she turned to face Mrs. Whereabouts. The librarian didn't seem to belong to an obvious class, so to be safe Candida treated her the same way she treated most of her teachers—with a casual indifference—but she was careful not to overstep the mark because more time in detention meant there was less time to be horrid to other people.

"I was seeing the nurse." Candida gave a half-hearted cough, and Mrs. Whereabouts raised a silver eyebrow.

"Casper, I hear, was in a piano lesson," Mrs. Whereabouts

continued, and Casper winced at the lie he had fed Mr. Barge. "But you, Leopold?"

Leopold picked up a book from the shelf next to him. "I was"—he paused—"reading."

Mrs. Whereabouts blinked. "Oh, really? About what?"

Leopold looked at the thesaurus he was holding and made a wild guess. "Theesysauruses. They're a type of dinosaur."

Candida rolled her eyes, then Mrs. Whereabouts lifted the book from Leopold's hands and, very calmly, delivered a detention. "Please report to the headmaster's office immediately. Tell him that you have no idea what a thesaurus is but you would very much like to copy out every single word inside one."

Then Leopold did what he always did when words finally failed him: He reached into his pocket. "Couldn't we just settle this with a nice crisp fiver?"

Mrs. Whereabouts was about to reply when there was a bellow from the doorway.

"DID THE MIGHTY SHANE HOGARTH THROW MONEY AT THE ROARING ROVERS WHEN HE WANTED TO SCORE A TRY?" Mr. Barge exploded as he marched toward Leopold.

Casper still hadn't a clue who the mighty Shane Hogarth was

(no matter how many times Mr. Barge mentioned him), but right now he loved him. Because suddenly, unexpectedly, there was a chance to run. And run Casper did. He tore down the length of the library—unaware that Candida was watching him like a hawk—and flung open the turret door. Then he closed it firmly behind him and for a moment or two he just stood there, panting into the quiet. With a sigh of relief, he climbed the cold stone steps to his flat.

The turret Casper's family lived in only had four rooms: a sitting room—with a sagging sofa, a threadbare rug, a broken grandfather clock his dad had promised the headmaster he'd fix, and a television that was far too old and small to be considered cool—a poky kitchen and two tiny bedrooms. There was another turret next door, which belonged to Mrs. Whereabouts and her cat, but Casper had only been over there once to borrow milk when they first moved in.

Casper placed his school bag neatly by the door before taking off his shoes and tucking them, at right angles, beneath the sofa. Then he pressed LISTEN on the answer machine. It was a message from his mum saying that she had forgotten her handbag in the village shop—again—but he mustn't worry because she would be home in half an hour. Casper looked out of the window and bit his lip. It was a drizzly afternoon, and the leaves on the trees left upright after the storms were still, but Casper knew that the sirens could sound unexpectedly on windless afternoons because, many miles away, the weather service had picked up the stirrings of yet another storm.

After the first hurricane hit the country at the beginning of the month, the headmaster had done a headcount in the hall and when he had confirmed that everyone was safe, a ripple of excitement had spread through the school. Pupils had whispered about lessons being canceled and term ending three weeks early while the groundsmen rebuilt the stonework and cleared away the fallen trees. But then the hurricanes had kept coming, roads had closed, train lines had been ripped apart, and the reports of fatalities had started. That was when the headmaster had told every year group that they must remain on school grounds at all times for their own safety. Teachers were allowed to leave if they wished, and it was possible to get to the local village, if you were prepared to clamber over toppled trees and edge past ruined buildings, but otherwise everyone was stuck where they were for the foreseeable future while the weather continued to behave in such an unpredictable manner.

Casper hated that his parents often volunteered to go to the village to stock up on what few supplies had made their way to the shop. What if there was another hurricane when his mum was walking home today? Casper tried not to think about it and instead consulted his timetable, then his watch. His dad was late back too. He had probably lost the keys to lock up his design and technology workshop—again—or was helping the groundsmen dig the underground bunker.

Casper decided he would allow himself a glass of juice to steady his nerves before embarking on a new to-do list—an activity that provided him with a satisfying sense of calm and control. But as he was crossing the sitting room, he heard the unmistakable creak of an old door opening. Casper tensed. His mum wasn't due back for another half hour, it couldn't be his dad—he always whistled his way up the stairs—and it was hardly likely to be another teacher because they knocked before coming up. But this person had entered quietly, sneakily, as if they didn't want anyone else to know they were there.

Casper swallowed.

For the first time in the six years he had been living at Little Wallops Boarding School, somebody had followed him into the turret.

Chapter 2

Casper stayed very still for several seconds. Perhaps whoever it was had made a mistake and would just clear off. But there were footsteps now, and they were climbing the stairs.

"Urgh. Even the staircase stinks of his mother's weird cooking."

Casper flinched. It was Candida; clearly she hadn't finished with him yet.

"Why does she insist on cooking African food?" she tutted. "Doesn't she know that over here we eat cucumber sandwiches and custard creams?"

Casper wished that he was brave enough to stand up for his mum, but he was too frightened, so he made a mental list of his hiding options instead.

Kitchen cupboard: not big enough.

Under his bed: too obvious.

Beneath his parents' bed: too messy.

Behind the sofa: really?

And then his eyes rested on the grandfather clock in the corner of the room. Casper had seen his dad open it up the night before—there was something wrong with the pendulum and both clock hands were stuck at twelve, he'd said—but a dodgy pendulum was the least of Casper's problems. He charged toward the clock, yanking the door open using the key slotted into the lock, then he snatched the key out and bundled himself inside.

It was dark within and it smelled of dust and secrets.

"Casper?"

Casper held his breath.

"I know you're in this poky little turret," Candida cooed as she tiptoed over the carpet. "And I know for a fact that your parents aren't. I saw your mother walking down the drive earlier and the lights are still on in your father's workshop." She paused. "And there I was assuming your door was always locked . . ."

Casper's heart beat in double time as he listened to Candida stalking through the flat. Cupboard doors opened and snapped shut in the kitchen, then Casper watched, through the narrowest crack in the clock door, as Candida returned to the sitting room and dug her nails into the back of the sofa.

"You think I'd let you get away with dumping Leopold in detention?" she hissed. "Do you have any idea how wealthy his family is? His father's so rich he can make people disappear with just one telephone call." She lowered her voice. "Your parents would never find you; you'd just wake up one day in Greenland or somewhere equally ghastly and that would jolly well be that."

Casper grimaced at the thought of such a drastic change to his timetable and tried to ignore the pendulum digging into his shoulder. Then his eyes widened. Candida was right outside the clock now. She looked it up and down, as if regarding a pile of dirty laundry, and Casper didn't dare blink. Then she flounced from the sitting room into Casper's bedroom.

Such was the way that Candida moved—dramatically, impatiently, like a spoiled little monarch—that in her wake a small gust of air slipped through the crack in the grandfather clock. The dust around Casper shifted and seemed to glitter in the half-light and it was then, in that hushed moment, that the Extremely Unpredictable Event occurred.

The key Casper was holding now looked altogether different. Without the layer of dust covering it, he could see that it was not simply a dull lump of metal anymore. It was silver and in its base there was a turquoise gem, which was glowing. And it was because of this glow that Casper saw he was not alone inside the clock.

There, sitting opposite him, was a girl holding a small white envelope, out of which she was pulling a note. The girl looked up and, upon seeing Casper, jumped before hastily shoving the note into her pocket and glaring at him.

Casper blinked. Then he blinked again and rubbed his eyes. But the girl was very much still there and she was unlike anyone he had ever seen before. She had tiny gold stars scattered over her cheekbones; she was wearing overalls with several wrenches and screwdrivers poking out of the front pocket; and, most disconcerting of all, she smelled strongly of the Outdoors, a place Casper tried to avoid at all costs because of the wide-open spaces and the lack of lost and found baskets, which made hiding from particular classmates very tricky.

The girl cracked her knuckles and Casper flinched. *Was she a burglar? Or an accomplice of Candida's? But what kind of burglar or accomplice dressed like this? And had she crept inside the turret after lessons or had she been sneaking around up here all day?!* Casper tried to gather his thoughts. *The clock isn't big enough for two people to hide in and the girl was definitely not here when I climbed inside because I would've sensed her or bumped into her, despite the dark. Wouldn't I?*

But as Casper stared ahead in disbelief, he couldn't help feeling that the inside of the clock looked somehow bigger now. Roomier. More like a cupboard, perhaps, or an old closet.

The girl narrowed her eyes, like a cat might do before pouncing, and Casper shrank inside his blazer. Was it safer in the clock with this odd girl or outside in the flat with Candida? He couldn't decide. So he did what most people in England do when they find themselves in an awkward situation: nothing.

It was the girl who spoke first. "So, *you're* the criminal."

Casper paled. If Candida overheard the girl talking, he'd be toast. So he closed his eyes and tried to pretend that what was happening wasn't. Because it couldn't be. Pendulums and hanging weights were what you found behind grandfather clock doors. Not strange girls in overalls.

A finger prodded him in his ribcage and Casper's eyes sprang open. The girl was dangerously close now and the gold on her cheeks glistened. She shuffled backward again, pushed her hair—which was white-blond and wild about her face as if she'd been shoved into a tumble dryer and pulled out mid-spin—back from her eyes, and glowered at Casper.

"I'd appreciate it if you didn't fall asleep mid-arrest. That's what dungeons are for."

Casper raised a shaking finger to his lips in an attempt to make the girl be quiet. Surely at any moment Candida would fling open the grandfather clock door if she heard the sound of a voice inside it? But nothing happened. Perhaps Candida was still rooting through his bedroom. He tried to think rationally. The girl inside the clock must be a pupil at Little Wallops—someone younger than him, someone extremely forgettable—and yet looking at her now, Casper couldn't help feeling that he'd remember someone like her.

"I . . . I don't recognize you from school," he whispered.

The girl wiggled her feet, which were bare and scuffed with dirt. "That's 'cause I'm usually too busy getting expelled from classes." She paused. "But they always let me back in, in the end. There's a shortage of bottlers in Rumblestar right now, so it's important I get a decent training." She frowned. "Stop distracting me. I'm trying to arrest *you*."

Casper felt sure that Candida would find him now—this girl was hardly making an effort to be quiet—but for some strange reason she didn't appear and Casper found himself whispering another question. "Where on earth did you come from, then?"

"The sky," the girl replied. "Obviously."

"The sky doesn't spit out children," Casper hissed. "That would be ridiculous."

The girl shivered. "You sound just like a grown-up."

Casper thought of Candida again. Was she rummaging through the kitchen cupboards now or had she given up and left the turret? "I don't know who *you* are or where *you're* from," Casper whispered to the girl inside the clock, "but I'm *not* a criminal—*you* are for trespassing onto private property! I'm just a Year Six boy hiding in a grandfather clock, and right now we need to keep quiet."

The girl snorted. "I'm only ever quiet when I'm sleeping, and even then I'm pretty sure I snore." She looked around. "Besides, you're inside a Neverlate Tree, not a clock. You really are a very stupid criminal not to know where you're hiding!

And not even bothering to disguise your face or your clothes to even *try* to look a tiny bit more like one of us!"

Casper was losing patience now. "If this is a tree, then why is there a pendulum digging into my shoulder?"

The girl looked faintly amused. "There's not. But the Neverlate Tree is a bit wonky inside, so I wouldn't be surprised if you're leaning against a crooked piece of wood."

Casper twisted his head round and his palms tickled with sweat. Where the pendulum had undoubtedly been there was now a gnarled wooden bump. And mingling with the smell of dust and secrets was the warm, wild smell of a tree. Casper swallowed. The situation was getting dangerously out of control. *What was going on?*

The girl folded her arms. "The Neverlate Tree grows excuses for those heading back to the castle late, but the envelopes only open if you climb inside to read them." She snatched the note from her pocket and held it up so that Casper could see:

Busy capturing criminal

Now, had she been a little less hasty and a little more thorough, the girl might have turned the piece of paper over and seen the words on the other side. But she was not that sort of girl; she moved fast, talked lots, and thought very little about the consequences.

"So," she said, "I'm going to drag you up the steps with me by your ears or your hair or whichever hurts more, then the Lofty Husks will punish you for tampering with the kingdom's marvels and"—she grinned—"reward *me* for being the hero to bring you in!"

Casper's eyes bulged—not at her words, though they made no sense at all, but at the lump wriggling past the wrenches and the screwdrivers in the pocket on the front of the girl's overalls. A blue-scaled, winged creature about the size of a fist poked its snout over the edge of the pocket and squinted at Casper.

The girl rapped the creature on the head. "Not now, Arlo. I'm extremely busy."

The miniature dragon—for that, to Casper's amazement, seemed to be what it was—let out a bored growl, then slunk back into the pocket.

The girl rubbed her hands together. "Now, where were we?"

Casper's pulse was racing. Overalls, dungeons, and now dragons called Arlo . . . He needed to put a stop to all this now, so he rammed his shoulder into the door. It didn't budge. He tried again, this time with his foot, but still the door wouldn't move.

The girl sniggered. "Neverlate Trees only open again for you if you're holding an excuse." She wiggled the note in the air. "Everyone knows that."

Casper ignored her and pummeled at the door with his fists. "Er, Candida? If you're still out there and now is a good time for you, I'd love to take that beating."

"I don't mind doing the beating myself," the girl in the clock said hopefully.

Casper flung himself at the door, but still it held fast. And then the girl pushed the door gently, and to Casper's shock and relief, it swung open. Light flooded in, drowning the turquoise glow, but as Casper scrambled out of the clock after the girl, he was surprised to find that his feet did not meet with carpet. They met with something cold and hard.

Stone.

Casper looked up and his stomach lurched. His sitting room was gone. Candida was gone. The grandfather clock was gone. In its place there stood a very old tree. And hanging from the twisted branches were—Casper gasped—not buds, not leaves, but dozens of small white envelopes.

Chapter 3

Casper raised two shaking hands to his mouth. He was standing on a vast staircase that narrowed as it climbed upward. But what made his insides churn was the fact that the steps disappeared into a cloud and that on either side of them there were clouds and that beyond the tree with the tangled roots that sprawled out over the steps, there were more clouds still.

Casper felt himself sway.

"Best not to get too close to the Edge," the girl said, nodding toward the cloud the staircase seemed to be resting on. "It's miles and miles down to the Boundless Seas and even though some of the most experienced ballooners have launched off there in their hot air balloons, no one has *ever* tried to jump."

Casper gave a shaky moan as the clouds around them shifted

and he took in an unforgivably long drop down to the ocean. The water glinted in the afternoon sun and seagulls swung on the breeze and, had Casper not been hundreds of meters up in the sky, he could have almost imagined that the scene below was somewhere out in the North Sea. But then there was the staircase with the tree. And he felt perfectly certain that the trees in England, or indeed the trees in any other country on the world maps lining Mr. Barge's classroom, did not sprout stationery, and they most definitely did not grow out of staircases in the sky.

The girl turned to face Casper and he was surprised to see she was small, probably the same height as him. Somehow her attitude had made her seem bigger. "Right, then," she said. "Have you decided whether you would like to be dragged up the steps by your ear or your hair? Both, I imagine, will be equally distressing."

Casper spun back toward the door leading out of the tree. But it snapped shut as he reached for it and no matter how many times he tried to pry the wood open, the way into the tree, or the clock, or whatever it was, had closed.

Heart galloping, Casper turned around.

The girl gave a wicked smile and the stars on her cheeks glittered. "I hope you're better with heights than Arlo."

Casper clung onto the trunk of the tree. "I'm not going anywhere until you tell me what on earth is going on. Where am I? Who are you? And on a scale of one to ten how dangerous is Arlo?"

The little dragon wriggled out of the girl's pocket, fluttered upward, then blew hard through his nostrils. A puff of smoke trickled out.

Even so, Casper gulped.

Arlo flapped up to a branch on the tree and the girl pierced Casper with a haughty stare. "He's a ten when he needs to be, but he's got a bad chest, so sometimes he finds breathing fire a bit of an ordeal." She grabbed Casper by the scruff of his blazer and dragged him up a step. "I'm Utterly Thankless, and I'm a bottler-in-training up at Rumblestar. I was *supposed* to be spending the afternoon in the castle, but I got kicked out of class for flicking rain into my teacher's face. Silly old Blustersnap should have seen it coming when she asked me to do group work—you'd think she and the rest of the Lofty Husks would know by now that I only ever work alone. Still, it meant I snuck out here for some peace and quiet, and when I realized I was late for dinner, I grabbed an envelope from the tree and was given a top-notch excuse for being out past curfew—capturing a criminal is important business what with everything that's been going on!" Utterly paused on the step and looked at Casper. "I was a *little* bit surprised at how easy you were to capture, though—just sitting there inside the tree looking hopeless—but perhaps you'll come into your own in the dungeons."

Casper yanked himself free and clutched his hair. "I'm not a criminal!"

Utterly rolled her eyes. "Do you think it'll be quicker if I drag you or push you?"

"N-neither," Casper stammered. "I'm staying right here because . . . well . . . I like rules too much to be a criminal, and I hate risks"—he grimaced at the staircase—"so climbing *that* is completely out of the question."

Utterly sighed. "You really are turning out to be a terrible disappointment, you know. I was expecting Morg's followers to be knife-wielding, karate-kicking, fire-breathing demons."

Casper tried to block Utterly's ramblings out because they were bordering on madness now. *This must be a dream,* a voice in his head whimpered. *You've seen the world maps in Mr. Barge's classroom and there's not a single mention of magical kingdoms. Surely you're just going to wake up any second and be back in Little*

Wallops, where— Suddenly, Casper thought of his parents. He imagined them coming back to the flat and finding him gone. They'd be worried sick!

Utterly shook Casper by the shoulders, and he snapped out of his thoughts. "And how *can* you be scared to go up into Rumblestar when you've been nosing around up there and tampering with our marvels for the past few weeks?" Her face darkened. "Do you have *any* idea how hard it is to catch marvels? They may look like ordinary old marbles, but they're flighty and fidgety—they're the purest droplets of rain, snow, and sunlight, after all!"

"I haven't been nosing around anywhere!" Casper cried. "I've been at school trying my best to hand in homework on time and avoid being hurled into a trash can. I know absolutely *nothing* about this ridiculous-sounding Rumblestar."

Utterly gasped at the insult, then her words tumbled out, hot and angry. "Ridiculous? RIDICULOUS? I'll have you know that without Rumblestar, the Unmapped Kingdoms would crumble! And then who do you think would send sunlight to Crackledawn, rain to Jungledrop, and snow to Silvercrag? The other kingdoms might *write* the weather scrolls for the Faraway, but none of the continents there would exist without

Rumblestar *gathering* the marvels in the first place! Imagine a Faraway without rain to nourish the land, sunlight to make the plants and trees grow, and snow to"—she paused—"cover Antarctica!"

Casper frowned at the mention of Antarctica. Why was this girl calling what sounded suspiciously like Earth the Faraway? He felt perfectly sure that Utterly was blurting out lies for one some reason or another—magical kingdoms didn't exist and the world's weather did not rely on them—and yet he was realizing that the angrier the girl got, the more information she gave away. So, if he could just keep baiting her, then maybe she'd come clean with what was *really* going on.

He took a deep breath and braced himself for the onslaught. "Magical kingdoms aren't real and there are no such things as marvels of snow, sun, or rain! Weather is based purely on scientific fact."

"AREN'T REAL?" Utterly spluttered. "DON'T EXIST?"

Up on his branch, Arlo covered his face with his claws.

"I suppose next you'll be telling me that none of the recent hurricanes in Europe happened? That there were no huge tornados in America? And that the whirlwinds in Africa and the typhoons in Asia and Australia were just rumors?" Utterly made a fist of Casper's shirt. "When you swan into Rumblestar and start tampering with our marvels, it disrupts the entire weather system! How does it make you feel to know that because of *you* a hurricane flattened half of England earlier this week and"—she hung her head—"*killed* hundreds of people?"

Casper was far from ready to accept that he had stumbled into a magical kingdom and that events there were behind the recent weather-related disasters, but his face lit up at the mention of home.

"England!" he exclaimed, untangling himself from Utterly's grip. "That's where I'm from! I go to a school there called Little Wallops—"

Utterly scowled. "I'll wallop you if you're not careful."

"Are you always this cross?"

"Cross is what happens when you forget an umbrella or burn toast." Utterly paused. "I'm not cross; I'm just unbelievably fierce." She looked Casper up and down. "You can't be from England. Everyone knows that those in the Faraway *stay* in the Faraway. They scurry around their continents doing non-magical things with non-magical people and non-magical creatures while those in the Unmapped Kingdoms *stay* in the Unmapped Kingdoms working away to make weather because sharing the magic is what keeps the Faraway *and* the Unmapped Kingdoms turning!"

At this outburst, Casper glanced around hopefully for a grown-up, but it was still just him and Utterly on the staircase and Arlo in the tree. Clearly making Utterly even crosser was not the way to get her to speak logically. So, in a desperate bid to stamp some sense and order onto the situation, Casper lifted the crumpled timetable from his pocket and gazed at it longingly. What he would give to be doing his homework now, or even to be crouched inside the lost and found basket or cornered in the library with Candida and Leopold. At least those situations made sense to him.

"What's that?" Utterly snapped.

Casper sighed. "My timetable."

"What's it for?"

"It tells me what to do when."

"Doesn't your temper tell you that?"

Casper sniffed. "I'd like to go home now, Utterly. To Little Wallops, where I'm from."

Utterly hauled him up a few more steps with her. "Criminals don't just go home. They get arrested, then tried, then fed to the dragons."

"WHAT?" Casper shrieked.

"Well, I'm not exactly *sure* that happens, but I'm pretty confident the Lofty Husks will want to put an end to you once they've tried you."

Casper stood rooted to the step. "In that case, I'm staying right here. On this step. Until everything goes back to normal."

"I wouldn't." Utterly smirked. "Things can get pretty dangerous outside the castle walls after sunset."

Casper looked out over the cloud-strewn sky around them—he could have sworn he could hear something rumbling, like thunder, only that didn't make any sense because the clouds around them were wispy and white. Where on earth was he?

He brushed the strange noise aside and took a deep breath. Then, gripping the cuffs of his blazer so hard his knuckles turned white, he followed Utterly up the steps because the grandfather clock seemed to have disappeared completely and if all this *was* actually happening and he really *was* in some sort of strange place far away, then he was going to need help getting home, so he had to trust that maybe these Lofty Husks, whoever they were, would be more understanding than Utterly and listen to him when he explained that he wasn't a criminal but a boy who had gotten hopelessly lost.

Casper tried to focus on Utterly's feet, anything to avoid looking at the terrifying drop. After a while he glanced up and noticed that Arlo was perched on Utterly's shoulder—and he was sobbing.

Utterly stroked his tiny blue wings. "Arlo's extremely sensitive," she whispered to Casper. "He can't bear unhappy endings, so if you're going to go and get all stressed out about being eaten by a dragon, I'd appreciate it if you could do it quietly so that Arlo doesn't get even more upset." She carried on climbing, straight through the middle of a cloud. "Chop, chop! Nobody likes a lazy criminal."

Casper inched through the cloud after her. It was wet and misty and so far removed from his timetable that he felt dangerously close to passing out, but before he could, they emerged on the other side and Casper saw that the clouds around them now were suddenly very, very, *very* different from the ones he was used to. They were vast, like sky-high icebergs, and those to his left appeared to have soily roots and vines dangling from the bottom of them while those on his right showed glimpses of rocks. Casper squinted. He could only see the undersides of these clouds, but the roots and the rocks seemed to hint at something bigger, something only partly glimpsed right now.

And then his gaze fell upon the towering stone wall in front of him. It curved away into the distance on both sides and from where he stood, Casper could just make out several arches carved into the stone in either direction and torrents of water gushing through them. *So it wasn't thunder I heard earlier,* he thought. *It was sky-tumbling waterfalls!* He looked at the large door in front of him. It was domed and wooden and crisscrossed with gold metal. *There can't possibly be a kingdom beyond this door responsible for the weather in my world. Can there?* He thought of his mum out buying the groceries. Had there been another hurricane while he'd been gone? And what if it had ripped through the village and the school and his mum had been caught in the middle of it? He felt suddenly very sick indeed.

In front of him, Utterly rummaged through her overall pocket, then pulled out what looked like a handful of Scrabble letters. "Since all the problems you've been causing with the marvels, Criminal, we've upgraded our security. Keys don't work on this door anymore, only passwords do." She threw Casper a smug look, then glanced at the letters in her palm, trying her best to shield them from Casper's sight. "Hmmmmm," she said as airily as she could. "This one I pinched from the porter's tower is proving a little harder to work out than most."

Casper stole a peek over her shoulder at the letters—I C P H U C—but couldn't make heads or tails of them.

Then Arlo hurtled out of a cloud and skidded to a halt in Utterly's hand, accidentally jumbling up all the letters there. But when the little dragon settled himself on Utterly's arm seconds later, Casper wondered whether his crash landing had been an accident after all. Because now that the letters had been rearranged, a word stared back at them—H I C C U P—and though Utterly quickly tucked it from sight, Casper could have sworn he saw Arlo wink at Utterly as she passed each letter in the correct order through the keyhole.

For a few seconds nothing happened, then the door creaked open and Utterly bundled Casper through it. His jaw dropped at the scene before him. Nestled among the clouds, there was a castle, just as Utterly had said there would be, but this castle was more splendid than any of the ones Casper had seen back home. It was a vast silver-stone maze of turrets and domes twisting into the sky.

Stone dragons clutching burning torches lined the turrets,

golden flags fluttered from the spires, and a moat of crystal-clear water fanned out in front of the castle before cascading, on the left and right, through arches in the walls. Casper glimpsed a river snaking through a forest on the left, then on the right what looked like mountain peaks in the distance. He shook his head in disbelief. The roots and the rocks he had seen from the bottom of the staircase earlier suddenly made sense. Was this really a secret kingdom tucked up in the sky? Surely there was some more reasonable explanation for all this. . . .

Casper turned his attention back to the castle. Inside the walls a few clouds poked through the water in the moat and dozens of humpback bridges connected them. On each cloud sat a stone tower, and while most of these were lit up and Casper could see the silhouettes of people moving around inside them, there was one tower lined with gargoyles holding black-flamed torches that none of the humpback bridges reached out to. And though Casper was in a castle in the sky that seemed a million miles from home, it didn't take him long to figure out what that building was.

"Excellent," Utterly said merrily. "I see you've spotted the dungeons."

Chapter 4

Utterly pointed to the humpback bridge in front of them. "Hold your breath when you cross the bridges, please. We try to avoid placing foundations on the backs of sleeping cloud giants because the slightest sound wakes them, but now and again it can't be helped because, let's face it, telling the difference between a cloud and a cloud giant is a tricky business." She shot Casper a daggered look. "Not that I need to explain that to you—you've probably worked out the castle's quirks with all your snooping around."

Casper chewed his nails. He wanted to dismiss Utterly's talk of giants in the sky, but given everything else he'd seen so far, he thought it best to bite his lip and take Utterly at her worryingly accurate word. "What . . . what happens if the cloud giants wake?" he asked.

"Things move. People get squashed." Arlo gave a panicked squeak from Utterly's shoulder and she lowered her voice. "Last year a boy sneezed on this bridge and the cloud giant beneath it rolled over in his sleep. The boy broke his leg and ever since, the bell tower has been at such a steep angle you have to use a rope to rappel up the stairs inside it. But once we're in the castle, you can kick and scream all you like." She surveyed the scene ahead. "You'll want to take the bridges at speed to maximize your chances of survival. A sort of running tiptoe is best."

Casper followed Utterly over the first bridge while frantically composing a to-do list in his head to try and keep himself together:

Try not to make Utterly angry
(could end in throttling)
Speak calmly to Lofty Husks
(beg and scream only if they bring out dragons)
When home, sit in dark room and breathe slowly

The sun was dipping behind the castle now and the torches scattered amber on the water in the moat. Casper gulped. How long had he been gone? And would his parents have noticed and started searching the school for him by now?

They passed two boys about Casper and Utterly's age, both with gold stars dotted across their cheekbones and clad in overalls with wrenches and screwdrivers poking out of their pockets, but their overalls, Casper noticed, were a great deal cleaner and less crumpled than Utterly's. The boys gaped at Casper in surprise, but they gave Utterly rather than him a very wide berth as they passed on the bridge—almost as if they were afraid of her.

Utterly glanced over her shoulder at them and for a second Casper thought he saw something in her expression that he recognized but couldn't put a finger on, but then her face closed up again, Arlo cuddled into her neck, and she ran on toward the castle.

On the fourth bridge they passed a woman in a leather jacket on which a large silver badge had been pinned with the word BALLOONER inscribed on it. Gold stars twinkled on her cheeks and she wore a leather hat lined with fur that tied up under her chin and a pair of goggles pushed up onto her forehead. Her eyes widened as she took in Casper, then she looked at Utterly with the kind of look that comes from a woman who has had children but definitely doesn't want any more.

"Who is *that*, Utterly?"

At her words, Casper felt the bridge beneath him shift—like sand underfoot as the tide comes in—and, realizing that she was seconds away from waking a cloud giant, the woman darted over the bridge, then disappeared into a tower. Utterly grabbed Casper's arm as they fled from the bridge and nipped beneath a stone arch leading into the castle. At the same time two enormous white arms carved from cloud stretched out in what looked like a yawn, knocking the roof of a nearby tower clean off.

Utterly winced. "Probably Slumbergrot; he's the lightest sleeper. But that was the ballooner's fault, not ours."

She tugged Casper into a large courtyard. The dragon statues that lined it were now silhouetted against the twilight, and in the middle of the courtyard there was a fountain spouting golden water and a group of girls—some dressed in overalls like Utterly and others in leather jackets and flying goggles like the woman they had just seen—were clustered around it. They were scooping mugs into the fountain and drinking the liquid pooled inside it, but they looked up on seeing Utterly and Casper.

One of the girls squinted. "*He's* not from Rumblestar . . ."

Another girl rubbed her flying goggles and peered through them at Casper. "You're right! He's not a ballooner *or* a bottler—he doesn't even have starlight scattered on his cheeks. . . . And I've taken flying classes over almost all of Rumblestar and he definitely doesn't look like anything out in the Beyond either!" She looked at Utterly, wide-eyed. "Is he from one of the *other* kingdoms? But then how did he manage to get *here*?"

Even though the girls were obviously curious, like the boys they had passed on the bridge, they didn't come any closer. Casper got the distinct feeling that they were keeping Utterly very much at a distance.

Utterly swaggered forward and the girls scuttled back a few steps. "While you lot have been sipping sunlight smoothies, I've been busy capturing a criminal." Utterly snatched Casper's arm and raised it high. "Here he is! The villain behind all the faulty marvels!" She puffed out her chest and Arlo did a victory dance on her shoulder. "Captured by yours truly."

An awkward silence followed, then one of the girls looked at Utterly. "Are you *sure*, Utterly? Didn't the Lofty Husks say the marvels were damaged because of faulty pipework in the Mixing Tower?" There was no malice in her words, but something about her tone made Casper wonder whether this was the first time Utterly had taken matters so completely into her own hands.

"The Lofty Husks just don't want to panic you with the truth!" Utterly shot back. "They—"

Casper sensed there could be an opportunity to be rescued here, so he forced his voice out over Utterly's. "I'm . . . I'm *not* a criminal," he spluttered. 'I'm just a boy from Little Wallops School who's gotten very lost indeed."

The girls whispered to one another. "Er . . . Utterly, do you think perhaps—"

"No time for chit-chat, I'm afraid." Utterly shoved Casper on through the courtyard before he could get another word out. "So long, girls!"

She marched toward the castle door and barged it open. Once again Casper looked on with gaping eyes. The hall was lined with doors, but none of them were the same size or shape. Some were round, others were rectangular and so large giants could have strolled through quite happily, while others still were so tiny perhaps only Arlo could've entered—and even then he would have had to stoop. Casper blinked. How could all this exist up amongst the clouds?

Utterly followed Casper's gaze. "When you live in a kingdom full of magical beasts, it's important to have doors for everyone. No point asking a cloud giant to enter a door fit for tiny river imps."

Casper tried to apply a shred of logic to the situation to keep himself sane. "Couldn't the river imp just go through the cloud giant's door instead?"

Utterly gave him a withering look. "That would hardly be polite. And when you're this high up in the sky, manners are very important. Without them, there would be all sorts of pushing and shoving and people tumbling to their deaths."

Casper thought it pointless to bring up the fact that Utterly seemed to have done a lot of pushing and shoving since they'd met, so he turned his attention to the enormous painting above the fireplace: a phoenix with magnificent ruby-red wings. There were Honors Boards surrounding the painting which, in large silver lettering, listed various awards for ballooners (*Biggest Marvel Haul, Most Daring Flight, Fastest Balloon*) and bottlers (*Most Ingenious Engineering Feats, Most Knowledgeable Blending, Quickest Bottling*). And Casper saw that down the "Junior" columns on the bottlers' boards one name kept appearing time and time again: "Mannerly Thankless."

"Thankless . . . That's your name, isn't it?" he said after a while.

Utterly glanced up at the boards, then back to Casper. "Shut up."

And Casper did. Because he knew, from experience, that there was a very fine line between "shut up" and being sat on or hurled into a trash can. He tried to concentrate on the walls which went up and up and up, past dozens of landings lining the floors, until eventually a glass dome roof closed over the top—but it only made him feel even more disoriented. How had climbing into a grandfather clock meant him straying so far from the comfort of his timetable? He watched the paper airplanes that now and again drifted down from above, disappearing beneath doors or slipping through letter boxes carved into them, but when one landed at Utterly's feet, Casper chanced a look as she smoothed it open. The contents were short and to the point.

You're late for dinner (again).
Mum

Utterly tore the note up and strode across the flagstones. "Right, we'll want the seventeenth floor. Most people will be having dinner in the banqueting hall on the twelfth, but the Lofty Husks usually meet in the Precipice at the end of the day."

Utterly led the way to an old-fashioned bathtub at the far end of the room. It was raised on two bronze feet, with matching bronze taps, and when Utterly clambered inside it and Arlo followed, Casper was relieved to find that it wasn't full of water.

"In you get, Criminal," Utterly snapped. "It's the fastest way up."

Throwing a wary look at the electrical pulley system the bathtub seemed to be attached to, Casper did as he was told and climbed in. "I presume there are various health and safety rules for traveling in a bathtub?"

Utterly thumped her fist onto a button on the wall, sending the bathtub shooting upward. Casper clutched the sides and screamed as the tub hurtled past numerous floors in seconds before jolting to a halt in front of a gap in the banisters circling the seventeenth floor.

Utterly climbed out and Casper, feeling nauseous and terrified in equal measure, followed. Various passageways led off from the landing, but only one was lined with carpet. Utterly hastened down it with Arlo and after adding one more item to his to-do list (*Use stairs on descent from castle*) and giving it a purposeful title (*Ways to Survive Today*), Casper made his way, rather shakily, after them.

"Oooh, what have we here?" cooed a female voice. "Important visitors for the Lofty Husks?" There was an excited giggle.

Utterly groaned. "Ignore the Red Carpet. She's a real social climber—only ever nice to wealthy, important people—and let's face it, you're just a measly criminal."

Casper looked down, aghast. Between his feet there was a tear in the carpet and it was moving uncannily like a mouth!

The carpet sighed. "Oh, it's just an ordinary little bottler-in-training and"—there was a sniff—"a shoeless nobody." Casper wriggled uncomfortably in his socks. "How dreadfully common," the carpet added. "When royalty walk along my silken threads—like the aristocratic river nymphs who passed this way last week—I can feel their class. They ooze glamour. But with you two—it's like being trampled on by a couple of ungainly hippopotamuses."

Utterly scowled. "Actually, Red Carpet, you're being trodden on by one of the most *dangerous* criminals known to Rumblestar."

Casper didn't catch the carpet's reply because he and

Utterly were long past the tear in the fabric now. They were standing in front of a very tall, very narrow door which bore a plaque with the following words:

Knock ONLY if you have something terribly important to say.

Casper thought about the doors in the hallway—how the shape reflected whoever walked through them—and he eyed this tall one nervously. "I . . . I thought the Lofty Husks would be like you," he said to Utterly. "A bit of glitter on their faces, maybe a few more miniature dragons, but really just the same sort of thing—only older."

Utterly looked at him, her head cocked to one side, then she eyed the door in front of them before turning her attention back to Casper—and had Casper known this girl a little better, he would have realized that there was a flicker of doubt in her eyes now. She'd gotten this far—right up to the Lofty Husks' door—and yet the criminal really did seem to know next to nothing about her kingdom. He could be bluffing, of course, but then there had been that episode in the Neverlate Tree, too, when he was just sitting there, undisguised, waiting to be captured. Would a criminal really act so foolishly?

Utterly shook herself. This was to be her moment in the spotlight—her chance to make her parents proud after . . . everything that had happened—and she wasn't going to back down now. But seeing as the boy really was proving to be a pretty hopeless criminal, she felt she could, at the very least, offer a begrudging explanation of what lay behind the door in front of them.

"The Lofty Husks are folk born under the very first eclipse and marked out by the very first phoenix as rulers of the Unmapped Kingdoms," she muttered. "They take a different form in each kingdom, so we're told, and up here in Rumblestar they're—"

Casper winced as he thought of all the tall and terrible creatures he'd seen in the book of fairy tales he'd come across when tidying his mum's bookshelves. "Oh, don't tell me. They're trolls, aren't they? Or ogres?"

"I wish." Utterly knocked on the door. "They're wizards. But they're stern as you like, especially if you forget to laugh at their jokes or you don't listen properly in class. They wear robes made from enchanted parchment and hats encrusted with fallen stars and apparently"—she lowered her voice—"they have starlight bubbling through their veins, which is why they're so wise." She raised an eyebrow at Casper. "What's running through your veins, Criminal?"

Casper's knees wobbled. "Common sense."

"Is that so?"

Casper and Utterly jumped at the voice. While they had been talking, the very tall, very narrow door had opened to reveal a very tall, very narrow man. His robes were indeed made from parchment—ancient paper covered in scripted words that seemed to be there one minute, then gone the next. His hat was tall and pointed and glittering at the base, where the fallen stars glowed, and on his little finger a mirrored ring flashed. Casper looked at the Lofty Husk's face. It was heavily wrinkled, like the skin of an apricot, and his nose was long and crooked.

Arlo slid back into Utterly's overall pocket while Casper focused on the second item on his to-do list. *Speak calmly.*

"G-good evening, sir. My name is Casper Tock and . . . and I'm from England . . . in the Faraway?" he said hopefully. "I would very much like to go home. Can you help me?"

The Lofty Husk was silent and still. Only his eyes moved, two pale orbs looking Casper up and down.

Utterly coughed. "Um, sir—"

The Lofty Husk raised his hand and Utterly fell quiet. "You found an object from the Unmapped Kingdoms somewhere in the Faraway, did you not? That is how you managed to get here . . ." His voice was low and soft, like the first stirrings of thunder.

Casper gave an enormous sigh of relief because here was someone, at last, talking almost sensibly and who seemed to believe that Casper was somewhere he definitely didn't want to be. His words tumbled out at the prospect of being shown a way home. "I was hiding in a grandfather clock and the gemstone in the key for it glowed and then . . . then . . . everything changed. Utterly just appeared out of nowhere and when I stepped out of the clock, I found myself on a staircase in the sky!"

Casper drew the key out from his pocket and the Lofty Husk's eyes stilled on the gemstone in the center. "It seems that you have found one of the immortalized phoenix tears."

"Phoenix tears?"

The wizard reached out a long, spindly arm and took the key from Casper. He turned it over in his hands.

"Interesting," he said quietly. "Very interesting. And where—"

A female voice interrupted from the room behind him. "Who, pray, has decided to call upon us, Frostbite? And what, pray, do they want?"

Frostbite nudged Casper out of the view of those in the Precipice, but not before Casper caught a glimpse of a room lined with old-fashioned street lamps burning blue. There were all sorts of weather-measuring instruments hanging from the walls—thermometers, barometers, hygrometers, and anemometers—as well as a huge telescope in one corner, then a large table scattered with leather-bound books. Around this sat men and women in pointed hats and parchment robes, and beyond them lay the open sky and a sheer drop down to the moat. *The Precipice,* Casper thought. *It made sense . . .*

Frostbite turned his head back toward the room very slightly. "Do not be alarmed, Blustersnap, it is only Utterly Thankless."

"Oh, what is to be done with that child?" Blustersnap muttered. "If we are to issue the"—she paused, as if choosing her next words carefully in Utterly's hearing—"*warning* across the kingdom, then we must do so in the banqueting hall immediately rather than waste our time disciplining bottlers-in-training.

Send her away at once; we have important work to do now we know"—another pause—"what we know."

"But—" Utterly started.

Frostbite closed the door, then he turned to Casper, and as he did so, Casper's skin crawled. Because he realized that he had stumbled across something more dangerous than a girl with explosive hair and an oversensitive dragon. This was one of the rulers of Rumblestar, but he had lied to his fellow wizards about Casper's presence as coolly as if he had been declining a cup of tea.

Chapter 5

Frostbite turned to Utterly. "I hope that you are able to produce an excuse for neglecting the curfew?"

Utterly reached into her pocket and drew out Arlo by mistake. She pushed him down, fumbled for the note from the Neverlate Tree, and held that up instead. "I know that we're living in uncertain times with Morg still alive in Everdark and that you and the rest of the Lofty Husks want to avoid scaring everyone, but, well, what if there's more to this business with the marvels than faulty pipework? What if someone, a criminal working for Morg, has found their way into Rumblestar and has been tampering with the marvels? The Neverlate Tree certainly seems to think so"—Utterly glanced at Casper—"and so, sir, I present to you the criminal *I* captured.'

Frostbite was silent for a few seconds and then, to Casper's surprise, he smiled thinly. "Congratulations, Utterly. The rest of the Lofty Husks will be delighted when I tell them that there has indeed been an intruder but that you have skillfully captured him."

Utterly grinned, then high-fived Arlo, then grinned again.

Casper, meanwhile, stared at Frostbite. "But . . . but you *know* I'm not a criminal! You said you believed I was from the Faraway earlier!"

Frostbite raised one wiry eyebrow. "I considered the possibility," he said coolly. "But then I decided . . . not."

He smiled at Utterly and she smiled back, and Casper knew then that there wasn't a chance Utterly would question what was going on; she had earned the praise she wanted and now she was basking in the spotlight.

"We shall have a feast tomorrow, Utterly," Frostbite added. "In aid of your magnificent capture—"

Utterly gasped. "Will there be snow pies and mist tea?"

Frostbite nodded. "It would not be a feast without them. Now, if you will excuse me, Utterly, I shall escort the criminal to the dungeons myself before returning to the Precipice to share the good news with the rest of the Lofty Husks."

Then, for a small moment, Utterly hesitated. "I hope you

don't think I'm being too bold, sir, but earlier you didn't mention the criminal to the other Lofty Husks, so I just—"

Frostbite sniffed. "Run along now, Utterly, or I shall change my mind about that feast and the speech I am planning to make entirely in your honor in front of every Unmapper in the kingdom."

"He's not going to—" Casper started. But Frostbite clapped a hand over his mouth and then threw Utterly such a stern look that Arlo burst into tears and Utterly scurried back along the corridor with him.

When she was out of sight, Frostbite withdrew his hand and glared at Casper. "How did you find the phoenix tear, boy? And how exactly did you activate it so that you could travel from the Faraway? I thought only dragons carrying weather scrolls could find and then cross the invisible links between our world and yours."

"So you *do* believe me?" Casper asked in a small voice.

Frostbite ignored him. "How did you do it?" He pursed his lips. "Because this could change everything."

"I didn't *do* anything," Casper replied. "I told you, I hid inside a grandfather clock and ended up here somehow. And now I *really* need to get home."

"Frostbite?" a voice from within the Precipice called. "We have important work to do tonight."

"I shall be with you very shortly," Frostbite replied. "I must just complete one small errand. Do carry on without me."

Casper thought back to his to-do list. No dragons had been unleashed yet, but even so, this seemed like a fairly appropriate moment to start begging and screaming. But just as Casper opened his mouth, Frostbite once again clamped a hand over it and with the other, he gripped Casper's shoulder and marched him down the Red Carpet. Casper made to struggle free, but the Lofty Husk was four times his size, and as Frostbite bounded down the stairs, one flight at a time, Casper tried to console himself with the measly knowledge that at least he had ticked one thing off his to-do list since arriving in Rumblestar: *Use stairs on descent from castle.*

Frostbite glided across the courtyard, then strode out over the cloud giant bridges. Night had now fallen, and as they passed the moat, it stirred with shadows. The Lofty Husk said nothing as they walked, but Casper could sense his mind whirring as he leapt from the bridge they were on, still holding Casper tight with a hand that was so wrinkled it was almost scaled, and landed on the walkway encircling the dungeon tower. The gargoyles clutching their black-flamed torches leered out from the stonework.

"Please," Casper whispered, edging away from the metal grate barring the entrance. "I accidentally found my way here. I don't want to cause any problems. I just want to go home."

"It may well have been an accident," Frostbite muttered, "but somehow you must have activated a phoenix tear, and if you have found a way to cross the links from your world to ours, then perhaps you can also find a way to cross from Everdark to Rumblestar." He paused. "Which makes you rather valuable to someone I know—until she decides to sever the links between the Unmapped Kingdoms and the Faraway, that is."

"Sever the links?" Casper cried. "But . . . that would mean I couldn't ever return home!"

"Silence!" Frostbite said curtly. "We would not want to awaken the cloud giants now, would we?"

The Lofty Husk yanked a lever jutting out from the tower wall, and as he did so, Casper noticed the ring on Frostbite's finger again. Only the mirror embedded in it didn't show a reflection, as it had done earlier; it showed something dark and feathered with a skull-like head. Frostbite tucked the ring beneath the cuff of his robes and then smiled as the grate cranked up to reveal a flight of steps leading into the gloom.

Frostbite pushed Casper inside and the grate slammed down over the entrance. "After I have told the Lofty Husks about Utterly's shocking admission that *she* was the one behind all the problems in the Mixing Tower—it is not like the child stays out of trouble for long, after all—I shall be back to question you, so you will not be alone *all* night." He paused. "You will have the gravestones, I suppose, but they are not the cheeriest of company—grave by name, grave by nature, I am afraid."

Frostbite moved the lever in various directions and a crunching noise, like that of a very large key turning in a lock, sounded. Then the Lofty Husk stalked back across the bridges to the castle.

Casper huddled against the bars and thought of his parents. His mum and dad were always encouraging him to step outside his comfort zone and to have another go at making friends, but he reckoned even they would have drawn a line at this. . . . He prayed again with everything inside him that his mum was safely back from the village and that a hurricane didn't come in the night and reduce their little turret to a pile of rubble. His dad could fix most things, but these storms were another matter entirely. What Casper would do to have his dad's strong arms wrapped around him right now. Hugging wasn't even an activity Casper usually factored into his timetables, but tonight he felt an overwhelming need to be held.

He looked out at the sky. It was stitched with stars, and a crescent moon hung over the castle. Many of the windows were lit up and there were all sorts of cranking, popping, and fizzing noises coming from an enormous tower connected to the castle by a humpback bridge. Three vast chimneys poked up from the roof of this tower, and hammered to the large door down by the moat was a sign just visible in the moonlight: THE MIXING TOWER (CONTAINS CHAOTIC ACTIVITY—ENTER AT OWN RISK). But Casper supposed even those running the machines in the tower would go to bed eventually. And then the lights and sounds would dim and it would just be him and the cloud giants—until Frostbite came back.

Casper felt a lump lodge in his throat. He had allowed himself a flicker of hope when Frostbite had believed his story, but now it seemed that even though the Lofty Husk knew he wasn't from here, Frostbite wasn't going to help Casper get back to Little Wallops—quite the reverse, in fact—it sounded like the Lofty Husk wanted to cut off the way home completely! Casper swiveled round, the impossibility of things weighing heavy inside him, and eyed the steps. They sank into darkness and he thought of the gravestones Frostbite had mentioned. Were prisoners left so long inside the dungeons that they died here?

"What am I going to do?" Casper sobbed, and then his jaw slackened because words were appearing, in golden ink, on the dungeon walls.

Casper brushed his tears away, stood up, then read the words aloud in a half whisper:

"THE MAPS YOU KNOW HOLD WELL-KNOWN LINES,
SHAPES SCORED AND INKED IN OLDEN TIMES.
CONTINENTS DRAWN AND OCEANS NAMED,
PEAKS CLIMBED AND COUNTRIES CLAIMED.
BUT MAPS HOLD SECRETS YET UNTOLD
OF PLACES YOU SHOULD INK IN GOLD,
UP NORTH, DOWN SOUTH, FAR WEST AND EAST,
KINGDOMS FULL OF MAGICAL BEASTS.

IT'S HARD TO TRUST IN WORDS LIKE THESE,

BUT TRUST YOU MUST IF YOU'RE TO LEAVE."

Casper stared at the words. It was as if they had been written specifically for him because this was an answer, of sorts, to the question he had just asked.

"Are . . . are the stones alive?" Casper's voice was so quiet it was almost just a breath, but as he spoke, the words on the wall faded from sight and then new ones appeared, glinting through the dark.

ALIVE—WHY YES—THOUGH WE'VE WORDS NOT BONES,

FOR WE ARE THE LEGENDARY GRAVE STONES.

WE SPEAK THE TRUTH AND ONLY THE TRUTH,

SO ASK US THINGS, YOU SHOELESS YOUTH.

Casper watched as the words vanished, then he took a step closer and ran his hand across the stones. "Can you help me?"

HELP, PERHAPS, THOUGH IT DEPENDS.

WE'RE HARDLY HERE TO BE YOUR FRIENDS.

OUR WORDS ARE FAMED FOR DOOM AND GLOOM,

SO IF YOU'RE SCARED, PLEASE LEAVE THE ROOM.

Casper threw his hands in the air. "We're in a locked dungeon! I can't leave!"

New words appeared.

THE WORDS YOU SPEAK ARE VERY TRUE,
BUT YOU TRY RHYMING RIGHT ON CUE.
SOMETIMES THE WORDS WE WANT TO SHARE
NEED RHYMES THAT ARE A REAL NIGHTMARE.
SO IF THAT HAPPENS WE JUST SHOW
WORDS OF DEEPEST, DARKEST WOE.

Casper tried to think clearly. "So, you're saying that all this is real—the secret kingdoms and the magical beasts—and if I want to get home, I have to believe in it all." He looked out at the sleeping cloud giants. "Well, if you speak the truth and only the truth, I want to know *how* these hidden kingdoms came about."

More words glittered on the stones.

THE EGG CAME FIRST, BRIGHT AND GOLD,
THEN THE PHOENIX, SO WE'RE TOLD.
ALONE IT WEPT, SEVEN LARGE TEARS

AND THE FARAWAY FORMED OVER THE YEARS.
AFRICA, EUROPE, ASIA, AND MORE,
ALL DIFFERENT SHAPES WITH DIFFERENT SHORES.
BUT THESE LANDS WERE DULL AND AWFULLY DARK,
SO THE PHOENIX LEFT ANOTHER MARK.
FOUR OF ITS FEATHERS TUMBLED DOWN
AND THE UNMAPPED KINGDOMS CAME AROUND.

Casper felt his knees wobble. He'd been half hoping the Grave Stones would mention the Big Bang and evolution, but they had spoken of a phoenix and magical tears instead. He tried to wrap his head around it all. So, had Utterly been telling the truth? There really were four secret kingdoms working away to share sunlight, rain, and snow with his world? It sounded impossible and unlikely and horribly full of risk, but then even the cleverest meteorologists hadn't been able to understand the strange weather of late. Could it be that it wasn't just climate change causing problems, but there were also damaged marvels tainting these . . . weather scrolls the Unmappers created? And was Utterly right when she'd said it wasn't simply faulty pipes behind the chaos but someone meddling with the marvels instead?

But Casper wasn't the criminal, and Utterly didn't seem to be either, so *who* was?

Casper thought of Sophie's cake sale to raise money for those who had lost their homes in London. Then he thought of the bus full of people in Ireland that had been blown from a cliff into the sea, never to surface again. And of the little village in Scotland that had been wiped clean off the map. The horror stories were endless. Was there something *he* could do up here to stop all the bad weather back home? Casper banished the thought almost as quickly as it had come. He wasn't cut out for saving kingdoms and righting worlds. Absolutely not. But whether he liked it not, he couldn't avoid the worrying truth of things before him now.

He collected his thoughts and arranged them, in his head, in a brief but purposeful to-do list:

1. *Trust the Grave Stones (because your life depends on it)*
2. *Only get involved in highly risky world-saving business if absolutely necessary and there are grown-ups in charge*
3. *Get home ASAP*

Then he straightened the collar on his blazer and looked at the Grave Stones. "I . . . I've decided to believe *you*," he said. "Partly because what *you've* said *sort of* makes sense but mostly because I want to go home—*right now*." He took a deep breath. "So, what do I do?"

The stones remained blank for a few minutes, then the following words glistened.

I'M AFRAID, YOUNG BOY, YOU MIGHT AS WELL CRY,
'CAUSE TOMORROW, FOR SURE, YOU'LL BE DRAGON PIE.

Casper narrowed his eyes at the stones. "Are *you* saying that because it's going to happen or because *you* can't find any good rhymes?"

But this time, no new words surfaced. *Perhaps even stones go to sleep eventually*, Casper thought. He sat down before the grate again and, shivering with cold and fear, he drew out his crumpled timetable. He had felt lonely back at Little Wallops at times, but that was nothing compared to being locked in the dungeons of a kingdom so far from home.

A tear trickled down his cheek, then a sinking dread

crept through him. Both Frostbite and the Grave Stones had talked about phoenix tears, and it did seem likely that the gemstone inside the clock key had been one—how else would he have come to be here?—but only now did Casper realize that this gemstone, the only thing that linked him to home, was still in Frostbite's possession.

Chapter 6

Utterly lay in her bed on the sixty-third floor of the castle. She listened to her mother mumbling in her sleep, but no matter how many times she tossed and turned, Utterly couldn't drift off. *Was it the excitement of the feast the next day?* she wondered. But somehow she didn't think so. Because where there should have been excitement, there was a tugging sort of feeling deep inside her belly that made her push back her quilt and sit up.

Utterly's whole family shared a bed, and had they lived in the Faraway, this might have been considered unfortunate. But in Rumblestar, it was quite the reverse. Because this bed was, in fact, a three-story bunk bed and instead of ordinary bunks there were three enormous four-poster beds carved from silver birch trees and built one on top of the other.

Utterly slept in the top bed, which was boxed in by billowing curtains spun from cloudwisp, and her parents slept in the bottom one, which was surrounded by velvet drapes. The middle bunk lay empty and had done so for three years, but, even so, every night Utterly paused on the ladder as she came to it and a longing inside her throbbed.

Each of the four trunks on Utterly's bed had a gold button with words carved into the wood below: **CALM**, **MOSTLY CALM** (WITH THE ODD BIT OF GIGGLING), **NOT VERY CALM** (EXPECT SUSTAINED PERIODS OF BREATHLESSNESS), and **HECTIC** (INVOLVES BUMPS AND JUMPS—NOT FOR THE FAINT-HEARTED).

They were dream choices, and although Utterly had broken with her tradition and selected **MOSTLY CALM** (WITH THE ODD BIT OF GIGGLING) to get a good night's sleep ahead of the feast, she had felt distinctly *un*calm since leaving Casper a few hours ago. She opened the shutters behind her bed to reveal a small circular window. Arlo, who slept inside an old knitted sock on Utterly's pillow and had done every night since he'd shown up at her window three years ago, opened one eye, and as Utterly peered out over the moat, the little dragon crawled up her hair and settled himself on the windowsill.

The stars were flickering over the kingdom, and the moonlight wrapped the clouds in silver. Utterly thought of her dad in his hot air balloon. A few days ago he had headed out for the mountains to the east of the kingdom, where the magical winds stirred, the ones that funneled down the Mixing Tower chimneys and nudged the marvels down all the pipes. No marvels grew in the Dusky Peaks, but by eavesdropping on her parents talking, Utterly had learned that her father had been sent there because this was a different sort of mission from ordinary ballooner work. Utterly's dad was among the most skilled ballooners in the kingdom and he had received a secret order from the Lofty Husks to investigate whether there was anything untoward going on with the magical winds that might taint the marvels when they poured into the Mixing Tower chimneys. And that was when Utterly had first suspected that perhaps the Lofty Husks were keeping things from the rest of the Unmappers.

It was no secret that the Lofty Husks were worried. Everyone in the Unmapped Kingdoms was frightened. Because even though Smudge and Bartholomew had stolen Morg's wings, a new phoenix hadn't risen from Everdark. Which could only mean one thing: Morg was still alive. And how long would it be before she found her wings and rose up out of Everdark?

No one had seen Smudge or Bartholomew since they stole

Morg's wings, and everyone knew harpies were greedy—notoriously so—and if Morg had stalled the rising of the next phoenix, it was because she wanted to steal every last scrap of Unmapped magic for herself. All the Lofty Husks and Unmappers lay in fear of this day—how could they not when with every year that passed, a little more of the Unmapped magic dried up? Crackledawn's water pixies were now extinct, Jungledrop's talking trees had stopped speaking, Silvercrag's glow-in-the-dark igloos hadn't glowed for decades, and here in Rumblestar the west wing of the castle had ceased its enchantments altogether—the coats of arms no longer told inappropriately scary ghost stories, the wallpaper no longer changed to suit your mood, and the tapestries hanging from the walls no longer led into hidden passageways.

Only a phoenix could fully restore all the lost magic, but the Unmappers had taken measures to try and protect the kingdoms from further harm and put an end to Morg. It was impossible to cross from one kingdom to another—only dragons carrying marvels could make such a journey—but the Lofty Husks in Rumblestar, Crackledawn, Jungledrop, and Silvercrag used their magical mirror rings to communicate with one another, and each kingdom had sent their best explorers to try to find

Everdark, the enchanted forest in a strange half-land between the Unmapped Kingdoms and the Faraway where every phoenix was rumored to be born. But every time, the boats and balloons returned from their voyages without success. Then there were the protection charms the Lofty Husks had conjured across the kingdoms to ward off evil, as well as the curfews and updated locks. And, earlier this evening, Blustersnap had made an announcement: There was to be a ban on ballooners roaming the skies in Rumblestar with immediate effect, and anyone currently out flying had been sent a message calling them back instantly. Even her dad, apparently. Which struck Utterly as odd because they'd only just sent him away, and if she really *had* captured the criminal who had been meddling with the marvels, then why were the Lofty Husks ramping up the precautions? Wasn't it time for a celebration? She had caught one of Morg's spies, after all.

Her mum hadn't seemed very convinced about the criminal when she told her. But then again, her mum hadn't seemed very enthusiastic about *anything* Utterly had to say since the . . . incident. She was all closed off and quiet now—nothing like she used to be. It felt to Utterly like her mum had given up on her, and even her dad seemed to look at her with sad, remembering eyes. So she had taken it upon herself to cause as much mayhem as possible until either she achieved something incredible that won her back the love and respect of her parents, or she achieved something outrageous that made someone, somewhere finally realize that deep, deep inside, she was falling apart.

Utterly gazed out into the dark and for a moment, she thought of another night—three years ago—filled with stars and comets and moonlight. A pain in her chest sharpened and tears burned behind her eyes, then she glanced at the dungeon tower and a familiar anger boiled inside her, drowning out everything else.

"Stupid criminal," she muttered.

But as she watched the dark shape huddled against the dungeon grate, she couldn't help feeling that capturing, arresting, and handing over the criminal hadn't felt quite as satisfying as she had expected. There had been Frostbite's slightly odd behavior, too. Why had he hidden Casper away from the other Lofty Husks? Utterly reached beneath her pillow and drew out the Neverlate note.

Busy capturing criminal

There it was, confirmation that she had done the right thing—that she had saved the marvels from further meddling—so why did she feel so unsure about it all? She folded the note up, but just as she was about to shove it back beneath her pillow, she noticed something: There was writing on *both* sides of the parchment. She gulped as she realized that she had only seen *half* of the tree's excuse earlier—and the full thing had *very* different implications.

Busy capturing criminal
creatures with Casper.
Back in a week or so.

Utterly gripped the note with shaking hands. The Neverlate Tree was one of the wisest magical creatures in the kingdom—she had heard the Lofty Husks talk of it giving messages to Unmappers when trouble was lurking—and trouble was most certainly lurking now: The marvels were in danger and, according to the note, there might even be *more* than one criminal skulking around the kingdom!

Utterly glanced out of the window again. The boy had said that his name was Casper. So the note implied that the person she had sent to the dungeons was in fact the very person she was meant to be capturing the criminal creatures *with*. . . . Utterly's skin tingled. A small part of her had wondered all along whether that timetable-clutching scaredy-cat could really be a criminal. But she had so wanted to make her parents proud and to be noticed by the Lofty Husks for the right reasons for once. Because maybe that would somehow undo what had happened . . .

Utterly reached for her dressing gown and bundled Arlo and a wrench into its pocket. Her mum hadn't given quite the reaction Utterly had been hoping for earlier, but then again Utterly hadn't quite captured the right person. So it seemed a journey beyond the castle walls to find the *real* criminals was the only thing to be done to make her mum and dad proud. But with Casper? He didn't seem a likely candidate for an adventure at all. *Still*, Utterly thought, *the Neverlate Tree doesn't lie, so perhaps Casper'll be good for something. Like bait for the criminal creatures, if things get really rough.*

She bent down toward her dressing gown pocket. "You know that boy that we thought was a criminal?"

Arlo poked his head up and blinked.

"Well, I think we should just quickly take another look at him."

Arlo covered his face with his wings. Utterly made it a rule never to admit defeat or apologize to anyone, but Arlo knew her inside out, so he could tell when she'd got herself into a pickle even if Utterly was adamant she hadn't. . . .

"I don't blame you entirely, Arlo," Utterly whispered. "I accept that a very small part of all this was my fault, too." She paused. "But now we've got a bit of sorting out to do. In the Beyond, I think. So I want your undivided attention."

Arlo thrust his snout into Utterly's hair and started chewing.

"Good." Utterly crawled over her bed toward the ladder. "Let's go."

Chapter 7

Casper stiffened at the sound of the footsteps pattering over the bridges. But these weren't the loping strides of a Lofty Husk; this was a small-footed scurry. Casper recoiled from the grate. What was coming for him now?

"Oi! Casper!"

Casper frowned. He recognized that voice, and as he edged back toward the grate, he saw a girl in a dressing gown standing on the bridge opposite the dungeon tower. A miniature blue dragon was hopping up and down on her shoulder.

"If you're hoping to watch me being eaten by dragons," Casper said miserably, "I think Frostbite has scheduled that for later tonight."

"Entertaining as that would be, that's not why I've come."

Utterly drew herself up. "After some careful thought, Arlo and I have come to the conclusion that—"

The bridge beneath her wobbled and Utterly clung to the stones as an enormous leg shaped from cloud stretched out, then crashed back down into the moat. Casper gasped, but Utterly simply rolled up her pajama bottoms, tied her dressing gown into a knot at the waist, then clambered off the bridge into the water.

"What are you doing?" Casper hissed.

"Rescuing you," Utterly snapped.

"Rescuing me? But you're the reason I'm locked up in the first place!"

Utterly maneuvered herself round a cloud giant's excessively large bottom, then waded on through the water. "Yes, well. That was an . . . oversight. Arlo's fault mostly." From her shoulder, Arlo let out an indignant squeak. "But we're here now to break you out and that's what matters."

Casper clutched the grate. "So you know I'm not a criminal?"

"Yes." Utterly hauled herself onto the stone walkway surrounding the dungeon. "After some further"—she paused as she searched for a convincing word—"calculations, Arlo and I decided you were innocent. And, well, there was also this"—Utterly pulled the note from her dressing gown pocket—"from a tree that never lies."

Casper shot a hand through the bars, snatched the note from the Neverlate Tree, and read it. "But—"

"So, you know what this means?" Utterly said breathlessly. "You and me—on an adventure beyond the castle walls to save Rumblestar and restore hope to those in the Faraway!"

She paused for effect and Casper looked suitably horrified.

"A week or so?" he spluttered. "But . . . my parents will be so worried! And . . . and . . . just think of how much homework I'll have to catch up on!"

Utterly grimaced. "You can't let *homework* stand in the way of an adventure! If Arlo's up for it, you should be too." Arlo scrambled to his feet and made a frantic beeline for Utterly's dressing gown pocket. "The Lofty Husks rule our kingdom and I know rules are there to be obeyed, but I also know that something is going on. My dad was sent on a secret mission to investigate the magical winds at the Dusky Peaks—which means the Lofty Husks *don't* think faulty pipework is the problem with the marvels, even if that's what they're telling us. And now there's a ban on ballooners flying anywhere and Mum told me Dad's coming home—which means the Lofty Husks don't think the winds are the problem, either! So, it *must* mean that they *do* now think someone or something is messing with the marvels, either in the Mixing Tower or outside the castle walls in the rivers, forests, and valleys where the marvels themselves are conjured." She lowered her voice. "And it's my bet Frostbite has something to do with all this. He's been acting strangely for the past few weeks: locking himself away in his study instead of teaching classes, whispering into his mirror ring far more than normal, and—"

"Knowing that I was from the Faraway," Casper said eagerly, "but for some reason lying to the other Lofty Husks and pretending I wasn't even there—then letting slip to me that he plans to tell the Lofty Husks that *you* were behind all the problems in the Mixing Tower . . ."

"ME?!" Utterly spluttered. "But . . . but . . . I was the one trying to help sort everything out—even if Arlo did go and arrest the wrong person." The dragon growled up at Utterly from her dressing gown pocket. "And why would I want to harm Rumblestar?"

Casper thought it best not to give the reason Frostbite had invented—that Utterly was always in some sort of trouble—because that was bound to end in him being throttled and at last he felt like he was almost getting somewhere. So instead he said: "There's more, Utterly. Frostbite asked me how I used the phoenix tear to cross the . . . link? He said I could be of help to someone he knew who wanted to find a way from Everdark to Rumblestar before severing the links between the Unmapped Kingdoms and the Faraway completely."

Arlo gasped and Utterly tucked herself into the shadows cast by the dungeon walls. "*Sever the links?* You're *sure* he said that?"

Casper nodded.

"There is only one creature who wants to rise up out of Everdark and sever the links between our world and yours." Utterly's voice was a trembling whisper now. "Morg. *She's* the reason everyone's so scared."

The shadows seemed to swell and into the darkness, Utterly told Casper about Smudge and Bartholomew stealing the harpy's wings in Everdark all those years ago. By the end of her tale, Arlo was shaking so violently Utterly lifted him into her palm and stroked his head.

"Our world *and* yours depend on a new phoenix rising and us Unmappers passing on its magic in the form of weather scrolls to the Faraway," Utterly whispered. "The dragons might be scattering moondust to keep the old magic going, but one day that will run out and we will be at the mercy of Morg and her dark magic! If she finds her wings and leaves Everdark, she will command the sun to scorch, the rain to unleash mighty storms, and the snow to cast the fiercest blizzards. . . . We'll all be doomed!"

Casper thought back to the mirror ring Frostbite had been wearing. "I . . . I saw something inside Frostbite's ring. Something dark and feathery with a skull for a head."

Utterly's face drained of color. "The Lofty Husks use their mirror rings to communicate with the rest of their kind in the other kingdoms. Only it seems Frostbite is using his to speak to—"

"—the harpy," Casper finished.

"Morg might not have found her wings yet, but somehow she's worked out how to twist someone from our kingdom into her control, someone who's now laying the blame at *my* feet! So does that mean Morg is planning to steal the magic in Rumblestar first?"

Casper was silent for a moment. "Could damaging the marvels break the link between Rumblestar and the other three kingdoms?"

Utterly nodded. "Marvels are only found here in Rumblestar, and the other kingdoms need them to write the weather scrolls. So if Frostbite is somehow damaging the marvels, then not only will the links between the kingdoms die but the Faraway will perish too." Arlo appeared to be on the brink of fainting now, so Utterly rocked him back and forth in her palm. Then she glanced at Casper warily. "Before this conversation, you didn't seem to believe anything I said, but suddenly it seems like you're not as freaked out by what's going on. How come?"

"I had a chat with the Grave Stones, who politely informed me that the only way I'd get home was if I believed all of this was really happening. So, I drew up an extremely detailed to-do list, made an even more detailed action plan, and now"—he took a deep breath—"I am setting events in motion." In reality, Casper had considered little more than his three-point to-do list, but saying all that to Utterly made him feel that he did, at least, have *some* control over the situation.

Utterly wrinkled her nose. "I suppose you want to save the Faraway and be crowned a hero?"

"Oh no. I could never be a hero," Casper replied. "I'm not brave enough. But the more I think about it, the more I realize someone needs to at least *try* to sort out the weather back home—and if what you're saying is true, my world won't exist soon if things carry on as they are here." He paused. "And if there's a chance that trying means seeing my parents sooner and checking that they're all right, I'll help—provided we get some sensible grown-ups to help us."

"Hmmmmm." Utterly tightened her dressing gown belt. "Well, I suppose it's good to know you put your dungeon time to practical use. But you can forget about the grown-ups."

"Couldn't we just tell the other Lofty Husks about Frostbite, though?" Casper asked. "They can sort it all out, then it's job done and I can go home."

"But by now Frostbite has probably told them all that *I'm* to blame for everything, so there's no way they'd listen to what we have to say!" Utterly scowled. "And besides, that's not what the Neverlate Tree told me to do. The note mentioned criminal creature*s*, as in more than one, and the two of us working together but nothing about telling the Lofty Husks or any other grown-ups for that matter." She pulled up her dressing gown hood. "It really does look like Frostbite is working for Morg, but it's our word against his, and the other Lofty Husks would never listen to us without proof. We need to be clever. We need to find out more about Frostbite, then capture *all* the criminal creatures lurking in the Beyond."

"The Beyond?" Casper asked nervously.

"The Beyond is everything outside the castle walls—all the mountains, rivers, forests, and valleys that make up the kingdom of Rumblestar."

Casper shuddered at the thought of so much outdoor space.

"The Neverlate Tree note says we'll be away for a week or so, so it has to be the Beyond we want; there'd be no point sniffing around inside the castle walls for days on end. But once we've found the criminals, put an end to them, and made sure the marvels are okay, I'll help you get home. I promise."

"But who knows what might happen at home while I'm gone if it's going to take us weeks to find the criminals!"

Utterly shook her head. "Time doesn't work the same way here as it does in the Faraway. It passes much, much more slowly for you. One day in your world is a month in the Unmapped Kingdoms—how else do you think we manage to complete the marveling process and write the weather scrolls in time for the dragons to deliver them at sunrise each day in the Faraway?"

Casper was silent for a moment. If time moved more slowly

back home, then perhaps his parents hadn't noticed he was gone yet and perhaps the afternoon was just as windless as it had been when he'd left. He held on to that thought as Utterly pointed to the lever on the dungeon wall.

"I'm afraid the Lofty Husks have hexed that lever so that only they can operate it."

Casper's face fell.

"But I've got a knack for picking locks. Even enchanted ones."

Utterly lifted the wrench out of her dressing gown pocket, slotted it either side of the lever, then began twizzling it this way and that. To Casper, there didn't seem any sort of method to what Utterly was doing, but he kept quiet just in case it worked.

Utterly had loosened the lever now, it seemed, and was twisting it round and round in circles. "Important to turn counterclockwise for this bit," she explained. "It's the only way to undo the magic."

After several minutes, there was, finally, a *crunch*, just like the one Casper had heard when Frostbite locked the grate earlier. He peered out through the bars eagerly.

"And now"—Utterly yanked down on the lever with her hand and the grate lifted up—"you're free."

Casper felt suddenly light and hopeful as he stepped out onto the stone walkway—but at exactly the same time a very tall, very narrow figure strode out from the castle.

Casper seized Utterly's arm. "Frostbite!"

Chapter 8

Frostbite's parchment cloak glittered in the moonlight, and despite the fact that there were many bridges between him and the dungeon tower, Casper knew that the Lofty Husk could bound over to them in moments.

"What do we do?" Casper hissed.

Utterly scanned the moat. "Swim toward the arches?"

"And take a chance on the sky-tumbling waterfalls?" Casper bit down on his blazer. "Any other ideas?"

On seeing the dungeon grate open, Frostbite lurched over the bridges toward them, and just as Casper was closing his eyes and wishing with every fiber of his body that he was back in Little Wallops, there was a noise—a yawn, it sounded like, only this yawn was deeper and louder than any Casper had ever heard before.

"Hold on!" Utterly cried, flattening herself against the dungeon wall. "One of the cloud giants is stirring!"

Casper clung to the stones, and just as Frostbite placed his boot on the bridge nearest the dungeon, the whole thing reared into the air. The Lofty Husk leapt back onto safer ground as the stones crashed into the water, and Casper felt sure that the whole castle would wake, but this was a kingdom used to the stirrings of cloud giants and they slept on as the colossal figure rose up from the rubble.

The giant was as large as the castle itself, with a mane of silver hair and knuckles the size of bowling balls. Its body had been carved from the clouds, and round the edges trails of mist unfurled. But this was not to say the giant wasn't solid. He was. He wore a silver breastplate decorated with ice-white patterns and an enormous belt buckled over his tassets. Casper swallowed. This giant was unmistakably armed. And only then did Casper notice that the air smelled suddenly different—of rain and thunder and very much of fear.

"It's Sl-Slumbergrot!" Utterly stammered.

And she shot back into the dungeons, dragging Casper with her. But the giant didn't turn his attention to the children. Instead it swung one arm toward Frostbite, who ducked just as the giant's fist careered over his head. For a moment it looked like Frostbite might retrace his steps and dash over another bridge toward Casper, but then Slumbergrot growled—a sound so low it might have come from the depths of a volcano—and thrust out his other fist toward the Lofty Husk.

Frostbite didn't look for a way toward Casper then. Instead he rushed back over the bridges, and just as Slumbergrot was about to close a fist around him, Frostbite flung himself through the nearest arch. Seconds later all that could be heard was the thrum of beating wings and then that too disappeared into the night and Slumbergrot turned to face Casper and Utterly.

The giant was not exactly pleasant to look at: He had a bulging nose, several missing teeth, and so many scars it was a wonder his face still hung together. But there was something wise about him. You could see it in his ears—which were big and raggedy where the mist unraveled from the tips and drifted into the night—the kind of ears that had listened to the very first moonrise and held the whisperings of a thousand secrets inside them.

Slumbergrot blinked and Casper jumped.

"I'm . . . I'm sorry we woke you up," Casper stuttered.

The giant said nothing. He simply stood silently before them, ribbons of mist trailing from his sides.

"Say you're sorry too," Casper said, elbowing Utterly. "Then maybe he won't eat us."

"Giants don't talk," Utterly hissed. "Everyone knows that. They just sleep and throw stuff and—"

"And what?" the giant asked.

Utterly froze. The giant's voice was even lower than his yawn and his growl, and both Utterly and Casper felt the ground beneath them shudder. Arlo clung to Utterly's hair as Slumbergrot spoke again.

"I am the first of my kind to speak for many, many years, but speak I must, for the kingdom is in grave danger and you are about to embark upon an adventure to save it."

Utterly's eyes shone in amazement while Casper's glazed over with fear. He stuck his hand in the air, as if asking for permission to speak in class. "I . . . I'm not ready for an adventure."

Slumbergrot's ears wiggled. "My boy, one is almost never ready for an adventure."

"But I like to be prepared," Casper went on. "For everything. I need to know whether to pack sunscreen and how many undershirts I'll need and where on earth I'll find toilet roll and—"

The giant cut in. "There is only one thing you need to pack for an adventure."

Casper wished that he had a notepad and a pen in hand. "Yes?"

"Courage."

"Oh," Casper said gloomily. "That doesn't bode well. . . ."

"And if, perchance, you have a little more room for one extra item, a sense of humor helps. Because adventures are unpredictable and often terribly badly behaved—a bit like pickled onions if you have ever tried to fork one on a plate—but they have a way of unlocking people and turning them upside down so that all the astonishing things fizzing around inside them start to tumble out."

"I really think you've got the wrong person for this," Casper replied. "I'm not even wearing shoes!"

"And yet, Casper, your name appeared on the note from the Neverlate Tree, did it not?"

"How do you know about that?" Utterly asked.

"My dear Utterly, giants know just about everything." Slumbergrot adjusted his breastplate. "But we can only stay awake for a limited amount of time—which has been inconvenient of late because there have been things I've heard that I've wanted to share—and no doubt you will have questions about what lies ahead. So ask away, children, before I fall back asleep."

"I really love your armor!" Utterly blurted. "Where did you get it from?"

Casper spun round. "He might go to sleep at any moment and you ask about armor?"

Utterly clapped a hand over her mouth, but Slumbergrot only smiled. "Frozen lightning," he said. "Forged in a sky cauldron by my great-great-great-great-great-great-great-great-great-great-great-great-great-great-great-great-grandmother. There is not a blade that can cut through this breastplate. Even fire does not stand a chance."

Slumbergrot sat down in the moat, sending water flying over the nearby towers, then he yawned and Casper hastily reached for another question. He wanted to ask if the giant knew a way for him to get home right away, but something about the way Slumbergrot looked at him—as if, possibly, Casper was a little more than just a small, unpopular boy who was afraid of almost everything—made him ask about the quest before them instead.

"Is Frostbite working for Morg?" he asked.

Slumbergrot nodded and wisps of cloud twirled from his hair into the dark. "Giant ears pick up on things that are not meant to be heard, and last night, because the creature *pretending* to be Frostbite was impatient and careless, I heard him"—he yawned again—"heard him . . ." And then to Casper and Utterly's horror the giant, while sitting bolt upright, began to snore.

"Heard him what?" Casper threw his hands in the air. "You can't just fall asleep mid-sentence! Only grandparents are allowed to do that!"

Utterly pulled Arlo out from her hair. "Please can you wake Slumbergrot up?"

Arlo curled into a ball—it was, after all, way past his bedtime—but when Utterly reached into her pocket and drew out a toffee, Arlo lifted his head and sniffed. Then he swallowed the toffee whole, fluttered over to Slumbergrot, and landed, with a burp, on the giant's nose.

Slumbergrot grunted and his large eyes opened. And then, as if he hadn't been asleep at all, he carried right on with his sentence. "—heard him talking to Morg. The Lofty Husks may use their mirror rings wisely, but the being imitating Frostbite is no Lofty Husk; he is a follower of Morg and he calls himself a Midnight. Morg is still trapped in Everdark, but somehow she has found a way to send these Midnights under her power into Rumblestar. Indeed, earlier today the Lofty Husks were sent word from the magical creatures in the Beyond, reporting sightings of unfamiliar winged beasts. The Midnight posing as Frostbite somehow found a way past the castle's protection charms and took on his disguise, but now I would wager that he has gone to join the rest of his kind and return to his true form. I hope its departure will lift the curse placed on the real Frostbite to keep him away, though where in Rumblestar the true Lofty Husk is I have no idea."

Slumbergrot stretched out his arms and Utterly could see that he was getting ready to sleep. "Have the Midnights been damaging the marvels?" she asked the giant.

Again, Slumbergrot nodded. "Somehow they have got their hands on a wind called shatterblast. When it blows, chaos follows—its bite is worse than fire and its breath lays waste to all in its path. The bottlers here at the castle assume only the benevolent winds—cometwhirl, starwisp, and moonbreeze—are funneling down the Mixing Tower chimneys, but really the Midnights are slipping shatterblast down there too, which is tainting the marvels and ruining the other kingdoms' weather scrolls. So *that* is why the winds in the Faraway are spiraling out of control."

Utterly huffed. "Nothing to do with me messing around in the Mixing Tower, as Frostbite will have told the Lofty Husks." She looked up at Slumbergrot. "So, how do we sort all this out?"

"To protect the marvels, you must destroy the Midnights, and to destroy the Midnights"—Slumbergrot looked up at the night sky, as if searching for something, then Casper felt a breeze rustle over the moat and saw the wind flit through the hairs hanging from the giant's ears—"you—Casper—must find a familiar face."

Casper squinted. "But . . . but that can't be right. It doesn't make any sense. I only just got here! I don't know anyone in Rumblestar!"

Slumbergrot waved his hand dismissively. "I am only passing on what the cometwhirl whispered to me a moment ago. And the winds are *never* wrong, my child."

Even Utterly was looking confused now. "Why am *I* the one helping Casper find a familiar face? I don't know who he knows!" She squinted. "Do you think that maybe the Neverlate Tree has made a mistake?"

Casper nodded. "I'm *definitely* here by mistake! It's not like I *want* to be in charge of saving all sorts of worlds!"

"Adventures happen to people who *need* them." Slumbergrot looked from Casper to Utterly. "Whether they *want* them or not is entirely beside the point."

"But . . . but that still doesn't answer how on *earth* I'm going to find a familiar face!" Casper stammered.

The giant yawned. "Seek out the drizzle hags who live along the Witch's Fingers; they have a way of unraveling the wind's secrets, so they might be able to tell you more." Slumbergrot laid his head down on his arms and made himself comfortable amongst the remains of the bridge. "The Lofty Husks will not believe you if you try to explain what has happened with Frostbite—even the wisest minds overlook children in a crisis, especially when they are being led to believe that the very problem lies with a child in the first place"—Utterly balled her fists—"and when I finally awake again, it will be too late, so you must take matters into your own hands. Immediately. Because if the Midnights are not stopped and the link between Rumblestar and the other kingdoms is severed, the Unmapped world *and* the Faraway will be in a great deal of trouble." Slumbergrot yawned again and closed his eyes. "And . . . on that sobering thought . . . I fear I am . . . falling . . . asleep."

"But how do we reach the drizzle hags?" Utterly cried. "The Witch's Fingers is a *very* long river!"

And possibly because he could still just hear the children in his sleep and was worried that the fate of the world lay in the hands of a shoeless boy and a girl in a dressing gown, Slumbergrot stretched in such a way that his hand fell, very conveniently, over the lock on the door of the tower next to him. Seconds later a wooden canoe bobbed out into the moat and Slumbergrot stretched one final time so that his hand once again brushed, very conveniently, against the door until it shut.

Utterly watched, riveted, as the canoe drifted toward them. "Ready for this, Casper? Because these things go seriously fast."

Chapter 9

Utterly leapt from the dungeon walkway into the canoe and landed with a thump between the two seats, which, to Casper's surprise weren't small and wooden, like the ones in the canoe his dad had once been asked to mend for the sports department at Little Wallops, but full-blown armchairs.

Casper wrung his hands as Utterly maneuvered herself into the first one by the bow, settled Arlo on top of an old suitcase at her feet, then seized a paddle and glared at Casper.

"Coming?"

Casper stood, rooted to the ground. Where was the health and safety briefing? Where was the instruction manual? And where on earth was the map to find the drizzle hags?

"What are you waiting for?" Utterly snapped. "We need

the night to get away unseen because who knows where that Midnight pretending to be Frostbite is, and if the Lofty Husks find me and lock me up, there'll be no one left to save your world and mine! We need to get going *now*."

"I'm not sure about this at all. Is this canoe even safe to travel in? And I'm worried about the drizzle hags," Casper added. "Are they very, very dangerous?"

Utterly shrugged. "If I worried about every single thing I wasn't sure of, I'd never do anything at all." She paddled the canoe up to the dungeon. "Sometimes it's best just to get on with things and hope for the best."

"But what if *the best* turns out to be a total disaster? I really think that maybe we should be a bit more organized about—"

"Will you just get *in* the canoe?"

Wincing, Casper stretched out a leg, hooked it over the side of the boat, then slid into the armchair behind Utterly. It was more comfortable than sitting on the dungeon floor but more alarming, too—what kind of canoe had armchairs in it? He glanced about him to find that there were racks of books lining the sides of the boat: *How to Fly Through Lightning (A Ballooner's Manual)* by Ethelred Frazzle, *The Big Decision: Bottler or Ballooner?* by Whoopsy Ditherlot, *Handling Magical Winds* by Delilah Slippergrip.

Utterly chucked a paddle to Casper. "The fact that you're from the Faraway is a bit of a worry, I must admit; it means you don't have the slightest grasp on magical things." She pushed the canoe off from the dungeon. "You haven't got any secret skills, by any chance? You can't turn invisible? Conjure up ice? Fly?"

Casper dug a shaking oar into the water. "No. Can you?"

"No. But I'm outrageously good at engineering, as you saw earlier when you were stuck in the dungeons. I can pick locks, take stuff apart, fix things, and build almost anything. What are you good at?"

Casper thought about it. "I . . . am never, ever late."

"Well, let's hope the drizzle hags are sticklers for timekeeping, then," Utterly muttered.

They drifted between the towers in the moat, then the wall came into view. Casper tried to rack his brain for what he'd seen out west beyond the arches, but all he could think about were the sky-tumbling waterfalls.

"As you may remember when you were posing as a criminal," Utterly said matter-of-factly, "most of the water sails through the arches and just carries on falling. I suppose it lands in the Boundless Seas eventually, but some of it flows on into a river known as the Witch's Fingers. And *that's* where we're heading."

"So, you've done this before?" Casper asked hopefully.

"Well, no." Utterly paused. "Under-sixteens aren't strictly allowed out into the Beyond without a grown-up, but we don't have time to worry about rules and chaperones." Utterly lifted her paddle out of the water and frowned. "Do you think we're meant to be moving quite so fast?"

Casper clutched the paddle to his chest as the current picked up even more speed and they charged toward the wall. "I thought you were in control?"

Utterly raised an eyebrow. "I am never in control, Casper. That's what makes me so exciting to be around."

"But you do know which arch we need to go through to avoid the sky-tumbling waterfalls, right?"

Utterly glanced from one arch to the next. The canoe was just meters away from them now, and at the realization Arlo started wheezing in panic. Then, just as they were about to glide through one of the larger arches, Utterly stuck her paddle into the water and the canoe swerved course.

"Hold on to the sides!" she yelled as the boat shot through a smaller arch.

For a second the canoe seemed to hang in the air, then it plunged down, down, down. Casper's heart thumped and his stomach swung to his throat but they didn't keep on falling, as Casper feared they might. The canoe smacked to a halt, water gushed over the sides, and mist sprayed around them. Casper's ears filled with the thunderous roar of the waterfall they'd just careered off, and, digging their paddles into the water, he and Utterly pushed away from the churn.

"That was amazing!" Utterly shrieked, wiping the water from her face.

"We could've drowned!" Casper panted.

Utterly sighed. "Having secret gills like the Unmappers in Crackledawn do when they eat a watergum would certainly be an advantage when attempting that kind of a maneuver—in fact, I bet Smudge ate a ton of watergums before she set out across the seas after Morg—but I thought we did pretty well, considering."

Casper tried to console himself with the fact that other than the starlight on her cheeks and her unforgivable temper, Utterly wasn't *so* different from the people in his world. Gills and watergums, on the other hand, sounded altogether terrifying, so he tried his best not to dwell on them. "You said the moat *flows on into a river*," Casper snapped as he wrung out his blazer. "That was hardly *flowing on*. . . ."

Utterly waved her hand. "It's hard to get your bearings when you're traveling so brilliantly fast." She patted Arlo on the back; he choked up a puddle of water, then was offered three toffees from Utterly's dressing gown pocket—which he accepted—to make up for the ordeal. "Still, I picked the right arch, in the end. Now we're properly on our way!"

Casper looked around him for any sign of a Midnight as they drifted downstream, but without knowing exactly what these Midnights *were*, other than that they might have wings, Casper wasn't really sure quite what he was looking for. There didn't seem anything untoward in their surroundings. Weeping willows lined the riverbanks, their leaves silver-blue in the moonlight, and past them there seemed to be more trees, large twisting trunks that might have been the start of a forest.

In the distance, Casper saw a collection of peaks, dark pointed shapes against the starlit sky. He shuddered. The Beyond looked vast and unorganized and dangerous; there were no doors or walls or grown-ups to hold it all together. Out here anything could happen. And, though currently Casper couldn't *see* any terrifying beasts crashing through the undergrowth, he could *feel* a sense of unease hovering in the air, as if Rumblestar itself knew that the link between it and the other kingdoms was hanging by a thread.

It was only when Casper looked up at the moon that he realized it was raining. The droplets were so fine it was almost like watching dust fall, but because of the moonlight, the rain was diamond-bright. Casper made it a rule to stay clear of rain back home; what with the skidding and the slipping and the umbrella spokes in people's eyes, the risks surrounding rain were hideously high. And as he looked at it now, he grimaced. Everything felt dangerous enough already—the Edge was probably beyond the forest and Certain Death was undoubtedly beyond that—but rain made things worse because it brought with it the risk of flash floods and impromptu drowning. Casper shivered inside his blazer.

Utterly, though, turned her head up to the rain and let the drops land on her tongue. "Every place in Rumblestar is responsible for a different type of marvel. In Shiverbark Forest it snows all year round, at Dapplemere it's non-stop sunshine, at the Smoking Chimneys there are tons of storms (though we don't bother collecting marvels there as not much good comes from gale-force winds and sheet lightning), and along the Witch's Fingers, it rains." Utterly stuck out a hand to catch the droplets. "Isn't it glorious?"

Casper flicked the water off his blazer. "No. I wish it would stop."

"It's ungrateful to complain about the rain when the drizzle hags spend hours conjuring it," Utterly replied sharply. "And that's only the start of the process. Ballooners then catch the rain marvels in spidersilk nets, bottlers blend them with benevolent winds before packaging them up in bottles for the dragons to carry to Jungledrop. Then the Unmappers there make ink with the marvels so that they can paint the rain scrolls, which the dragons take on to the Faraway." She paused. "Same thing happens before *you* get *your* sunlight and snow, only the Unmappers in Crackledawn use their ink to write musical symphonies onto the sun scrolls and the Unmappers in Silvercrag write stories. But the paintings, symphonies, and stories are all weather scrolls for *your* world, so *you* could try being a bit more *grateful* for the rain and everything else that falls from the sky!"

Casper was having trouble letting all this talk of marvels and magical scrolls override the scientific facts about weather he'd learned back home. "How come *I've* never seen a weather scroll?" he asked.

"Because dragons are clever and secretive, so they leave them in the overlooked corners of your world—like cracks in the wall, hollows of trees, and deep inside caves—then, just as you are waking up, the scrolls vanish into thin air, leaving you your weather for the day."

Casper thought about all this happening without the people in his world knowing a thing. "I know you said the magic here has to be shared with my world otherwise it turns bad, but four kingdoms' worth of Unmappers working away to create weather for us—what do *you* all get in return? Money or something?"

"Money?!" Utterly spluttered, then she threw back her head and laughed. "We get to live in a kingdom filled with magic, Casper—dream choices on our bedposts, exploding gobstoppers in our banqueting halls, skies full of dragons—and the wonder and joy of all *that* counts for more than any money ever could."

Casper wondered what Candida and Leopold would have to say about money coming second to wonder and joy. He straightened himself up. The key to keeping sane in Rumblestar, Casper decided, was probably allowing himself to believe a few impossible things every hour. So to manage the extraordinary statements that Utterly kept coming out with, Casper conjured up a timetable in his head for just that; Utterly's explanations about the weather scrolls could sink in from now until sunrise, then he'd brace himself for the next hurdle. And to balance all that out, he would also spend an equal amount of time focusing on the task ahead as the impossible things. Most importantly, he needed to work out who the familiar face was that he was meant to find. Could either of his parents have followed him into Rumblestar through the grandfather clock? Or Candida? He shuddered at the thought, then he realized that the Midnights—whatever they were—would be a far worse threat than a girl with a love of custard creams.

"What kind of winged creatures do you think the Midnights are?" Casper asked quietly.

"Won't be dragons," Utterly replied. "They never bend to the command of dark magic. And definitely not unicorns—they're an endangered species and far too responsible to get mixed up with Morg. Maybe manticores?"

At the word, Arlo choked on his toffee.

"Manti-*whats*?" Casper asked, although he was almost afraid of the answer.

"Manticores. Tail of a scorpion, body of a lion, bat-like wings, and shark teeth."

Casper swallowed several times. The thought of being dragged into Everdark by a manticore was almost enough to make him cry there and then. He swiveled in his armchair to check their surroundings again and his eyes caught on dozens of lights burning in the sky around the castle. They weren't stars—these were brighter and bigger somehow—and they were moving.

"What are those?" Casper whispered.

Utterly spun around, and Casper could tell then that behind all the bravado there was a girl just as frightened as him. Utterly peered out through her maze of hair, then she breathed a sigh of relief.

"Good job we left when we did. Those are ballooners returning to the castle on the Lofty Husks' orders. Their hot air balloons are powered by dragon fire and that's what you can see burning."

Casper tried not to dwell on the fact that experienced ballooners were abandoning the Beyond and here he, Utterly, and Arlo were sailing out *into* it. "How old do you have to be to fly a balloon?" he asked instead.

"When you're ten, you decide whether you want to be a bottler or a ballooner—or, if you want something with a bit less pressure, there are castle jobs too, like running the kingdom's newspaper, researching spells in the library, and liaising with the magical creatures who come to stay. But with bottlers and ballooners, it's a lot of classes with the Lofty Husks—and far too much homework—then you qualify at the age of eighteen. And that's when you can start flying balloons solo or manning all the incredible machines inside the Mixing Tower." Utterly's eyes lit up. "There are cauldrons the size of cars, chimneys so long and twisting it takes the wind days to travel down them, and bottles every possible shape and size you can imagine. I once saw one the shape of a pineapple."

"And before you're ten years old," Casper asked, "what do you do then?"

"Explore the castle and have fun, really. There are go-karts on the twenty-third floor, haunted turrets, a vanishing library (it appears on a different floor every week), and apparently there's even an ice rink somewhere, though I've never found it." She paused. "But maybe that's because it's in the west wing and no one goes there anymore because all the magic's dried up." She looked at Casper. "What do you lot do before you're ten?"

Casper considered. “Spelling tests, mostly.”

Utterly grimaced, then she settled Arlo into her lap, lifted her wrench from her pocket and began using it to twist all the nuts and bolts that scored the length of the suitcase in front of her. A minute later, the suitcase sprang open.

“Told you I was great at unlocking things,” she said smugly. “That would’ve taken my classmates *ages*.”

Utterly drew out the only two objects inside the suitcase: an old-fashioned telephone with a round dial and a notepad.

“Are you calling a grown-up?” Casper asked hopefully.

Utterly looked horrified. “No, I am most certainly not.”

Then Casper realized that actually there was no hope of calling anyone because the telephone wasn’t even connected to any sort of wiring. “Would’ve been helpful if the suitcase contained a *working* telephone.”

“It’s not a suitcase,” Utterly replied. “It’s a just-in-case. And it’s *incredibly* helpful, actually.”

She opened the notepad and over her shoulder Casper read the following words:

For food, whisper a secret

For drinks, share a memory

For dry clothes, state the time (and your size)
For scented candles, decorative pot plants, side lamps, and other furnishings, crack a joke

Utterly closed the just-in-case, but Casper saw that she didn't bolt it all up again. She squinted at the sky, then lifted the handset and said: "The time is seven stars past moonrise. And we're eleven-year-old sized. Bigger than sun scamps but smaller than snow trolls."

There was silence on the other end of the line. Utterly hung up.

"That went well," Casper muttered.

And it turned out it did. Because when Utterly knocked three times on the just-in-case, then lifted the lid again, a jumble of clothes that definitely hadn't been there before—duffel coats, overalls, woolly sweaters, boots, and a tiny knitted waistcoat for Arlo—lay inside.

Casper was too stunned to speak, so he just accepted the dry clothes Utterly chucked at him and put them on. It felt strange peeling off his blazer and slipping into overalls. Even outside school hours Casper liked to keep his blazer on; it made the gap between childhood and adulthood a little less depressing.

Utterly buttoned up her duffel coat, then slumped into her armchair. "I suppose when the Lofty Husks realize I'm not in the castle, they'll assume I've run away out of guilt because I meddled with the marvels."

"But when they discover Frostbite has gone, they'll know there's more to it, won't they?"

Utterly shrugged. "I don't exactly have a good track record with behavior, Casper. They'll probably think Frostbite has left, out of concern, to bring me home."

"But when Frostbite doesn't come back and doesn't message and seems to have vanished altogether, then the Lofty Husks will know that something's afoot and that you're innocent." Casper's eyes lit up. "And then they'll rush out to help us."

"Or tell us off." Utterly turned away. "We should get some sleep. It won't be long before the Midnight pretending to be Frostbite has reported back to his demon pals and the whole lot of them are on our tail." She propped Arlo up on the bow of the canoe. "Wake us at the first sign of any danger."

The dragon straightened his knitwear, then looked out over the river.

Casper bit his lip. "How will Arlo know what to look for?"

"Arlo is extremely clever, so if the slightest danger comes our way, he'll let us know."

Casper watched despairingly as Arlo scampered round in a circle, chasing his own tail. "I think I'd feel better about the whole situation if I wrote a to-do list out, so please can you ask the just-in-case for a pen and paper?"

"Why do you need to write a to-do list?" Utterly said, baffled. "Isn't it obvious what we've got to do? Find the drizzle hags and ask them where in the kingdom you'll find a familiar face."

Casper shifted in his seat. "Yes, but there are several other things on our agenda—"

"What's an agenda?"

"Like a plan."

"Can't we just wing it?"

Casper quivered at the thought. "We should be writing the things we've got to do down so we don't forget them. Things like, sorting out accommodation, sourcing multivitamins and hand sanitizers . . . buying umbrellas . . ."

Utterly considered. "You're right about the umbrellas, Casper. No point being in dry clothes if we're out in the rain, but no need to *buy* them."

She rummaged beneath her armchair. There was a *click*, and a metal rod shot out the back of her seat and opened above her as an umbrella. Casper peered beneath his own armchair to find three labeled buttons:

SWIFT EXIT

SHELTER

SLEEP

He guessed Utterly must have pressed SHELTER, and although he was tempted by SWIFT EXIT, he wasn't altogether convinced that would get him back to Little Wallops, so he pressed SHELTER to activate an umbrella of his own and then SLEEP, which made his armchair recline a little and begin a gentle massage that seemed to dry the fabric as the chair moved. But Casper found that he was too hungry to sleep—lunch in the dining room back in Little Wallops seemed a long, long time ago.

"We need to dial in for some food, Utterly."

There was a snort from the armchair in front. "You should've eaten at the castle instead of messing around in the dungeons. Canoe food is only to be used in an emergency."

Utterly rooted through her discarded dressing gown, pulled out a toffee, and lobbed it back to Casper. Casper briefly considered launching over Utterly to make a grab for the telephone himself, but then he calculated the risks involved and settled for the toffee instead. He closed his eyes and thought about his parents—he missed them more than he would have ever thought possible—and while the canoe sailed on down the Witch's Fingers, farther and farther into the Beyond, Casper did, finally, drift off to sleep.

Chapter 10

But past the Edge and across the Boundless Seas, in the heart of a tangled forest, there was somebody who was very much awake. Not a magical firefly—the last of those had left Everdark many years ago. Not a diamond tree—the forest no longer shone at night. And not a silver panther—they were all long gone.

No, only the harpy named Morg remained in Everdark, and now she was clawing her way out of a nest draped in cobwebs. Her talons were cracked, her body was gray and shrunken—only a few feathers still hung from her puckered skin—and her wingless arms drooped either side of the pointed skull she wore over her head.

She dragged herself down through the branches, stumbled across the clearing, and drew her hunched body up in front of a tree that held a dozen doors carved into its trunk. Morg reached out a spindly hand toward the one that bore a plaque reading TO FINAL ENDINGS and held her precious wings, but no matter how many times she clawed at the handle, it wouldn't open. It never did.

But every night Morg visited the tree because although the girl, Smudge, and her wretched monkey had trapped the harpy in the forest, Morg was slowly gaining strength, and while she couldn't reach her wings, she had worked out a way to summon the feathers from her wings to life as followers—her Midnights. Morg couldn't beckon the creatures out into Everdark because the door in the tree was hexed shut, but she had commanded her followers to find *another* door, one that might lead on to the Unmapped Kingdoms. And, in the last few weeks, they had. . . .

Morg wanted nothing more than to find a way through this door so that she could follow her Midnights out into Rumblestar, but no way opened up for her, so through the tiniest of cracks in the door TO FINAL ENDINGS, the Midnights updated Morg on their progress.

The harpy listened eagerly as they spoke of wreaking havoc with Rumblestar's marvels tonight, but at the news that a boy from the Faraway had found his way into this kingdom, Morg cackled in delight. Because here, suddenly, was someone who could cross the links between worlds and kingdoms, someone who could free her from Everdark and lead her into Rumblestar!

The harpy pressed her cracked lips up to the hole in the door. "Bring me the boy from the Faraway, but do not turn your back on the marvels. Ruin them, every last one, because when I join *you* in Rumblestar, I want the kingdom on its knees so I can steal all its magic and begin my rule."

For a moment there was silence and Morg looked at the door with haunted eyes, then there was a fluttering, whirring, whirling sound inside the tree and the harpy's fingers twitched. Next came a scratching of talons and claws and a high-pitched screech, then that din faded, too, and only a quiet ticking—like that of a clock—ate into the silence.

But at this, Morg smiled. The Midnights were stirring inside the tree and soon they would be tearing through Rumblestar again.

"Fly forth, my winged ones," Morg screeched. "Fly forth."

Chapter 11

Casper woke to a short, sharp jab in the stomach. His eyes shot open. Was the canoe crawling with Midnights? Were they being ambushed by drizzle hags?

It was neither of these things. Utterly had twisted round in her seat and she was wielding a paddle like some sort of spear to poke at Casper. And although he could think of many more restful ways to be woken up than having an oar rammed into his intestines, Casper was glad of Utterly's presence. It was not because of the conversation (she was far too fierce to say anything sensible). And it was not because he harbored any sort of hope that they might become friends (their spending time together was purely practical). But her being there, along with Arlo, meant Casper felt ever so slightly less alone.

For a moment, as his brain cleared the fog of sleep, Casper thought of his parents and prayed hard that they were both still safe from the winds. Then he turned his attention to Arlo, who, true to Utterly's word, was still faithfully watching the river for danger.

It was a cloudy morning and the rain was pattering onto the umbrellas. There were no longer weeping willows lining the river; instead reeds and rushes grew alongside it and now and again a flash of fur or feathers could be seen between the foliage. The animals, it seemed, were on edge, and though they tried their best to stay hidden, Casper glimpsed a kingfisher tucked under a branch and blinking at the front page of a tiny newspaper, a cluster of ducks hiding in the reeds dressed in miniature wellington boots, and a heron wearing spectacles as it poked its head up above the reeds and then vanished from sight.

Utterly followed Casper's gaze. "The animals here can't talk, but they're pretty civilized, unlike the magical creatures who jabber away but are often far from polite."

Casper shrank into his duffel coat at the mention of magical creatures. He looked around him. This was the first time he had ever woken up outside, and the absence of walls, doors, and alarm clocks made his pulse skitter.

Utterly reached inside the just-in-case for the telephone and, after whispering a secret into it (Casper caught the words "banana skin," "Lofty Husk," and "unconscious"), Utterly closed the case, knocked three times on it, then pulled out a piping-hot breakfast.

Casper crossed his arms. "So, *this* is an emergency, is it?"

"No," Utterly replied. "But missing breakfast would be. It's the most important meal of the day, according to my mum, so although she'll be furious with me for supposedly messing up the marvels and running away, at least I'll be able to tell her I ate breakfast if the Lofty Husks come for us and we're dragged back to the castle."

Utterly pulled out two plates piled high with scrambled eggs, buttered toast, crispy bacon, and sausages, then after sharing a memory with the just-in-case (something about handling cometwhirl in the Mixing Tower for the first time) and taking out two freshly squeezed orange juices, she and Casper ate breakfast.

"Best to keep a low profile when passing these rushes," Utterly said through a mouthful of food. "I've only been to these parts once, on a field trip, though sadly things look a lot less magical around here than they did last year—the reeds used to play music when the wind stirred, and there were stepping stones that made you laugh when you trod on them. The boy I was partnered with ended up being held captive by a jailbird for an entire day. It wasn't *technically* my fault, but then again I don't suppose the jailbird would've left its nest if I hadn't hollered at it." She looked back at Casper. "They're incredibly vain, so if you end up catching a jailbird's eye, pay it a compliment, then you'll be fine. I learned that trick *after* Rudi got captured."

Casper scanned the reeds. "What's a jailbird and does it have claws?"

"They're a bit like swans, but angrier and more antisocial—they hate being disturbed. And yes to claws. Big ones, I'm afraid."

Utterly bundled their empty plates and glasses into the just-in-case, then raised a finger to her lips and pointed to the rushes ahead. They were taller now and they didn't just line the banks of the river but rather grew in clumps across the water, channeling it into narrow passageways. And there were nests scattered amongst these rushes. The kind of nests herons might sit on. Only the birds that sat on these nests were most definitely not herons.

They were larger—much larger—with white, scooped

necks and wings made from shards of mirror instead of feathers. And every single one of them was gazing at his or her reflection in their wings.

Arlo buried his head beneath his waistcoat and Casper tried to keep focused on dipping his paddle in and out of the water as the boat slipped between the rushes, but when the jailbirds began to call to one another—low, hollow hoots—he couldn't help glancing up. His eyes met with the shining eyeball of a jailbird on a nest just past the end of his paddle. It hissed at him.

"Pay it a compliment," Utterly whispered. "Quick!"

"You . . . you have a lovely beak!" Casper stammered.

The jailbird hissed again, but it didn't move. It stayed exactly where it was, eyes narrowing at Casper and Utterly. Then, just when Casper was thinking perhaps he'd got away with it, there was a chinking sound as the jailbird ruffled its mirror wings and soared up into the sky.

"Another compliment!" Utterly cried, cowering beneath her umbrella. "It's getting ready to dive!"

But the jailbird didn't dive straight away. It circled high in the sky, then let out another low hoot. At its call the rest of the jailbirds shot off their nests and flew up into the sky.

Arlo squeaked in terror at the whirl of glinting mirrors,

then frantically began trying to puff flames from his nostrils—to no avail—because he knew, as well as Utterly and Casper, that no amount of flattery could keep them safe now.

"They must be *really* mad if the whole flock have left their nests!" Utterly gasped. "I've never seen that happen before!"

"What do we do?" Casper yelled as the jailbirds wheeled above them.

"If we press the SWIFT EXIT button under our seats, we might lose the canoe!" Utterly shouted.

The jailbirds tucked in their wings and plunged down toward the boat. Utterly snapped the umbrellas shut, tossed one paddle to Casper, and held the other up with shaking hands.

"We're just going to bash them with our paddles?" Casper screamed.

The jailbirds tore through the sky and then, when they were only meters away from the canoe, they spread their wings, stalling their descent, before forming a ring around the boat and spinning round to face upriver.

"What . . . what are they doing?" Casper stammered.

And then his face paled. Because as the jailbirds hovered around the canoe, a reflection appeared in their mirrored feathers:

a dark, winged shape growing larger and larger by the second. Utterly had seen it too and she and Casper whirled round.

Then they realized the reason that *all* the jailbirds had left their nests at once was because the one that Casper had angered had seen something as it circled in the sky and it had called down to the rest of its kind because it knew where the real fight lay—not against two children disturbing their peace but against an unfamiliar beast advancing toward them.

The creature had jagged wings, shining talons, and the body and tail of a lion. This was a griffin, Casper knew that much from books of myths he'd read, but its wings and coat were so black it was as if the very darkest parts of the ocean had been stitched together to make it. And as it flew toward them, at speed, the air turned suddenly hot.

Not just *a griffin*, thought Casper. *A Midnight come to drag him into Everdark to face Morg!*

Utterly scrambled out of her seat and pulled Casper down into the body of the canoe with her and Arlo. "Keep as low as you can!" she cried. "And trust in the jailbirds' wings!"

Casper flattened himself to the bottom of the canoe as the Midnight hurtled closer, its yellow eyes glowering. It stretched out its talons and Casper watched in horror as it yanked the first two jailbirds out of its way before plowing on through two more and thumping a claw down onto the stern of the canoe. The boat jerked to a halt.

"Get to the bow with me!" Utterly shouted to Casper.

Casper launched himself toward Utterly as the Midnight clambered over his armchair and then, just at the moment it opened its terrible beak and the air turned even hotter still, until even breathing felt hard, it slid upward as if pulled into the sky by some strong but invisible force.

"What's happening?" Casper panted.

"The jailbirds' wings," Utterly gasped. "They're working their magic!"

A blinding white light flooded from the birds' wings, dragging the snarling Midnight closer and closer toward them until suddenly the griffin was screeching before the mirrors of the largest jailbird. The light flashed and Casper watched, open-mouthed, as the midnight was sucked into its mirrors until it vanished from sight and the only clue that it had been there at all was that the wings of the largest jailbird had turned completely black.

Casper staggered to his feet. "The Midnight . . . it's gone!"

Arlo lay on the bottom of the boat panting while Utterly sat back down shakily in her armchair and Casper followed suit.

"Trapped in the wings," Utterly replied, "but not gone—a jailbird's prison doesn't last forever. Tomorrow that Midnight will be on the loose again. We were lucky it didn't carry you off to meet Morg."

The jailbirds sank to their nests and Casper shivered as he took in the one with black wings. The Midnight had been even worse than he had expected, and he knew that Utterly had been just as rattled by it because she was unusually quiet now. They took up their paddles again and whispered as many compliments as they could think of to the jailbirds they passed before sailing on through the rushes until the nests petered out.

Eventually the river widened and the rushes gave way to blossom trees. There were hundreds of them, their branches so full of bloom the water itself had turned white from their reflection, and to Casper it seemed like paddling through milk.

"I've never been this far west," Utterly said quietly. "It's Beyond the Boundary for Safekeeping. It's beautiful here!"

Casper shuddered. Utterly was trying her best not to mention the Midnight, but his mind was swimming with yellow eyes and black feathers and all he could think about were the risks ahead. *What if there was another Midnight lurking in the trees nearby? What if it attacked and there was no one around to help them? What if it managed to haul him into Everdark, then somehow Morg used him to cross the links into the Unmapped Kingdoms?*

"The Midnight was terrible," he said finally. "Like something out of a nightmare. And I got the strangest feeling when it opened its mouth, as if the air around us was growing hotter and hotter—at one point I could barely breathe!"

The rain fell harder, hammering onto the umbrellas and denting the river.

"You were probably so scared you were just sweating more than normal." Utterly sniffed. "It's time to stop being a wimp."

But Casper could tell from the way Arlo was still nuzzling into her hair that Utterly was shaken too.

Maybe even brave people feel a little bit wimpish sometimes, Casper thought.

The canoe trundled on through blossom trees surrounded by bluebells and wild garlic and eventually the rain eased until it was merely spitting.

"Why is the river called the Witch's Fingers?" Casper asked after a while.

"Because witches only have three fingers and the river breaks into three tributaries. But I don't think that happens for miles yet."

She tickled Arlo as the river bent left, then widened.

Casper squinted downstream. There were rapids ahead and past them, the river seemed to fork into three gushing tributaries. He tapped Utterly on the shoulder, then pointed. "Umm . . . is that the river splitting?"

"Don't be daft. That's just a few rocks breaking things up; the river will join again shortly afterward."

Casper craned his neck to get a better view and his heart started to thump. "But if it all joins up, then why is there a signpost wedged into the rock in the middle of the river just before the fork?"

Utterly peered closer then, her eyes widening as she took in the signpost. Three signs fanned out from it, each one pointing to a different tributary:

HERE

THERE

ANYWHERE

Utterly grimaced. "Now would be an *excellent* time to make a swift decision on where we go next, Casper."

"But . . ." Casper gulped as the canoe charged on into the rapids. "There's no sign for the drizzle hags! They could be anywhere!"

"Good thinking!" Utterly cried as the canoe clipped a rock and veered onto one side. "We'll go for Anywhere!"

Before Casper could reply, Utterly dug her oar into the water and the canoe swerved past the signpost, then bumped down the rapids toward **ANYWHERE**, sending Arlo head-over-heels into Utterly's shin.

"We need a map and a compass!" Casper spluttered.

The boat sped on down the river and Utterly scrabbled around beneath her seat. "Here, have a soggy toffee instead."

Casper scowled as they continued downstream past a meadow full of poppies. Then there was a plop as something white and soggy landed in the canoe. It was a paper airplane and on seeing it Utterly cringed. "Mum's clearly realized I'm nowhere in the castle. . . ." She picked it up. "I'm all for wireless communication, but now the whole kingdom has SkyFly, there's no getting away from parents. I like hearing from Dad—it's kind of cool that even though he's a ballooner and he's out in his hot air balloon catching marvels most days he can just whisper a message into a piece of paper and it shows up, via paper airplane, wherever I am a few hours later—but Mum's messages are always so"—she paused—"grumpy—and this one'll be no exception."

She opened the paper and read the words aloud:

"My darling Utterly,
I'm worried sick about you.
Wherever you are in the Beyond, please, please come back."

For a moment Utterly's face softened. There was no mention of her being the criminal behind all the troubles with the marvels. Then she read on and a hardness Casper was growing to recognize closed around her.

"This morning the Lofty Husks revealed the news we've been living in fear of: Morg is growing in power and her followers have found a way into Rumblestar. Unfamiliar beasts have been reported out in the Beyond, Frostbite has disappeared, and the castle is in lockdown. We have an emergency supply of marvels so nobody needs to be outside the castle walls. Least of all you, whatever you might have done in the Mixing Tower before you left. We know you, Utterly, and we know

that you wouldn't have meant to cause the kingdom harm. Come back home. Your father and I love you dearly, despite everything, but you cannot fix what you have started—only the Lofty Husks can—and you cannot fix the past.

"Mum

"PS I hope you have had breakfast today."

Utterly's words grew quieter as she reached the end of the note, and as she finished reading, she scrunched up the paper and hurled it behind her. "What I have started indeed," she spat.

But Casper caught the note, unbeknown to Utterly, and pressed it open in his lap. "What did your mum mean by fixing the—"

Utterly cut across him. "It sounds like if we don't find this familiar face *fast*, your world and mine are both done for."

Casper looked at the note again. There were things Utterly wasn't telling him. "Something happened, didn't it? Something bad—"

Utterly's eyes flashed. "Shut it or I'll throw you overboard."

Casper stared at the note, then, very quietly, he said: "Shouldn't we send a message back to your mum telling her you're okay—and innocent?!"

"We're in a race against time, Casper. Not a letter-writing club. I need to show everyone back at the castle that I'm innocent by getting on and saving the kingdom myself!"

But Casper was determined to approach this quest as systematically as possible, whatever Utterly's pride had to say. He knew there was no point messaging the Lofty Husks and begging them to come and sort everything out. Even Slumbergrot had said that the only way to fix things would be for Casper to find a familiar face. But those in the castle *needed* to know about the shatterblast so that they could check the pipes or change the cauldrons or whatever bottlers did inside the Mixing Tower. Perhaps on learning this valuable information the Lofty Husks would come to assist Casper and Utterly on their quest instead of assuming Utterly was somehow tangled up with the Midnights. Casper rummaged around the side pocket of the canoe until he found a half-rotted pencil, then, making sure that Utterly wasn't watching, scribbled a hasty message on the back of the paper:

Safe, well, and INNOCENT. Morg's followers called Midnights (Frostbite one of them—he framed me). Have it on authority Midnights pouring deadly wind called shatterblast into Mixing

Tower. Am trying to stop them with message from the wind and boy from the Faraway. Back soon. PS Midnights are griffins. PPS Had breakfast.

Casper whispered "Utterly's mum" into the paper before folding it up into the shape of an airplane and letting it float, unseen by Utterly, back toward the castle. Casper looked at the alder trees crowding the riverbanks. They were bent so far over the water on either side that their branches joined where they met in the middle, closing the river off into a shaded cage. And still the rain pattered onto the leaves.

"We're definitely going the right way," Utterly said after a while. "This is drizzle hag territory, for sure."

"How can you tell?'

"Because there's a distinct smell of magic in the air."

Casper sniffed. "What does magic smell like?"

Utterly considered. "Musky—like the way pine trees smell when the wind rushes through them."

Casper sniffed again. And then again. And on the third sniff he smelled it. "Ha! There it is!" he exclaimed. Then all of a sudden he realized that several hours had passed and all sorts of impossible things had happened and he hadn't stuck to his timetable for *Managing and Processing Impossible Information* at all. He shook himself. It was important that he didn't lose a grip on things. "But then again," he said to Utterly, "it might just smell this way because there are pine trees nearby."

Utterly shrugged. "But then why has the river turned silver?"

Chapter 12

Casper jumped. The water had indeed changed color! Beneath the tunnel of branches it was a gleaming silver, like molten steel. Arlo climbed into Utterly's coat pocket until just his ears poked out, swiveling this way and that in case danger was close.

"I've been told the drizzle hags keep themselves to themselves," Utterly added. "The waters here are hexed with river nymph tears to put people off from visiting; even ballooners have to take extra care when they come to collect the rain marvels."

A breeze sifted through the trees, jostling the leaves free from the branches and sprinkling them on the river as words:

If you drink from silver tears,
rich you'll be for all your years.

But you must give up something dear
to own this gift of silver cheer.

The leaves broke apart and floated downstream.

"Hexed silver is pricier than gold," Utterly muttered. "But it's best to ignore it. Drizzle hag magic is *not* to be trusted."

But now even the trees around them were silver, and no matter how hard Casper tried to focus on the task ahead, he found himself thinking about Candida and Leopold and the horrible things they always said about his family being poor. This amount of silver could change all that if he ever did get back to Little Wallops. It could bring smart clothes, a new car, and fancy holidays. . . . It would mean fitting in. At last.

Utterly knocked his paddle with her own and Casper's thoughts scattered. "Drinking enchanted silver never ends well," she told him. "In class we learned about a storm ogre who swallowed a whole jugful and now he's the richest ogre at the Smoking Chimneys, but he's never seen his silver because the river took his sight. And then there was the marsh goblin who got tons of silver but lost his voice. Trust me, it never ends happily."

They paddled on, but Casper wasn't used to the tricks of

magic and his eyes kept being drawn back to the river and the promise of riches. He thought of the time Leopold had locked him in the school toilets the day his class had gone to the cinema as an end-of-term treat. He thought about the day Candida had egged his parents' car. He thought about all the hours his mum and dad spent working overtime so that they could afford to buy him a present for his birthday and for Christmas. And he felt an uncontrollable urge to cup a hand into the river and have a taste. Surely that wouldn't bring any harm?

He lowered his hand into the river, slowly, gently, so as not to alert Utterly, and let it trail through the silver. The water was warm and it seemed to cradle his palm and all at once Casper saw his mother's face in its reflection. His heart filled with longing. But the image before him was blurred—like a partly drawn sketch—and as Casper tried to fill in the blanks, to remember the way his mother's dark hair fell and the way her eyes sparkled as she smiled, he met with a strange emptiness.

Is the river getting ready to steal my memories, Casper wondered hazily, *as payment for the silver?* But he felt so calm all of a sudden that he kept his hand where it was. *What if it's not such a bad thing to forget? What if having money is more important?*

Mum always wanted me to make friends, he said to himself, *and if I was rich—really rich—I wouldn't stick out anymore. Everyone in Little Wallops would want to spend time with me, and Candida and Leopold would stop being mean.*

The image of his mum in the water began to disappear, then Casper felt something land on his knee. He snatched his hand away from the river and in that split second, his mother's face appeared in his mind—clear and bright and full of warmth. Casper looked down at his knee and was surprised to see Arlo perched there. The dragon snuggled his head against Casper's leg and in that second Casper felt less sure that the answers to his problems lay in new cars and fancy holidays. Perhaps there was something to be said for unexpected dragons, and—he slid a glance at Utterly—furious girls in overalls.

And for a wild moment, Casper found himself hoping for friendship instead of silver. Because the bruised and lonely part of his heart recognized something in Utterly, something in the way she had looked at the boys who passed her on the bridge over the moat and in the way that she had approached the girls in the courtyard. Utterly didn't fit in either. She was an outsider, just like him, and though he wasn't quite sure how to build a friendship with anyone, let alone a Rumblestar girl and an oversensitive reptile, he decided that it wouldn't be entirely dreadful if one somehow ended up happening anyway.

Utterly swiveled round, raised an eyebrow at Arlo, then mumbled, "We need to keep our wits about us at all times. So just keep your head down and carry on paddling no matter what sort of magic is fizzing away either side of the canoe."

The silver waters petered out and the river once again ran crystal clear beneath ordinary alders, but the branches were now so tightly interwoven that almost all of the daylight was shut out. And in that gloomy tunnel, Casper felt sure that he could hear a sound that didn't quite fit—a slithering sound coming from the bottom of the canoe.

"Can you hear that?" he asked.

"Keep paddling, Casper. Remember what I said."

The slithering noise came again, and from what Casper could tell, it seemed to be coming from beneath the canoe. Casper listened harder, then he peered over the side of the boat to see weeds twisting up from the riverbed—long and green and trailing algae—but these slippery tendrils seemed to move quite independently from the pull of the current. Casper tried to ignore them and carry on paddling, but when one slithered up out of the water and wound itself around Casper's paddle, he shrieked.

Utterly thumped her oar down. "What is it now?!"

"The weeds are alive!"

Utterly glanced at his paddle. "Stop overreacting. You've got a tiny bit of riverweed tangled round your paddle. Nothing more."

She turned away and Casper watched, his face white with horror, as more weeds wrapped themselves around his paddle and yanked it under the water.

"They took it!" Casper cried. "They took my paddle!"

Utterly turned around. "You mean you lost it."

"I didn't lose it! *They* took it!" Casper pointed to the river, but the weeds swayed with the current as if nothing had happened at all.

"You are useless!" Utterly rolled her eyes. "Now keep quiet and leave the paddling to me."

Casper sank into his seat, all thoughts of friendship draining away. Maybe he imagined the weeds moving. Could he have been such a coward that even the thought of enchantments had set his mind reeling? Arlo climbed up onto Casper's arm and patted it, and though it was only a pat, Casper saw something in Arlo's eyes then. *I believe you*, he seemed to be saying. *I saw it, too.*

Utterly paddled on through the tunnel of trees and once again the river began to stir. The weeds shivered, even though the current was sluggish, then they twisted and turned before stretching up toward the surface and bursting over the sides of the canoe, grinding it to a halt.

And then Utterly took notice.

Her paddle clattered into the canoe and she screamed as the weeds coiled round her stomach. Arlo flapped toward her, trying, unsuccessfully, to puff fire, and at the smoke trickling from his nostrils a few of the weeds wilted, then snapped and fell back into the water. But then more poured over the sides, curling round Utterly so that she couldn't grab her paddle and reaching out toward Casper, too. Casper flung them back, then lunged toward Utterly to do the same, but at the same time, a thicker weed reared up from the water and snatched Arlo. The dragon yelped, gave one last unproductive go at blowing fire, then vanished beneath the surface of the river.

"Arlo!" Utterly screamed, her face white with panic.

But the weeds only tightened their grasp, winding round her feet and wrapping themselves over and over her legs.

"Do something, Casper!" she yelled. "I can't lose Arlo, too!"

More weeds slid over the edge of the canoe toward Casper, and for a moment he was paralyzed by fear. He wasn't brave! He didn't launch into rivers full of enchanted weeds! Then, suddenly, he found himself kicking away his doubts and standing up—despite his pounding heart and wobbling knees—and doing something very out of character. He threw off his coat and, shouting Arlo's name, he jumped from the canoe into the river.

The water was writhing with weeds—and though they grabbed at Casper's arms and feet and face, he pushed down through them until his hands met with something small and scaled. Arlo was thrashing against the weeds, but they held him fast and no matter how hard Casper hauled, he couldn't tear the dragon free. His lungs were aching and his heart was thundering, but still he didn't try to surface, not even when the weeds took advantage of his weakening limbs and curled around him, too. Instead, he stayed down by the riverbed—eyes wide with fear as he snatched at the weeds—until, finally, he managed to pull Arlo free. And then, clasping the dragon, he slammed his boots against the riverbed and pushed up with all the strength he could muster.

The weeds snapped and fell away and then Casper was spluttering at the surface and Utterly, who had somehow managed to saw the weeds in half against the sides of the canoe, was dragging him and Arlo into the boat. Once they were safely inside, she paddled on—fast—and then the trees opened up, the weeds trailed away, and the canoe drifted out into a screen of mist. And though Casper couldn't see a great deal ahead of him, he could see Utterly holding Arlo close as the little dragon coughed and wheezed and gasped and sobbed.

She turned around in her seat and, in a surprised voice, she said: "You saved him. You saved Arlo."

Casper blinked back. He was as shocked as Utterly. And then he blushed, because there was a curious tingling in his chest all of a sudden. It felt a little like scoring full marks in a math test, only this feeling ran deeper than that, all the way down to his soaking-wet toes.

Utterly shook her head in disbelief. "You were actually kind of brave rescuing Arlo like that." She paused. "I mean, not as brave as me fighting free from those weeds, obviously. But I'm uncommonly courageous—"

Arlo nipped her ear and Utterly shut up.

Casper blushed again. He was clever and rational and always

on time. But he had never considered himself brave. And for a moment he was surprised at what courage looked like. It wasn't big and grand and full of purpose. It was haphazard and chaotic and involved a considerable amount of sweating.

Casper squeezed the water from his jumper. "I wouldn't get used to it; it was probably just a one-off."

Utterly nodded. "Probably."

And Casper couldn't help feeling a little stung by that because he had secretly been hoping that his actions might have sparked the beginning of a friendship between him and Utterly after all. But it was clear Utterly didn't seem to think so.

She dug her paddle into the water as Casper wrung out his overalls. "I read about mudgrapple in a history book once, but I thought it only grew in the streams over at Dapplemere. That's why I didn't believe you. But the drizzle hags must have snuck some back here for unwanted visitors. . . ."

Casper realized that this was an apology of sorts—or half of one, at least. Then Arlo slid down Utterly's back, hopped onto Casper's lap, and folded himself into a ball there.

"I didn't know dragons purr," Casper said after a while.

Utterly looked at Arlo, then she looked up at Casper and said, very quietly, "Only when they feel safe."

And, as Utterly turned back around, Casper wondered whether it was possible to say sorry in stages, because this felt very much like the other half of Utterly's apology.

As they traveled, the mist around them started to thicken, and only by peering could Casper and Utterly make out the dank marshland either side of them.

"When Arlo was snatched by the mudgrapple," Casper said, after a while, "you said you couldn't lose him, too." He paused. "And, well, I wondered if maybe it had something to do with a name I saw on the honors boards in the castle." He paused again. "Mannerly Thankless."

Casper left his words hanging in the air, not wanting to risk asking a question directly—he had realized by now that Utterly didn't react well to them—but he didn't say anything else either just in case Utterly wanted to talk.

But she kept paddling in silence, even though she had definitely heard Casper because Arlo had settled on her shoulder and was now tugging at her hair to respond. It didn't help, though. And while silence was an improvement on earlier, when Utterly had threatened to throw Casper overboard when he asked about her mum's note, it still didn't mean Casper understood her any better.

They sailed on through the mist, then Utterly pointed to a dark shape on the right-hand side of the river. "There," she whispered. "Some kind of building . . ."

She let the canoe drift closer as a house on stilts over the river came into sight. Most of the windows were broken, the thatch on the roof was rotted through, and the planks of wood that formed the house had been so badly put together the entire thing seemed to slope to the left. But puffing out of a chimney was what looked to be blue smoke.

Casper read the weather-beaten sign that had been jammed, lopsided, into a pile of mud next to the house.

WELCOME TO THE DAMP SQUIB.
WE WILL ENDEAVOR TO MAKE YOUR STAY
AS UNPLEASANT AS POSSIBLE.

Chapter 13

Casper held his breath as the canoe drifted toward the Damp Squib, because on the porch jutting out from the house there were three old ladies sitting in rocking chairs—and all around them the air misted with drizzle. The women wore rags over their hunched frames, their hair was strewn with mud, and their feet were webbed. Back and forth the rocking chairs creaked, and the drizzle hags stared ahead with empty eyes.

"I think they might be asleep with their eyes open," Casper whispered. Then he leaned closer to Utterly. "Whatever you do, don't wake them up before we've decided on a plan."

Utterly nodded, then she fumbled for the mooring rope and chucked it round the Damp Squib sign. And it was all going well—Casper even had time to tidy the canoe a little, which it needed after the business with the mudgrapple—until Utterly yanked the rope to pull the canoe closer to the house and it bumped against the ladder leading up to the porch and the drizzle hags stopped rocking.

Utterly winced and Arlo scuttled up the sleeve of her coat as one by one the hags blinked and three sets of gray eyes fixed on the canoe.

"Well, well, well," crooned the hag in the middle. She was the tallest of the three and her chin was so pointed you could have cut a piece of toast with it. She cricked her neck and Casper shuddered as the bones inside it clicked, but then something far more disturbing happened. The woman's neck craned out from her shoulders and grew longer and longer, and though the drizzle hag remained slumped in her chair, her neck slid down the ladder like an old snake until her head was hovering before them.

"So," she said, her neck curling around the children as she spoke, "you passed through the Silver Tears *and* all the mudgrapple?" She smiled, revealing toothless gums, then she glanced up at the porch. "Come on down, ladies. We have company. It is time to make our guests feel as *un*welcome as possible."

There were several more cricks as the bones inside the necks of the other two hags loosened and then, moments later, their weathered faces coiled around the canoe. Casper tried not to gag at the smell of their breath, a revolting mix of rotten eggs and mold.

"Allow us to introduce ourselves," the tallest of the hags smirked. "I am Hortensia Quibble and these are my dear friends, Sylvara Buckweed and Gertie Swamp. It is our displeasure to greet you on this beautifully drizzly afternoon."

Sylvara and Gertie gave wheezy sniggers.

"So, how long have you two burplings been friends?" Gertie asked.

"We're not friends," Utterly replied sternly. "We're . . . work colleagues. Things are purely practical around here."

Casper nodded nervously. At least Utterly was clear on the subject. Saving Arlo had confused things a bit, but it seemed there really was no hope whatsoever of them becoming friends. Casper comforted himself with the realization that he could spend more time thinking about lists, timetables, and staying alive instead of worrying about being Utterly's friend.

Sylvara twisted her neck up to Casper's face. "Come

about a message you got from a magical wind, have you? Most people do . . ."

"Y-yes," Casper stammered. "And if you're able to help us, we'll be on our way immediately so as not to bother you a moment more."

Sylvara hissed with displeasure, then Hortensia stretched her neck right up to Casper's face so that their noses almost touched. And Casper realized that the drizzle hags did have teeth. They just weren't in their mouths. They were dangling on a piece of string around their necks.

"You break our enchantments," Hortensia spat, "you wake us up, and then you expect us to simply send you on your way with the information you require?"

Beads of sweat prickled through Casper's forehead.

"Just because we have sensed dark magic in these parts of late and a handful of disgusting griffins managed to sneak past our enchantments and steal a few marvels this morning—"

Casper's heart skipped a beat at the thought of Midnights in these parts that very morning.

"—does not mean that we will yield our wisdom for free. We are the drizzle hags and any answers we give come at a price."

Casper thought back to the silver waters. Would finding out where this familiar face was mean losing his sight or his voice or, worse, his memories of home?

In front of him, Utterly straightened up. "What will it take to make sense of these words from the cometwhirl: 'find a familiar face to destroy the Midnights'?"

Hortensia, Sylvara, and Gertie slid up close to Utterly, their rotten breath pulsing against her cheeks.

"I think you had better come inside," Hortensia sniffed.

Casper glanced at the ramshackle house. A Spanish phrase he'd heard of before had been painted onto the front door, only the wording wasn't quite how he remembered it: MI CASA *IS NOT* SU CASA.

Casper leaned over toward Utterly. "Going in might mean never coming out."

"It might," Hortensia wheezed. "But staying out might mean never going home."

With that, the drizzle hags wound in their necks and, with their heads in place, rocked back and forth in their chairs. Casper, Utterly, and Arlo nodded to one another warily before climbing out of the canoe and making their way up the ladder and onto the porch.

The drizzle hags rose together, their joints clicking so many times it was like listening to a bunch of twigs snapping, and led the way into the Damp Squib over a doormat that bore the words HOME IS WHERE THE HEART IS, except the words HEART IS had been painted over so that really the mat said HOME IS WHERE THE ARGUMENTS HAPPEN instead. They entered a gloomy sitting room in which sat two damp sofas that were stained with mud and scattered with cushions embroidered with decidedly glum messages like HOME MISERABLE HOME. And at the far end of the room, rather than a fire crackling in the hearth, there was a cauldron filled with bubbling blue liquid that rose up the chimney as tiny blue droplets and looked exactly like a stream of marbles.

Casper blinked. So *this* was where the world's rain was conjured and what he had seen earlier puffing out of the chimney wasn't blue smoke but marvels—rain in its purest form, caught by ballooners in spidersilk nets.

Sylvara and Gertie busied themselves with the cork-stoppered bottles on the shelves either side of the cauldron, tipping the contents of a small bottle labeled OGRE TEARS (WARNING: SPICY) inside, then adding a few drops from a larger bottle entitled PITTER-PATTER OF SPRITE FEET (BEST BEFORE YESTERDAY). The mixture hissed blue smoke, then more marvels floated up the chimney while Gertie poured in a bottle of DAWN DEW (KEEP REFRIGERATED AFTER OPENING) and Sylvara stirred.

Casper gawped as Gertie reached for yet another bottle—WATERFALL ESSENCE (HANDLE WITH CARE)—and emptied it into the cauldron. He had no idea there were so many magical ingredients in rain. . . .

Hortensia, meanwhile, slumped down onto one sofa, motioning for Casper, Utterly, and Arlo to sit on the one opposite, then lay her toothy necklace on the coffee table between the sofas.

"Cometwhirl is often easier to understand once you get your teeth into it," she croaked. "And I will throw my teeth to give you an answer *if* you can solve my riddle."

"And if we can't?" Casper asked.

"*When* you can't," Hortensia corrected him, "because we at the Damp Squib are here to make your stay as unhelpful as possible, then we shall pickle you."

"*Pickle us?*" Utterly cried.

Casper gasped. "I thought only onions and cucumbers got pickled!"

"And irritating children." Hortensia's eyes flicked toward

a collection of jars wedged into wooden pigeonholes in the far corner of the room. "We do so like to keep mementos of our guests."

Casper's toes curled as he read a few of the labels on the jars—PICKLED EYEBALL (TROLL); PICKLED TONGUE (NYMPH); PICKLED TOENAILS (OGRE); PICKLED LEFT ELBOW (ANONYMOUS)—then he tried his best to focus on why they had come. "What's the riddle?"

Hortensia snapped her neck loose and it swam close to Utterly and Casper. "*The more you take, the more you leave behind.*" She blinked two dull eyes. "*What am I?*" She nudged a bowl of greenish-brown gloop toward them. "And do have a bite to eat while you mull that one over; lunch today is river slug with a side of marsh weed."

Utterly turned to Casper. "But . . . but that doesn't make sense. How can you be carrying more and more but then leaving more and more behind?"

Hortensia glanced over at the cauldron. "I think it would be wise to begin measuring our guests for the Pickling so that we can look out for the right-sized jars because these children are not going anywhere."

But Arlo, as it turns out, was. He hopped off Utterly's

shoulder onto the coffee table and began pattering back and forth across the surface.

"Not much of a dragon, is he?" Hortensia snorted as Gertie hobbled over with a measuring tape, wrapped it around Casper's head, and noted down the circumference.

Casper watched as Utterly's hands balled into fists and her spine straightened, but just as she was about to unleash a torrent of abuse at Hortensia, Casper butted in.

"The more *you* take, the more *you* leave behind . . . what about cake? That would work! You'd leave crumbs behind if you took lots."

"Not if you were greedy." Hortensia curled her lip. "A pathetic attempt."

Sylvara held another tape measure up to Utterly's hair. "Can you pickle hair, Hortensia? I never know."

Hortensia smiled. "My dear, you can pickle just about anything." She glanced at the clock above the door, then glared at Casper and Utterly. "You have until five o'clock to give me your answer, then we shall commence the Pickling."

"But that's in one minute's time!" Utterly cried.

"Precisely," Hortensia snapped. "So, if I were you, I would stop wasting it."

Utterly and Casper exchanged panicked glances while the clock ticked on into the silence and Gertie and Sylvara continued to hobble around with their tape measures.

"I can't think of anything!" Casper groaned. "My mind's gone blank!"

And then he noticed that Utterly had gone unusually quiet and was watching Arlo pacing back and forth across the coffee table. Every now and again the little dragon looked up at Utterly and Casper before continuing his steps. And then Casper's heart quickened and Utterly's eyes lit up. In the dust on the surface of the coffee table lay the answer to the drizzle hags' riddle, only Arlo had worked it out long before they had—just like he had with Utterly's password for the door leading into the castle!

Hortensia clapped her hands together as the clock struck the first of its five chimes. "Well, that concludes this afternoon's miserable affairs. I suggest you—"

"FOOTPRINTS!" Casper and Utterly blurted out together, pointing to the little claw marks in the dust. "The more you take, the more you leave behind!" Hortensia's face contorted and for a moment Casper wondered whether she was going to be sick.

"It's right, isn't it?" Utterly cried. "Arlo solved your riddle!"

Hortensia's eyes shrunk to slits, then she sent her neck down to inspect Arlo's footprints. She blinked in surprise, then she scowled at the dragon. "You think you are clever? Well, what is thirteen thousand five hundred sixty-five divided by two thousand seven hundred thirteen?"

Arlo was thoughtful for a moment, then he pawed his answer into the dust: 5.

Hortensia gasped. "He's right!"

"What's the chemical symbol for sodium chloride?" Gertie asked.

Arlo grinned as he wrote four letters onto the coffee table: NaCl.

Sylvara leaned closer. "What's a pentasyllabic word for rain?"

Arlo rapped his tail on the table as he thought, then he wrote "precipitation" into the dust.

"The dragon is a genius," Hortensia muttered. "And just think how splendid it would be to pickle the brain of a genius dragon. Like Christmas come early!"

Sylvara and Gertie licked their lips and their necks rose once more and curved around Arlo like a noose. But as they did so, Casper thought of the way Arlo had nuzzled into his legs as they passed through the Silver Tears and of how he had purred in his lap after the mudgrapple attack, and before he could stop himself, he found that he was on his feet.

"You will *not* pickle Arlo! How *dare* you even say such a thing, you miserable old toads!"

He paused to catch his breath—no one had warned him quite how exhausting being brave was—but then Utterly was on her feet, too.

"Casper's right," she snarled. "We beat you fair and square and you have to honor your word and help us." She scooped up Arlo and held him close. "So, we'd very much like to know where in the kingdom Casper can find a familiar face. Then we'll be on our way."

Like a sulking child, Hortensia slipped her teeth off the string she'd fashioned into a necklace, shook them in her crinkled palm, then rolled them across the table.

To Casper and Utterly the scattered teeth looked like what they were—scattered teeth—but Hortensia, Gertie, and Sylvara were crowded around them now, twisting their necks this way and that and tutting as they thought. Then, finally, Hortensia looked up.

"At the mouth of the river, take a right. If in doubt, keep climbing."

"That's it?" Utterly cried. "Couldn't you be a bit more specific?"

Casper nodded. "*When* will we reach the mouth of the river? *What* are we climbing? Do you at least have a map you could give us?"

"We will send a message to the castle to let the Lofty Husks know your progress, if only to stop them hounding us for news of a missing bottler-in-training called Utterly Thankless."

Utterly looked suddenly hopeful, then tried her best not to show it. "Do they know I'm not guilty of working with the Midnights, then?" she mumbled.

Casper thought back to the note he'd sent Utterly's mum. Had it already arrived? And had Utterly's mum told the Lofty Husks that her daughter was innocent and *that's* why they were hounding the magical creatures in the Beyond for news? Casper didn't want to tell Utterly he'd gone behind her back, so he said, "Maybe the Lofty Husks realized there was no way you could be bound up in all this really." He paused. "When they read the drizzle hags' message, though, they'll know for sure, and then I bet they'll rush out here to help us in any way they can."

Out of pride, Utterly pretended not to care. But Casper had

seen her face back with the Midnight and the mudgrapple, and he knew that both times she'd felt far, far out of her depth.

Hortensia, meanwhile, eyed the children with contempt, then swiped up her teeth from the table. "If you leave now, you will reach the mouth of the river by sunrise tomorrow morning. If you leave any later, you will risk immediate pickling—starting with the angry girl's bottom. Now, be gone!"

And so, keen to avoid the Pickling and anxious about the Midnight escaping the jailbird soon, Utterly, Casper, and Arlo left the Damp Squib.

Chapter 14

Utterly paddled them downstream, and within minutes the mist had lifted, the drizzle had cleared, and a cloudless evening sky stretched above them. It was orange in parts and pink, too, but the sun itself was blocked by rocks that rose up to form a craggy gorge either side of them. And as they left the drizzle hags' enchantments behind, the river started behaving more like a river ought to: An otter (albeit in long johns) splashed in the shallows, and dragonflies (albeit carrying minuscule briefcases) flitted between rocks.

Casper leaned toward Arlo, who was keeping a lookout for Midnights from Utterly's shoulder. "You were brilliant back there."

The dragon blushed and Utterly tickled his chin. "You

really were. I knew you were clever, but that was really quite something!" She looked over her shoulder at Casper. "Did you see Hortensia's face when she realized Arlo had helped us with the answer? And her neck—it went all wobbly!"

Casper nodded. "You could say Arlo solved the riddle at break*neck* speed."

The corners of Utterly's mouth twitched. "He really made the drizzle hags wind their *necks* in."

"I'd love to see Hortensia in a turtle*neck*."

And they laughed then, great belly-hugging laughs, and Casper realized that it had been a very long time since he'd done so because there wasn't an awful lot of time left for giggling what with hiding in lost and found baskets and double-checking his timetables. But he made a mental note to schedule a few minutes of it into each day when he got back. Because laughing felt even better than crossing the last thing off a to-do list. It was like trampolining for the spirit, and as Casper looked across at Utterly, he wondered whether this was the first time she had laughed properly for a long time too.

She looked different somehow. The stars on her cheeks glittered brighter, her eyes bent into half-moons, and even her hair seemed to be having a ball (though possibly that was down to Arlo skipping in and out of it). And every time Utterly laughed, it set Casper off again and vice versa. *Perhaps laughing is best enjoyed* with *someone*, Casper thought, which was something to consider when timetabling it back home.

He wiped his eyes. "We should upgrade ourselves from work colleagues." He stiffened as he realized he'd said the words aloud; all the giggling had knocked his common sense sideways. "Or not," he added hastily.

Utterly thought about it. "Acquaintances?"

Casper relaxed a little and then nodded. "Acquaintances."

Yes, he thought to himself, *that would do very well for now. A bit more friendly than work colleagues but not so intense that I need to start panicking about messy emotions.*

They sailed on through the gorge, ordering two pepperoni pizzas and a miniature garlic bread from the just-in-case and (thanks to Utterly cracking a half-decent joke) three much-needed hot water bottles because the air was growing colder the further downstream they traveled.

But as night fell, the jolly mood in the canoe fell with it, and the three of them listened carefully for the slightest noises from the crags either side of them. It was their second night out in the Beyond and they couldn't help feeling they'd been lucky up until now. The Midnights were bound to be on their scent. If they were *stealing* marvels now, as well as damaging them in the Mixing Tower, it could well mean they were growing in numbers or power, or both.

Casper thought about the paper airplane he'd sent Utterly's mum and the fact that she'd not written back. And even if his note hadn't reached the castle, surely the Lofty Husks knew of Utterly's innocence through the message the drizzle hags had said they'd send? So why hadn't the kingdom's rulers raced out into the Beyond to help Casper and Utterly on their quest? Or at least sent their best ballooners, like Utterly's dad, to the rescue? But no one had come. Was Utterly so much of an outsider everyone had given up on her, even her mum? Maybe the Lofty Husks had only been hounding the magical creatures for news because they were cross? But Utterly's mum had sounded *desperate* to see her again in her message. . . . Something didn't make sense, but Casper couldn't see how talking to Utterly about any of it would help—it would mean admitting that he'd written back to her mum, for a start.

The canoe floated on through hundreds of lily pads, which opened as the stars came out to reveal a river full of flickering candles, but despite the beauty around them Casper's mind would not stop whirring and he could tell that Utterly was finding it impossible to relax too. The night felt full of watching eyes and unwanted shadows, and though they did eventually fall asleep, their dreams were full of beating wings and yellow eyes.

Casper woke to birdsong, so he assumed it must be sunrise, but as he opened his eyes, there was no sign of the sun itself, which was strange. There were no clouds in the sky, so the sun should have been obvious, and yet there was nothing at all—only a faint glow beyond the gorge farther upstream that hinted at the sun down at the horizon, but it seemed to show no sign of rising. Casper waited a little longer, but the glow didn't move and the morning didn't brighten, so he nudged Utterly awake.

"Something's not right," he said. "It feels like sunrise, but it's all gloomy, like dusk, and no matter how long you watch that light behind the rocks, it doesn't budge."

"You're right," Utterly replied, rubbing her eyes. "That glow *is* in the east, where the sun should rise, but . . . is it *stuck* down at the horizon?"

Casper thought for a moment. "The drizzle hags said the

Midnights are stealing marvels, so perhaps they're trying to cut the magic off at the source as well as tainting it in the Mixing Tower—a two-pronged attack to break the link between Rumblestar and the other kingdoms! That could cause the weather here to change. . . . With fewer sun marvels, maybe it means the sun won't shine as much and might even have trouble rising. . . ."

Utterly shifted in her seat. "But the sun scamps over at Dapplemere are the hardest working of any magical creature. I know they'd work double time and overtime to produce enough marvels in their mills to replace anything that's stolen." She glanced up at the sky. "Unless the Midnights aren't just stealing the marvels . . . What if they're attacking the creatures making them?" She bit her lip. "I hope the sun scamps are okay. I visited Dapplemere with my mum and dad a few months ago for my birthday—I wanted to see the wishing trees again because you never know where in the kingdom the magic might dry up next—and the sun scamps who showed me around were so friendly and kind. But they're tiny; they won't stand a chance against the Midnights!"

Casper grabbed the remaining paddle. "Then we need to

move faster. Your mum said there's an emergency supply of marvels in the Mixing Tower, but that will run out eventually and if the Midnights really are starting to attack the creatures that *make* the marvels, then we're really in trouble. If we don't stop them, there won't be anything left to save."

Casper paddled quickly down the river, which was narrower now, the crags either side of them towering slabs of rock. It was even colder here, so Casper buttoned his duffel coat right up to his chin. He eyed the enormous pile of boulders blocking the river some way ahead. There was something organized about the way they lay: two protruding round rocks, then a long pointed one below them, and beneath that, a gaping hole where the river rushed through.

Casper pointed at the boulders with a shaking finger. "It's . . . it's a head."

Utterly leaned forward to get a better look. "A witch's head, by the look of that nose."

The canoe hastened toward it and then Casper gasped. "The drizzle hags said to take a right at the mouth of the river. The water following through that hole—*that's* the witch's mouth *and* the mouth of the river!"

Utterly's eyes widened, and Arlo zipped himself into her

overall pocket as they drew closer still. "And beyond that there seems to be . . . NOTHING! We've reached the Edge!"

Casper rammed the paddle into the water, the way he'd seen Utterly do before the tributaries, to try and slow their course. But the canoe spun wildly and showed no sign of stopping.

"Swift Exit!" Utterly screamed, reaching over her seat to slam a fist on the button under Casper's armchair, then swiveling back to activate her own escape.

Before Casper could react, the springs in their seats burst through the fabric, propelling both children out of the canoe, up into the air and smack down onto a ledge of rock jutting out of the gorge to the right.

Utterly whirled round to Casper. "Are you all right? Are you hurt? How many fingers am I holding up?" Arlo curled into her neck and Utterly bit her lip. "I should've given you more warning, Casper. It's my fault—all over again—if *you're* broken beyond repair too."

Casper struggled to his feet. He was bruised all over and his lip was bleeding, but he was, generally speaking, all right. He looked at Utterly and saw a gentleness there that he hadn't noticed before. "Was that you *worrying* about me?" he asked.

Utterly breathed a sigh of relief on hearing his voice. "Phew.

You can talk *and* move." The softness went out of her at once. "And no. I wasn't worrying about *you*. You're obviously dazed and confused from the crash landing."

But Casper knew Utterly had been worried—she'd looked almost vulnerable when she thought Casper might be truly hurt—and he wondered whether, perhaps, she had acted like this because of something that had happened in the past. But as he readied himself to ask, Utterly narrowed her eyes.

"If you even *think* about throwing personal questions at me now," she snapped, "I'll hurl you back into the river."

"I was also going to thank you," Casper said, "for remembering the 'Swift Exit' button and saving both of our lives."

Utterly gave a moody shrug.

Casper thought of the canoe, which had now vanished from sight. He'd been deeply suspicious of it to begin with, but during their journey he'd grown almost fond of it, so he was a bit sad to see it disappear so suddenly. All the same, he, Utterly, and Arlo were alive and they had a job to do, so he gathered his breath and looked at the boulders above them. "'If in doubt, keep climbing,'" he said, echoing the drizzle hag's words.

Utterly nodded. "Somewhere up there has to be your familiar face."

Casper's mind spun with the possibilities: who from his world had managed to follow him through the grandfather clock? With everything inside him, he hoped that it was his mum or his dad, that somehow they had known he'd hidden inside the clock and climbed in after him. Or had one of them found another phoenix tear and entered Rumblestar a different way? He clambered up the boulders after Utterly and Arlo, his heartbeat quickening the closer they got to the top.

But when they did, finally, haul themselves up onto the last boulder, Casper's eyes didn't meet with a familiar face. Instead they met with a dense forest. Suddenly the drop in temperature made sense, because the tightly packed spruce trees before them were sprinkled with snow.

"But it was spring farther upstream," Casper panted. "How can it be winter here?"

Utterly gathered her breath. "This must be Shiverbark Forest, where snow is conjured. It's winter all year round here." She peered into the trees. They were dusted with white flakes but nothing like as much snow as she had seen in the pictures of her schoolbooks. "Back at the castle we were taught that it never stops snowing here, that every single day snowflakes the size of dinner plates fall and snow piles up as high as houses."

Her voice turned dark. "Either the magic has already dried up in these parts or the Midnights have been stealing marvels from here, too."

Arlo zipped between the first few trees, ears pricked, eyes peeled, then Utterly and Casper hurried on after him. But they whispered as they ran because the forest felt unnaturally quiet: No birds sang, no animals stirred—it was as if the forest itself knew that there were Midnights nearby.

"What kind of creatures conjure snow?" Casper asked Utterly, anything to keep himself from thinking of the griffins.

"Trolls, apparently. Though only the legendary ballooner, Gilbert Gatherpace, has ever caught a glimpse of one, so almost nothing at all is known about them. But you never know, we might get lucky."

Casper raised an eyebrow. "I hope we don't. . . ."

Utterly stopped suddenly and hoisted herself up into a tree. "'If in doubt, keep climbing.' . . . We should be heading *up* the trees, not *through* them!"

"But how do you know the drizzle hags meant for you to climb *that* particular tree?" Casper hissed. "There are hundreds of trees in this forest! What if you climb all the way to the top and it's the wrong one?"

"Climbing trees is *never* a waste of time, Casper." Utterly pointed to a spruce a few meters from hers. "Try that one."

Casper placed a tentative foot on the first branch, then swung for a handhold and missed.

Utterly rolled her eyes. "You've never climbed a tree before, have you?"

Casper swiped for another branch and pulled himself up off the ground. "'Course I have."

But the truth was, he hadn't, and as he climbed now, he couldn't help wishing he had a helmet and a safety harness, but this was a kingdom in the sky, and the more time Casper spent in it, the more he realized that health and safety wasn't just taking a day off in this strange land—it was permanently on holiday.

He tried his best to keep up with Utterly, but she seemed to know instinctively which branches would hold her weight and which to avoid, and she scrambled upward in the manner she did most things: quickly and crossly.

"Can't you go any faster?" she called down.

Casper steadied himself on an icy branch. His hands were numb and the tree seemed to go on forever. "Are you just expecting me to find someone I know sitting conveniently on a branch?"

"There's no point *expecting* anything—especially when you're dealing with magic. I'm just *hoping*." Utterly paused. "Only you're so slow that even *hoping* seems a bit optimistic."

They climbed higher and higher. The forest was so tightly packed with trees their branches crisscrossed like a frozen web. If you were feeling brave, you could probably leap from one tree to the next, but Casper wasn't, so he carried on climbing at a sensible, if perhaps slightly cautious, speed.

"Come *on*, Casper!" Utterly yelled. "Even Arlo is climbing quicker than you!"

"Arlo's got wings! I'm going as fast as I can!"

"It's not fast enough!"

Casper tried to think of something reasonable to say, but he was tired and cold. "Why are you always so impatient and angry?"

"Why are you always so scared?" Utterly shot back. "And slow! And boring!"

Casper slumped against a branch—he'd had enough—and the words that had been bubbling inside him for a while now tumbled out. "You're being mean, Utterly. It's no wonder all your classmates stay clear of you! You're foul-tempered and forever in a grump!"

"If you weren't such terrible company, I wouldn't *need* to be in a grump!" Utterly snapped.

"*I'm* not the reason you're always in a mood!" Casper cried. "It's all this business with whatever happened to you in the past, only you're too closed up and stubborn to talk about it!"

There was silence for a few moments and tiny flakes of snow began to fall. Utterly scowled down through the branches. "You don't know *anything* about me, Casper. And all this trying to make friends with me and Arlo is pathetic." From the branch below Arlo gave an indignant squeak, then began tugging at Utterly's boot with his claws. But she shook him off and plowed on. "Is it because you don't have any pals back in the Faraway? Too much of a coward for anyone to like you?"

"That's not fair!" Casper retorted. "I saved Arlo back with the mudgrapple and I stood up for him in the Damp Squib!" He could feel his temper rising again, and though back in Little Wallops he would have let people walk all over him, out here in the forest he felt suddenly bold. "I'm a million miles from home, Utterly, but I'm giving this quest everything I've got even if *you* make me want to pack it all in every few minutes. I *may* be scared at times, but at least I admit it! Unlike you! It seems to me that the thing you're most *scared* of is losing people, but *you're* so horrible to everyone that it's not surprising people can't wait to be rid of *you*! Is that what happened with Mannerly that you won't talk about? Did she run off and leave you because *you're* so mean? It's probably why no one has bothered to come and help us from the castle too, because you're always so horrid!'"

There was a pause from above, then Utterly's reply came, cold and stony. "I'm going on without you."

Casper snorted. "How will you know whether a face is familiar to me or not? You need me whether you like it or not."

But Utterly was done listening and thinking sensibly now. "I'll find another way to beat the Midnights. A way that doesn't involve spending time with someone as useless as you." She reached down a branch and snatched Arlo into her pocket. "And just so you know, Casper: *Never ever being late* isn't a skill. Find something else to be good at."

Utterly stormed off up the tree and Casper blinked after her, fighting back the tears that were threatening to fall. He hadn't meant to say all of that, but then again, he hadn't expected Utterly to be so quite so cruel. He sighed. Even having an acquaintance was turning out to be extremely stressful. He dreaded to think what dramas a real friendship might involve and felt glad that he didn't have plans to embrace one.

Casper carried on climbing through the maze of branches, and he was surprised to see that the tree was less icy now. There wasn't so much snow up here either and, strangely, the air felt ever so slightly warmer. He paused to try and make sense of it all and to see if he could make out Utterly chattering away to Arlo. But what he heard instead was something else entirely.

The steady *whrum* of wings.

Chapter 15

The hairs on Casper's neck bristled as the *whrum* of wings grew louder. It was too great a noise for a solitary forest bird, like a pigeon or a pheasant. These wings beat in chorus, a throbbing din of feathers that shook the air and rustled the trees. This was a flock of something very large indeed, and it was coming closer and closer to where Casper crouched.

"Utterly!" Casper whispered. "Can *you* hear that?"

No reply, save the moan of a gathering wind.

"Utterly?" Casper whispered again.

The wings beat faster, the wind began to howl, and Casper scuttled on up the tree, grabbing at the branches in the hope of catching sight of Utterly or Arlo. But neither of them was anywhere to be seen now. Utterly's anger must have propelled her up the tree even faster than normal, and he had no idea how far she and Arlo had climbed.

Until he heard Utterly scream.

Casper froze. That scream hadn't been filled with Utterly's usual fury; it had been loaded with fear. He scanned the branches above him—which shook and creaked as the wind roared—to see black shapes zipping through the trees, and every now and again a flash of yellow eyes.

Casper's blood pounded. Midnights!

A griffin hurtled through the trees, ducking and weaving to avoid the branches, and in its scaled talons it held a screaming girl in overalls. Utterly locked eyes with Casper for a split second, and Casper saw her terror and felt a punch of guilt. It was *his* fault that Utterly had stormed off and been captured. But Utterly didn't cry out for him; instead she kicked and bit and struggled to wriggle free. He realized that she was determined not to give him away, because she knew—even if she had been too angry to admit it earlier—that they *had* to find the familiar face, and it would never happen if they were both carried off by the Midnights.

The griffin swerved and a tiny blue scaled thing dropped from Utterly's pocket and landed on the branch next to Casper. It was Arlo. And he was whimpering.

Casper scooped the dragon into his palm. "We'll get her back," he whispered. "I promise."

He pinned himself to the tree trunk as the forest around them quaked with wind and the sound of screeching griffins. He could hear Utterly shouting too as she was dragged farther and farther into the forest. Knowing that he couldn't possibly take on a flock of Midnights on his own and also that he couldn't possibly let his acquaintance or his work colleague or whatever Utterly was be snatched away by the Midnights, he took a deep breath. Because Casper was beginning to learn a little more about adventures and that, like laughter, they were better when shared.

Casper tucked Arlo into his coat pocket, braced himself against the wind, then scuttled out along the branch he was hiding on. Not daring to look at the drop below, he leapt into the next-door tree. He landed with a thud, steadying himself against a gust of wind. From somewhere deeper in the forest, the griffins called to one another with grating shrieks. Casper hurried on toward the next tree, then the one after that, jumping the gulfs between them as he charged through the forest after Utterly. He wouldn't let the Midnights take her. Even if she was the most unreasonable person he had ever met.

He flung himself on, slipping and stumbling against the wind, right up to the moment a griffin burst out from a tree in front of him and settled on the end of the branch Casper was careering down.

He skidded to a halt as the griffin opened its wings. They were dagger-sharp at the edges and blacker than soot, and as the creature hissed through its hooked beak, Casper felt a terrible heat pulse inside him, and all at once the melted ice and snow made sense and he knew that he *hadn't* imagined the heat back in the canoe when the Midnight appeared. Somehow the air really *did* turn hot when the griffins came close.

The Midnight narrowed its yellow eyes and Casper realized they were the same eyes he and Utterly had encountered on the Witch's Fingers. This was the Midnight the jailbird had held. It must have been lying in wait for Casper, while the rest of its flock flew on, because it knew that there had been *two* children riding in the canoe!

Casper clung to the branch as the Midnight opened its mouth and screeched. And though the sound rocked the marrow in Casper's bones, it was the stiflingly hot breath now burning against his cheeks and spreading out inside him that frightened Casper more. Something was pouring from the griffin's beak—something invisible but hot and fierce all the same, and it made Casper's limbs feel horribly weak.

He found his thoughts reaching back to Slumbergrot's words about shatterblast: "Its bite is worse than fire." Then he gasped. Did the griffins *breathe out* shatterblast? And was that what was whirling through the forest and sucking the strength from Casper now?

He scrambled backward, but a talon clamped down on his shoulder and ground him still. Casper twisted and turned, bit and tore, but he was weaker now and the Midnight's hold was steel-strong and Casper knew he had little chance of escaping. The griffin continued to let the shatterblast pour from its beak, gripping Casper in its talons, and Casper felt his limbs grow even more drowsy then. The griffin surged upward, its formidable body snapping every branch it struck. Casper tried to break free with what strength he had left, and even Arlo did his best to help, but the griffin was answering the call of its flock now and it was smashing a way deeper into the forest—toward Everdark and Morg.

Then the unexpected happened.

Something long and wooden and tipped with silver shot through the air and went *thwunk* into the griffin's side. The

Midnight reeled, one of its talons raking against Casper's leg, then its grip loosened and it clattered down, down, down through the trees. Casper and Arlo fell too, but they reached out and grabbed at the branches until one held and they swung themselves into its trunk. But the griffin kept falling, a tangle of feathers and claws, until, after several minutes, Casper heard a distant thud as it hit the forest floor.

There was a grunt from somewhere close by and, clutching his leg, Casper clambered upright to see two hairy feet disappearing up the tree.

"Hey, wait!" Casper gasped. "Who are you? You saved us!"

But the feet pattered on until they vanished from sight. Then the calls of the griffins and the moan of the shatterblast ceased too, and once more it began to snow. Casper felt his strength return to his body, but as the silence of the forest took over again, broken only by Arlo's little sobs, one thing became horribly clear: Utterly was well and truly gone.

Chapter 16

Arlo padded down the length of the branch and looked out into the falling snow.

"Can you see her?" Casper asked as he slumped against the trunk.

He knew the answer even before Arlo shook his head. The Midnights had taken her, but did that mean they would put an end to Utterly here in Rumblestar, or would they take her back to the harpy in Everdark? Casper winced at the pain in his leg where a talon had cut his skin, but it was nothing compared to the pain of knowing that if he'd climbed just a little bit faster and kept up with Utterly, perhaps none of this would've happened. Casper felt almost dizzy with guilt as Arlo traipsed back toward him, a tear smudging down his snout.

They were alone now. Completely alone. And it didn't seem

like anyone at the castle even cared. Arlo climbed into Casper's lap and Casper hung his head. Things were spiraling out of control and there didn't seem to be any way to fix it all. He thought about composing another to-do list in his mind, but then he realized that he didn't want to. All he wanted, really, was to see Utterly again. Things had felt a lot more hopeful with her around. And even though they'd both said some truly awful things earlier and Casper had tried to convince himself that he didn't need Utterly, or indeed anyone else, as a friend, he knew he did. Because it wasn't enough to go through life just with acquaintances and work colleagues. It was important to have *real* friends, too. People to open up to and laugh with and to make you feel less lonely. And little by little those things had been happening with Utterly—until he'd blown it . . .

Tears rolled down Casper's cheeks, and as he held Arlo close, he thought of home. He missed his parents so much the pain in his chest was almost unbearable. And suddenly his mum's forgetfulness and his dad's inability to wear a watch didn't seem quite as irritating as they had back in Little Wallops. Because at the end of the day—when you were alone in the forest and down on one knee—those things didn't matter. His parents had been right all along: What counted, really, was love and friendship. Casper hadn't wanted to make friends in case Candida and Leopold ruined it again, but it turned out that he was capable of mucking up friendship all by himself. And now he was coming to terms with the truth: Making friends *was* painful and messy and frightening, but it was worth the trouble because life was a whole lot better when you lived it alongside a friend.

Casper took a deep breath and tried to think like Utterly. If she was the one left behind, she wouldn't stand for the Midnights getting in her way. She'd keep going after the familiar face. And so that's what Casper would do, hoping hard that there was a chance Utterly could be here in Rumblestar still, especially if the Midnights were keeping her as bait to catch him.

Casper wiped away his tears and looked down at Arlo in his palm. *If in doubt, keep climbing.* Arlo brushed his own tears from his snout and tried to look brave, which Casper took as a sign that the tiny dragon agreed they needed to keep searching, whatever might have happened to Utterly.

Casper grimaced as he hauled himself up. A dark red patch had seeped through his overalls, but he pushed on up the tree with Arlo flopped miserably on his shoulder. Casper tried not to think about how high up they were now. The trees back home stopped eventually, but these trees seemed to keep going forever. And it wasn't just the height that made the trees seem odd: The farther Casper climbed, the smoother the trunks became, and the branches grew less frequent so that Casper had to stretch farther between each one.

He paused for a moment and stared at the trunk more closely. The wood looked as if it had been smoothed and buffed and chiseled into shape rather than growing this way naturally. Casper blinked. The tree seemed just like the fancy table and chair legs back in the dining room at school. He climbed farther and saw that above him now was a rectangular platform made from slats of wood positioned through the trees. . . .

He turned to Arlo. "I think we might have been climbing up a gigantic table leg."

Utterly had said that snow trolls lived in Shiverbark Forest. What if this sky-high furniture belonged to them? The trolls Casper had come across in fairy tales back in England didn't seem the sort of creatures who would busy themselves with carpentry, but here in Rumblestar he was learning to expect the unexpected.

He continued to climb until finally he reached the wooden platform and heaved himself over the top. As Casper had guessed, he found himself on a giant tabletop. There were numerous board games open on its surface, including a Scrabble board that Casper had accidentally blundered into the middle of, scattering the letters in all directions. He looked up to see that the branches had been completely cut away above the table for a good few meters, creating a pocket of space right up to where the forest canopy started.

Suddenly, his head began to spin and the pain in his leg made it feel close to buckling, and though Casper tried to focus, the more he concentrated the more his vision blurred. And the last thing Casper saw before he blacked out completely were ten very hairy and very surprised faces staring down at him.

Casper knew he hadn't died because of the voices: a male voice and a female voice talking in parenty whispers.

"Make sure he's warm enough, Bristlebeard. Light more lanterns."

"What on earth *is* he?" the male voice replied. "He's much smaller than the ballooners that pass this way, and he doesn't have those whatsiblobs on his cheeks."

"I think he's an imp gone wrong, but best not say anything. Wouldn't want to offend him."

Casper's eyes fluttered open and for a few moments he had trouble piecing everything together. He was lying in a hammock strung up between the trees and bundled with blankets. It was snowing still, and dark now, but dangling from the canopy of the forest above them there were lanterns that cast warmth as well as light. There was a little wooden platform below him on which there was everything that might be found in a bedroom: an exquisitely carved side table with a book entitled *Goodbye Crossbows, Hello Mindfulness* on it; a wardrobe bursting with fur coats and leather boots; an armchair; a rug; and a mirror hanging from a nearby branch. There was also a bow and a quiver full of arrows propped up on a higher branch, which perhaps weren't quite so bedroom-appropriate.

All around the table he had clambered onto—which still bore the remains of the game of Scrabble alongside several other unfinished rounds of chess, backgammon, and Monopoly—there were wooden platforms filled with different types of beds: chaise longues, futons, double beds, single beds, bunk beds, rocking beds, and even one bed in the shape of a sleigh.

Arlo crawled onto Casper's face and hugged his cheek, and the memories of the day's events crashed in. Utterly. Carried off by the Midnights. Because Casper had failed to keep up, and he had failed to look out for her, and now, probably, he was going to fail at finding the familiar face and both Rumblestar and the Faraway would crumble. Casper tried to block those fears out and as he did so, an idea surfaced: What if *Utterly* was the familiar face he was meant to find? What if the wind always knew she'd be carried away by the Midnights? What if he was supposed to rescue her and in doing so destroy the Midnights?

Casper made to sit up, but the moment he moved, two incredibly hairy faces leaned in.

"Careful now," a creature with red, backcombed hair urged. "Easy on your tootlepegs. That was quite some cut." She tutted. "You were lucky Bristlebeard and I had a spare tub of shiverbark sap lying around."

"A few more hours and you'll be as right as rain," the creature beside her added. He was a little bit taller than Casper, and much plumper, and he had a red beard that was so long he'd tied it in thirteen knots, but it still reached the floor. "Or, as we like to say, as aglow as the snow."

"You . . . you're snow trolls?" Casper asked weakly.

The bearded troll, who was dressed in furs just like the female troll beside him, bowed. "Bristlebeard and Brushwick at your service."

He gestured behind him to a wood-slat conveyor belt chugging through the treetops. There were burlap sacks loaded onto it and they had been tied up with tags that read: CRUSHED DIAMONDS, MOON SYRUP, CLOUD WISP, SKYWEBS.

"Ingredients for the snow marvels," Brushwick explained.

Several other snow trolls—all relatively short, plump, and red-haired—were tipping the contents of these sacks into open hatches that ran down a large and perfectly cylindrical tree. They slammed the glass doors shut over the hatches and yanked on various switches and levers, and the ingredients spun around inside to form perfect white droplets of snow.

"The marvels pump out of the cylinder above the canopy," Bristlebeard explained, "and the ballooners come by once in a while to collect them. Snow is whoopsihard to catch otherwise."

Casper glanced at the bow and arrow hanging from a branch nearby. "You rescued us, didn't you? You used an arrow on that griffin that captured me and Arlo?"

Bristlebeard picked up his bow. "I used to be a bow and arrow kind of guy, but then I read this book on mindfulness. I passed it around the gang, and we decided to give Scrabble, knitting, and vegan Saturdays a go. We haven't looked back"—he paused—"well, not until the griffins started coming these last few days—tearing through the trees and stealing our marvels. Then, tonight, breathing that ghastly shatterblast that all of us snow trolls had assumed was locked away in the Smoking Chimneys. So when I saw you being carted off by one of the griffins I decided to step in." He stroked his bow. "And I have to say it was rather a nice feeling wielding a weapon again."

Brushwick put a hand on his arm. "Now, now, love—*Sudoku over savagery; carpentry over killing*. You know the rules."

"But that was before the griffins, Brushwick. And if those creatures were being subtle about things before by *secretly* tampering with the marvels at the castle, now they're not afraid to be seen, so we *need* to be armed to protect our marvels."

Brushwick nodded. "You're right, of course." Then, rather mischievously, she opened her fur coat to reveal a shining sword hanging down from her belt, together with a row of glinting knives. Her husband blinked in surprise. "I suppose I just haven't wanted to admit it these last few days."

Bristlebeard patted her arm. "I know, dear. I know." He looked back at Casper. "My arrow was dipped in deadly nightshade, which will stun that griffin for a day or so, but the dark magic the creature is conjured from will break through eventually." He sighed. "We haven't worked out a way to kill these beasts for good."

Casper didn't feel up to telling Bristlebeard that the hopes of the kingdom lay in his incapable hands, so instead he said: "You ran off before I could thank you."

Bristlebeard reddened. "Truth be told, I didn't quite know what you were. Clearly not from the castle. Definitely not a magical creature from around these parts. So, well, I'm afraid I turned tail and ran."

Casper took a deep breath. "My name is Casper. I'm from the Faraway."

Bristlebeard and Brushwick gaped at him, then Bristlebeard blew through his lips. "You're a long way from home, boy. . . ."

Casper nodded. "The wind sent me to Shiverbark Forest to find a familiar face—apparently it's the only thing that will destroy the Midnights."

"Midnights?" Brushwick asked.

"The name Morg gives the griffins; they're her followers."

Bristlebeard growled. "We thought as much."

"When I started out on the journey," Casper went on, "I thought I was meant to be keeping an eye out for someone that I recognized from home, but now I wonder whether I'm meant to be searching for a girl I met at Rumblestar Castle and who got snatched by the Midnights earlier today. She's called Utterly. You didn't manage to rescue her, too, did you?"

"*Utterly?*" Bristlebeard looked at Brushwick. "Wasn't that the name on the paper airplane you found on the forest floor this morning? The one from the Lofty Husks?"

Casper's eyes widened as Brushwick drew a piece of paper from her pocket and read the words aloud:

"Dear Utterly and guest. Notes from you and drizzle hags received. Know you are innocent. Sending search party to the Witch's Fingers immediately to help you on your quest. Yours in haste, the Lofty Husks."

Casper blinked at the knowledge that the Lofty Husks *had* been searching for them—that he and Utterly *did* matter—then he frowned. "The Lofty Husks did write back! But why didn't the note reach us? And why didn't the search party arrive?"

Bristlebeard shook his head. "Maybe you had left for the forest by the time the search party reached downstream, so they turned back for the castle to make another plan?"

"Or maybe the Midnights intervened," Brushwick said quietly.

"It's strange that the airplane didn't make it to you, though," Bristlebeard said. "And come to think of it, we haven't heard a word from the Lofty Husks today. We carve messages into the bark of the trees up here, you see, and our words appear, moments later, in the mirrors of the banqueting hall in the castle."

Casper peered more closely at the trees around them and saw that there were words—thousands of them—carved into the bark, only he had missed them before.

"But we sent them a message about finding this note and another about the Midnight attack and finding you, but there's been no reply to either," Bristlebeard said.

Brushwick shivered. "Something's afoot, I'll warrant, but as for who is in the forest now, Casper, it's only us and the Wild Ones."

Casper shrank inside his quilt. "Wild Ones?"

"Wolves made of snow, bears who breathe stardust, and reindeer with antlers so tall and grand several woodland birds can nest in them at once." He paused. "No children at all, except you."

Arlo burrowed into Casper's chest, and Casper watched the snow fall steadily around them. Where *was* Utterly and what on earth was happening back at the castle that meant the Lofty Husks hadn't messaged the snow trolls back? Casper blinked back his tears again and Brushwick opened one of the lanterns dangling nearby and held a mug of something steaming up to the flame. A wisp of fire curled into it. She handed the mug to Casper, then held another to the flames, which she gave to Bristlebeard.

"Spruce needle tea, brewed with a wisp of forest flame to warm the most troubled of souls," she said. "Have a drink of that and I'll fix you up some shiverbark stew."

She hurried along the walkways to a small platform filled with pots and pans, a stove, and a rack full of woodland spices, while Casper tilted his mug toward Arlo to give him the first sip. The dragon swallowed, then purred, and then Casper drank too. The tea was warm and spicy, like swallowing sunbeams, but even that couldn't drown out what had happened. And, little by little, Casper began telling Bristlebeard about the grandfather clock and Frostbite and the girl from the castle whom he had lost in the forest.

"Usually I manage to hold things together with my lists

and timetables," Casper said, "but now, without them, everything's gone wrong. Utterly's been kidnapped, the Midnights are sending more and more faulty marvels into the Mixing Tower, the weather in the Faraway is spiraling out of control, and I'm not sure I'm ever going to get home. Everything's such a mess and I don't even think there are lists and timetables big enough to sort it all out anymore."

Bristlebeard sat down in the armchair by the hammock and took a good long sip of tea. "Life, Casper, is wigglysplat."

"*Wigglysplat?*"

"It means complicated," Bristlebeard said. "Lots of bumps. Plenty of bruises. And so many unexpected problems that it's a wonder any of us bother getting up in the morning."

"So why *do* we bother?" Casper mumbled.

Bristlebeard leaned back in his armchair. "Because life is a little bit like snow, boy: frequently disruptive, hopelessly unpredictable, and often quick to fade. But my word is it beautiful while it lasts." He smiled. "We can't always know where we're heading, when we'll get there, or even who we'll meet along the way, but we can choose how we travel—and I'd say it's best to journey with friends alongside us and hope tucked firmly in our pockets."

Casper shook his head. "But what hope is there now? With Utterly gone?"

"She's gone for now," Bristlebeard said quietly, "but perhaps not gone for good, especially if this familiar face you are destined to find belongs to her. I can take you to the outskirts of the forest before dawn tomorrow—I would come with you, but the marvels here are in grave danger and I must protect them—but you will keep going and you will scour the kingdom for Utterly. She's your friend, after all."

"Acquaintance, really," Casper said glumly. "She was quite firm that we *weren't* friends." And then he added: "But I think we might've been working our way up to friends. Possibly. Hopefully. If I'd kept my mouth shut about things." He paused. "Though I've not really had a friend before, so perhaps what me and Utterly had was still miles off. She was always so cross. With me, with life . . . with everything and everyone really."

Bristlebeard sighed. "People rarely snap and scowl because of others but rather because there is a storm raging inside them. By the sound of it your Utterly has swallowed a whopperific storm and though it's hard to be friends with stormgulpers, Casper, they're the ones who need friends most."

They were silent for a while, and as Arlo snoozed on Casper's tummy, Casper watched the lanterns flickering between the trees as a group of snow trolls tipped a few more sacks of moon syrup into the hatch in the tree. He thought of his life back at Little Wallops. Hiding in the lost and found basket to avoid Candida and Leopold seemed silly compared to everything that had happened to him since stepping inside the grandfather clock.

"Are friendships always complicated?" Casper said eventually. "Or just the ones involving stormgulpers?"

Bristlebeard chuckled. "No friendship is buttersmooth. How can it be when every person is so wildly different inside? Friendships are, however, very good at sticking around even when tempers fly and doors are slammed. In fact, I'd say friendships are stickier than jam—and if you've tasted Brushwick's snowberry tarts, that's really saying something." He paused. "The thing about friendships, especially the ones with stormgulpers, is that they stretch you."

"I'm tiny, so that'll be handy."

Bristlebeard twirled his nose hair. "It's a different kind of stretching, Casper. Not the sort you'd need a tape measure for. Friendships push you and pull you in all sorts of surprising directions and the stretching is all done in here." The snow troll lifted a hand to his chest. "It sounds to me like your heart is not the same shape it was before you entered this kingdom—and it's my bet neither is Utterly's—because the thing that makes friendships stickier than jam is also the thing that makes hearts stretch. Loyalty. It grows slowly and quietly, almost without you noticing, then before you know it you're a little bit better at listening and a little bit kinder than you had been before all the stretching started." Bristlebeard sat forward. "You must go on after Utterly, Casper, however tricksyhard that sounds, because I think the Midnights will be holding her alive as bait to get to you." He glanced up toward the canopy. "Brushwick will keep watch tonight for any sign of the griffins, then perhaps we'll have a lead by the morning so you'll know which direction to go."

Casper looked down. "But . . . but I'm not sure I'm brave enough to go on alone. I was terrified back there with the griffin!"

"And yet you raced through the trees after Utterly anyway—and from what you were telling me about your adventure so far, you saved little Arlo from the mudgrapple. Life is built up of opportunities, Casper, and when you're ninety-four and wrinkled through—"

"Are you *ninety-four*?"

"Yes, but I have remarkably good genes. Anyway, that wasn't the point I was trying to make. I was saying that when you're ninety-four and you find yourself looking back on everything, it is nice to know that you lived your life fully. That you took chances and risks, that you pushed open doors and even grandfather clocks, and above all that you seized every minute of every day with every fiber inside you. Because life moves a great deal faster than most of us realize. Utterly is your opportunity here, Casper—and you *are* brave enough for it."

Casper watched the snow fall. "I'm not *properly* brave, though, like the heroes you read about in stories and history books. If anything, I'm just brave by mistake."

Bristlebeard smiled. "Courage is three parts fear and one part grit, but that one part grit is made of thunder. I saw your courage up close with the griffin, Casper, and its thunder shook my bones."

Casper didn't say anything for a moment or two because Bristlebeard's words were so different from the ones Candida and Leopold had flung at him back in Little Wallops and he wanted to remember this conversation if he ever got home.

Because here, up in the tallest trees of Shiverbark Forest, there was a snow troll saying he was brave.

"The drizzle hags told me to keep climbing and I'd find a familiar face, but Utterly isn't here."

"No, but I am." Bristlebeard winked. "Maybe the drizzle hags sent you here to collect something from me to help you *find* the familiar face? Magic is never straightforward, after all." He paused. "Many years ago, when snow trolls loved fighting as much as storm ogres, the two used to have raging battles to prove who was the mightiest of magical creatures. For a long time the ogres won, thanks to the shatterblast they conjured from the scorching ashes of their volcanoes. If given enough time, shatterblast worms its way inside victims—hot and deadly—weakening their limbs and minds until they sink into an eternal sleep." Bristlebeard shuddered. "Only the Lofty Husks have the power to wake from such a sleep—so we discovered when Blustersnap came by to try and halt one of our particularly long and bloodthirsty fights—and even then it takes a Lofty Husk weeks to summon up the strength."

Casper's pulse raced as he thought of Utterly. Had the shatterblast done its worst or were the Midnights keeping her alive and awake so that, on seeing her, Casper would go after her and fall straight into the griffins' clutches? Casper tried to think clearly. "So, did the Midnights get the shatterblast from the storm ogres?"

Bristlebeard nodded. "We think so. And that means the ogres didn't keep their promise after we snow trolls were victorious in the greatest battle of them all: the Battle of the Brutes." He smiled as he recalled it. "We fought on the brims of the Smoking Chimneys, the volcanoes to the east of the kingdom where the storm ogres live, and our defeat was so magnificent we not only cast a Victory Seal after the battle—which means that if the ogres ever try to leave the volcanoes, they themselves will crumble to ash—but we also forced the ogres to lock the shatterblast they had conjured inside a trunk. They vowed never to open it for fear of us snow trolls waging war again, but on seeing it tonight as the griffins tore through the forest after you, it's my guess the Midnights bribed them for it. Storm ogres *never* say no to bribes."

Casper thought of the ogre Utterly had told him about who had traded in his sight for the river's silver.

Bristlebeard lowered his voice. "A few hours ago, while you were resting, we sent our bravest snow troll, Pucklefist, to the Smoking Chimneys to try to convince the ogres to call the shatterblast back—winds like that answer to those who conjured them, you see. But whether Pucklefist will have any luck, I don't know. It's not easy negotiating with storm ogres, and the Midnights don't seem afraid to kill magical creatures standing in their way."

"How did you win the Battle of the Brutes?" Casper asked.

"We came across something extraordinary to use in the fight," Bristlebeard whispered. "We've always kept it a secret, but since the Midnights arrived in Rumblestar, I've had a feeling—a hunch—that I need to pass our secret on, and Brushwick agrees. A snow troll's hunch is never wrong, after all."

Casper leaned closer. "What was the secret that helped you beat the storm ogres?"

Bristlebeard's eyes twinkled. "Armor, boy. Armor built with magic."

Chapter 17

Bristlebeard reached inside the drawer of his bedside table, then drew out a key and slotted it into a door leading into the tree his hammock hung from. He opened it and pulled out two hooded capes, made from silver fur, which had ice-white patterns that looked a little like tree roots running down their lengths. He held them up. "Made from the furs of a silver panther and decorated with—"

"—frozen lightning!" Casper cried.

Bristlebeard cocked his head. "How do you know about frozen lightning?"

"The cloud giant who helped us back at the castle was wearing a breastplate made from it," Casper explained. "He said that no blade could cut through his breastplate and even fire didn't stand a chance."

Bristlebeard nodded. "Frozen lightning won us a war and now it's going to help you against the Midnights, because by wearing these you'll be protected not only from their talons and their beaks but also from the shatterblast they breathe." He handed the capes to Casper. "One for you and one for Utterly—because you *will* find her—and when you do, I want you both to give those Midnights the wallopsmashing they deserve."

He glanced at the cupboard in the tree again, looked over his shoulder to check they were alone, then drew out a crossbow and an axe and handed them both to Casper, too.

Casper gulped. Up until this moment the most dangerous thing he'd ever held was a Bunsen burner in chemistry lessons.

"Don't tell Brushwick about this just yet," Bristlebeard whispered. "Armor's fine, but she's never been keen on handing out weapons to under-agers. I *can* tell that she's coming round to the idea of taking up arms again to protect the marvels, though—the woman's got a sword and a dozen knives tucked into her knickers, for crying out loud, and she hasn't practiced mindful breathing for at least a week. . . ."

Casper turned the crossbow over in his hands. "I *really* don't think this is a good idea."

"The crossbow might look frightening," Bristlebeard replied, "but all troll weapons are enchanted so they're easy to use—even for a newcomer, like you. The bolt here is attached to a rope that unwinds when you fire using this trigger"—he showed Casper so that he understood—"so you'll never lose it, and it's been dipped in deadly nightshade, like my arrows, so it'll stun any Midnight upon impact."

Casper nodded shakily.

"And the axe—Sir Chopalot, I named him—is the trustiest weapon I've ever fought with. It slices anything it comes into contact with. So don't you go holding back, boy. Blow the Midnights to smithereens!"

"Who's blowing the Midnights to smithereens, darling?"

Bristlebeard whirled round. Brushwick was standing behind him with a bowl of steaming stew, so he hastily tucked the weapons beneath the blankets in the hammock and gave her a kiss on the cheek.

"We will be," Bristlebeard replied, "if they *dare* steal any more of our marvels."

Brushwick nodded. "And there I was worrying you had handed out all your prized weapons to young Casper here. The capes are one thing, but crossbows and axes are quite another."

Casper twiddled his fingers nervously, but thankfully, Bristlebeard changed the subject before he had to reply. "Ah, vegan stew. Your finest."

Brushwick produced four spoons from her apron pocket. "One for Arlo, too," she said, and at his name, the little dragon opened an eye.

They ate quickly and quietly, for there were things on their minds and when they had finished the stew, Brushwick cleared the bowls away. "I'll be up in the lookout post all night. With my sword and my knives," she added under her breath, "in case the Midnights come snooping. So, you and Arlo get some sleep because if you're going after your friend tomorrow and attempting to put an end to these griffins, you're going to need your energy for what's ahead of you—it's a big old kingdom out there."

Brushwick rubbed a little more of the sap into Casper's leg, which miraculously now only bore a dark bruise, and while Bristlebeard and the rest of the snow trolls busied themselves with their sacks of snow, Casper and Arlo tried their best to sleep before the journey onward.

In the early hours of the next day, when the forest was still dark and full of snoring trolls, Bristlebeard woke Casper.

"Best to leave under cover of darkness," he whispered. "Brushwick hasn't *seen* the Midnights, but she nipped down earlier to say she'd *heard* them calling out across the heath beyond the forest. Maybe they're searching for the griffin I took down? Whatever the reason, it's your only lead on Utterly, so it's worth following." He held up a blank wad of paper, then smeared it with a handful of snow. Instantly, words appeared and Bristlebeard's face lit up.

"The *Unmapped Chronicle*," he said. "The kingdom's newspaper. But ever since Morg took the place of the last phoenix, it's been hexed so that the words only appear if you're a trusted Unmapper *and* you dip the paper in water—though out here in Shiverbark Forest, snow works too." He squinted at the newspaper. "Yesterday only the last page of the newspaper showed up for some reason—rather unhelpfully that happened to be the seaball results from the kingdom of Crackledawn—and today it seems we just have the first page."

"But important stories usually come first," Casper said eagerly, "so this could be useful. What does it say?'"

The snow troll scanned the first paragraph. "Doesn't look like it's good news. . . . The emergency supply of marvels in the Mixing Tower is running out."

"Can't the Lofty Husks leave the castle and bring a few more back? Surely *they* know ways to stay one step ahead of the Midnights?"

Bristlebeard read on, then his mouth fell open. "They can't leave the castle, Casper. . . ." He pointed to the article on the front page, written by an Unmapper called Bertie Flitterquill. "Look . . ."

"Can't *leave*?" Casper whispered, taking the newspaper from Bristlebeard.

Then he saw why. Dozens of Midnights were patrolling the castle walls now. No one was able to get out—not ballooners, bottlers, *or* Lofty Husks. Everyone was trapped inside. And suddenly it made sense why the Lofty Husks hadn't sent out another search party for him and Utterly. They *couldn't*.

Casper read aloud from the newspaper:

> "This may well be the last chronicle for a while. Not satisfied with disrupting our SkyFly so that paper airplanes hurtle out to the wrong destinations and our newspaper only shows a quarter of our news, now Morg's followers have hexed the castle walls to stop messages from leaving altogether and to prevent word from the magical creatures reaching our mirrors."

Casper gasped. "That would explain why you can't contact the Lofty Husks!" he said to Bristlebeard. "And why the message for me and Utterly was delivered to the wrong place and the *Unmapped Chronicle* only shows a fraction of the news!" The snow troll nodded gravely and Casper read on.

"It's only a matter of time before the Midnights shut down this newspaper completely.

"The Lofty Husks continue to cast every kind of spell to prevent the Midnights breathing shatterblast down the Mixing Tower chimneys, but last night Blustersnap confirmed that Morg has filled these beasts with the darkest magic and it will take a very rare kind of spell to stop them, which, so far, they have yet to find. Our rulers will pore over *every* book in the castle for it and our bottlers will try to get rid of the shatterblast in the Mixing Tower, but everyone's thoughts are with the only two children still out in the Beyond"—Casper's heart skipped a beat—"a mere bottler-in-training called Utterly Thankless and, according to Utterly's mother (who received a note from Utterly before the SkyFly was halted), a young boy from the Faraway. Having been forced to abandon a search mission for Utterly and the boy after only narrowly escaping an ambush by the Midnights on the Witch's Fingers just before the castle walls were hexed, the Lofty Husks have now confirmed that the future of the Unmapped Kingdoms and the Faraway lies in the hands of these two children.

"Mrs. Thankless had this to say to her daughter: 'My darling girl, your father and I are so proud of you out there in the Beyond, and we know in our hearts that if anyone can save Rumblestar now, it is you and your friend. We love you and we miss you and we will scour the kingdom for you at the very first chance we get.'

"And from all of us back at the castle to Utterly and her friend: Wherever you are, you two, keep believing in yourselves and know that every single Unmapper is willing you on."

Casper stared at the words. He felt almost dizzy at the thought of so many people hoping and trusting in him. And that was just here in the Unmapped Kingdoms. He felt even more overwhelmed when he thought of the consequences back home if he failed. . . . Casper looked at the article again and his guilt sharpened. All those people knowing Utterly was innocent and willing her on—and Utterly's mum believing her daughter could save Rumblestar—when he'd already let her be carried off by Midnights . . .

"I always thought the Lofty Husks would come to the rescue in the end," Casper said softly, "but it really is just down to me—and Utterly, if I ever find her—to save the Unmapped Kingdoms *and* the Faraway." Arlo sat up on Casper's shoulder and straightened his waistcoat. "And you, Arlo, of course."

Bristlebeard put a hand on Casper's arm. "And other than the ogres, it would seem you have the magical creatures on your side too." He paused. "The chronicle says the Unmappers can't get out of the castle, but perhaps there's a way *in*. I thought my fight lay here in the forest, but maybe—if Brushwick and the others can spare me—I could try to find a way to sneak our marvels past the Midnights while you go on to find Utterly."

Casper nodded. "Rumblestar and the Faraway need *all* the help they can get." He looked at the message from Utterly's mum again, then he ripped it off and shoved it in his pocket. Then, taking a deep breath, Casper swung himself out of the hammock. He had been expecting the pain in his leg to throb, but it had vanished completely and as he rolled up his overalls, he saw that even the bruising was gone!

"Works wonders, that sap does." Bristlebeard handed Casper a rucksack. "Nut roast, together with five portions of fruit, a flask of water, capes, crossbow, *and* Sir Chopalot, the finest axe around."

Casper peered over the edge of the platform. They were so high up in the trees that he couldn't even see the ground.

Bristlebeard winked. "Don't worry, boy, going down is a great deal quicker and easier than coming up."

He pointed to a tree beside the one in which the trolls had shoveled the ingredients for the marvels. The trunk wound down in the most extraordinary manner—spirals, loop-the-loops, swerving corners, diagonal steps—and a small door had been carved into it at their level. Bristlebeard led the way over the walkways through the trees toward it, then he pulled the door open.

Casper bit his lip. "I was afraid it might be this door you were after."

"Best to descend in a sack," Bristlebeard said, grabbing one from a hook on the back of the door. "Increases speed, which right now we need more than ever." And before Casper could say anything in reply, the snow troll shuffled into his sack and pushed off into the hollow.

Casper took another sack down and slipped his feet inside it, but Arlo was so impatient to get on after Utterly he kept fluttering in Casper's face, which eventually made him lose his footing altogether and tumble headfirst into the woodland flume. Casper shrieked as they careered through the dark, jostling over bumps, spinning in a circle, and at one point flipping head over heels in a somersault before—many minutes later—shooting out into a pile of leaves.

Bristlebeard was already dusting himself down. "Not the most stylish of descents, Casper, but full marks for attempting the ride headfirst."

Casper pulled a leaf out of his ear. "It was completely unintentional."

And though Casper had been nervous on seeing the flume and was now rather shaken after the ride, he hadn't thought once about a helmet or crash mats or anything like that. He'd just got on and done it (with a little help from Arlo), and knowing that really did make him feel a tiny bit brave.

Bristlebeard pointed east through the forest. "Come on—this way."

Now that they were down on the forest floor again, and beyond the safety of the snow trolls' hideaway, Casper started at every twig-snapping, leaf-rustling noise. And he could have sworn he could see creatures stalking between the trees: something silver-white first, then something tall and dark with huge, twisting antlers. Were they down amongst the Wild Ones now? Amongst wolves built of snow and deer with enormous antlers . . .

Casper peered through the trees. It was mostly dark still and the snow fell soundlessly, and though there was no sign of the Midnights, Casper had the distinct feeling that he was being followed. Once or twice he thought he saw a shadow out of place—a part of the darkness in the distance that seemed to be moving in a way that was quite unlike the wolves and the deer—but whenever he nudged Bristlebeard or tugged Arlo's wing, there was nothing there to see. They walked on for a while more and then it was Bristlebeard who stopped.

"What can you see?" Casper whispered.

"Not see, boy. *Hear* . . ."

He was silent for a few seconds, then he looked to their right, through the snowy trees. Casper tensed. He could hear twigs snapping, leaves rustling, and the faintest patter of footsteps.

"A snow troll?"

Bristlebeard shook his head, then Arlo squeaked and dived into Casper's pocket. Because the footsteps were getting louder now and they were accompanied by the raggedy breath of somebody running, or stumbling, through the forest. Casper clutched Bristlebeard's arm as the snow troll drew out a knife from his coat and held it up.

"Who's there?"

The footsteps hurried closer, the breathing became louder, and then a very tall, very narrow man staggered through the dark toward them. His robes were made from enchanted parchment, but they were muddied and ripped, and his pointed hat, studded with fallen stars, had a large hole in it. Casper blinked. This was a Lofty Husk, one that he recognized all too well, only his eyes were kinder than they had been back at the castle.

"The *real* Frostbite," Casper murmured.

Bristlebeard bowed and Casper dipped his head, but Frostbite waved his hand.

"There is no time for formalities now, though I thank you for your respect." He leaned against a tree for support. "Two weeks ago a Midnight ambushed me as I was departing the castle in my hot air balloon. He stole my mirror ring and with it, my identity, and though his shatterblast sent me into an endless nightmare from which I could not awake, I did, finally, last night." Frostbite coughed, which forced his words into gasps. "My hot air balloon must have been adrift in the sky for many, many days, but when I awoke to snow, I realized that I was close to Shiverbark Forest." He looked at Bristlebeard. "The Midnight has drained almost all of my magic and my strength, but I have heard that you snow trolls have healing balms to lift the darkest curses. Perhaps you can help me before it is too late."

Bristlebeard nodded. "We'll do everything we can."

Then Frostbite's gaze fell on Casper. "In the lanterns in the Precipice we Lofty Husks can see into the Faraway," he said quietly, "and you, my child, look very much like a boy from those lands." And though his voice was weak, he smiled. "In the last meeting I chaired before I left the castle, I felt the moonbreeze trying to tell me something—about help against Morg and her Midnights coming from unexpected places."

He looked Casper up and down. "So am I right in thinking that you, boy, are here to help?"

Casper nodded, but he couldn't help feeling ashamed because surely Frostbite was expecting someone brave and capable. "I'm sorry if I'm not what you were hoping for."

The Lofty Husk slumped down to his knees so that he was level with Casper. "You should not be apologizing, my boy. You are here, with all your limbs intact, alongside a miniature dragon." Arlo saluted Frostbite from Casper's pocket. "You seem to be doing rather well."

Casper looked down. "Except I've lost my friend, Utterly. The Midnights took her."

"Utterly Thankless? A stormgulper if ever I knew one, but a stormgulper with heart and spirit and a brilliant mind for bottling." Frostbite's face darkened. "I heard the griffins shrieking across the heath last night," he wheezed, "but they're not there now."

Casper felt what little hope he had been clutching at slip through his fingers.

"They flew on north," Frostbite rasped.

"North?" Bristlebeard asked. "Toward Dapplemere?"

"That would make sense," Casper said slowly. "Utterly and

I noticed something strange back on the Witch's Fingers: We never saw the sun. Not once. Even when the rain and clouds had cleared off. Just a hazy kind of light trying to push through down at the horizon." He paused. "Maybe the Midnights have a roost at this place Dapplemere and maybe the sun isn't appearing"—he paused again—"because of what Utterly said to me: The Midnights have done something terrible to the creatures living there."

"The poor sun scamps," Bristlebeard said, clenching his fists. "If the Midnights have taken Utterly to Dapplemere, you shouldn't waste time on the heath. You need to get there—fast—"

"Then once the snow trolls have helped me gather my strength"—Frostbite's breathing was becoming shallower now—"I'll work on a way to get a message past the Midnights to the other Lofty Husks, then come on after you."

Bristlebeard shook his head. "It'll be a while before you're fit to travel, sir. And the kingdom doesn't have a while. It's already on the brink of ruin!"

Frostbite held Casper's hand though his grip was weak and his skin was cold. "Then you are our only hope, boy. Follow the path I was on to the edge of the forest." He drew in a lungful of air, then choked it all the way out. "You'll find my balloon." He gasped. "And you must fly it to Dapplemere without a moment's delay."

Casper's eyes widened and Arlo let out a frightened squeak. "I can't even fly a kite! Don't I need a license or at least a lesson first?"

"Not if you want to put an end to the Midnights"—Frostbite coughed—"before they put an end to Rumblestar and the Faraway."

Bristlebeard put an arm out to help Frostbite to his feet. "There's no time for caution."

"But . . . is it easy to steer a hot air balloon?" Casper asked.

"I wouldn't say it's so much about"—Frostbite coughed again—"steering as telling." He forced the next words out, wincing through the pain. "Just know your mind"—his voice was just a rasp now—"and say it."

Bristlebeard reached out his other arm to hug Casper. "You'll be grand, boy. And if you're worried about a thing, don't you hesitate to reach for Sir Chopalot."

"Thank you for being such a good friend," Casper said. "I hope we meet again."

Bristlebeard smiled. "As do I, Casper. As do I. And if we

manage to get through all this, remember that you're welcome back for a game of Scrabble or a bowl of tofu any time you like." He lifted Frostbite's arm up over his shoulder. "Let's get you up to the warmth now and see about that healing balm."

Too weak to speak more, Frostbite clasped Casper's hand, then he and Bristlebeard turned back into the forest, and Casper and Arlo were alone once more. They hurried down the path the Lofty Husk had taken, and as they drew up to the edge of the forest, the snow petered out and Casper peeped round a tree at the heath beyond.

It was an open expanse of bracken, gorse, and heather—and though there was a cloudless sky above, it was lit only by a faint trickle of light down at the horizon. Were there still a few sun scamps free from the clutches of the Midnights working away to create the marvels? Casper hoped so. Because what would all this mean for his parents and everyone else back home? A world plunged into darkness as well as chaos from the winds?

Arlo tugged on his sleeve and pointed through the trees to their right. Tethered to a tree trunk at the very outskirts of the forest was the hot air balloon. Only it wasn't floating in the air all ready to go, as Casper had hoped it might be. The balloon was a great sagging red shape dotted with stars, sprawled across the heather, and the basket was turned on its side.

Casper took a very deep breath. Somehow he had to get this hot air balloon up into the sky.

Chapter 18

Casper unknotted the rope that tethered the balloon to the tree, then peered into the basket. There was no extremely helpful telephone inside, like there had been in the canoe, and there didn't seem to be anything obvious that would make a balloon like this fly. There was only a large and finely woven silver net, which Casper supposed might be used to catch marvels, buckled to one side, and a cork-stoppered bottled labeled FUEL—which was empty.

Casper pushed the basket upright, then he clambered in and turned to Arlo, who was perched on top of the unlit burners. The balloon itself draped down to the ground behind these burners, but watching Arlo there, Casper recalled something Utterly had said when they were in the canoe on the Witch's Fingers: "Hot air balloons are powered by dragon fire."

Arlo looked at Casper with eager eyes, as if to ask the boy whether he thought the little dragon was up to the task. Casper thought back to the time Arlo had tried to blow fire on the steps outside the castle (without luck), then again in the canoe at the jailbirds (again, without luck), then once more when the mudgrapple snatched him (yet again, without luck). But, Casper thought, just because someone wasn't obviously very good at something, didn't mean they couldn't surprise *you*. He hadn't imagined himself much of an adventurer, but he had survived a flock of jailbirds, three dreadful drizzle hags, *and* dozens of Midnights.

Casper nodded at Arlo. "Let's see what you've got, then."

The dragon drew in a lungful of air, then blew hard. There was a croaky noise, which sounded suspiciously like a burp, then a wisp of smoke. Arlo tried again, huffing and puffing at the burners in front of him until he disappeared in another cloud of smoke. But Casper knew smoke wasn't enough to power the balloon, and when it faded, he saw that Arlo was sitting in a ball with his wings curled over his face.

Casper thought of the Midnights circling the castle and the supply of marvels running low. How long did they have before the marvels ran out completely and the link between

Rumblestar and the other kingdoms died? But he spoke kindly to the little dragon because he knew what it felt like to feel small and hopeless.

"You can do this, Arlo. The kingdom depends on it and I believe in you. And so would Utterly if she were here too."

And at his words, Arlo picked himself up and tried again. He blew and he blew and he blew until his wings shook and Casper felt sure that he was going to keel over and faint. But he didn't. He kept blowing until, eventually, a snort of fire burst out of his nostrils—and set the burnings roaring.

"Well done, Arlo!" Casper cried, scooping him up and holding him close. "What a magnificent dragon you are!"

Arlo gave a shy smile then, exhausted from the ordeal, collapsed in Casper's palm, and went to sleep. Casper looked at the burners. He had expected the flames to carry the balloon up into the sky after a few minutes, especially since he had untethered the basket earlier. But the balloon stayed exactly where it was.

Then Casper spotted a small microphone jutting out from the front of the basket that he had missed before. He narrowed his eyes. "Just know your mind and say it," Frostbite had told him. Could that mean simply instructing the hot air balloon where to go?

He gave it a try. "Dapplemere, please."

The microphone crackled, then a woman's voice—firm and to-the-point—sounded through it. "This is your captain, Zip, speaking. Welcome aboard the SkySoar9000."

Casper blinked in surprise.

"Please confirm your route preference," Zip added. "Safe and scenic or fast and blurry?"

Casper thought about being hundreds of meters up in the air in a tiny wicker basket and his legs wobbled. Then he thought of Morg getting ready to steal the kingdom's magic and Utterly in the clutches of the Midnights. He took a deep breath and summoned up every ounce of courage he could muster. "F-fast and blurry."

No sooner had he finished speaking than the balloon lurched upward, rising so blisteringly fast into the sky that Casper and Arlo clattered to their knees and tears streamed down their cheeks. Casper clung to the side of the basket, his knuckles white, his eyes wide. He was out of control, out of his depth, and very probably out of his mind, too. But right now, there was not a lot he could do about it, so he simply held on as the hot air balloon rose beyond the tallest trees in Shiverbark Forest, then soared out across the heath.

The microphone sputtered into life again. "We are cruising at"—there was a pause—"an unspeakably high altitude. There are emergency exits on all four sides of your basket—just tip yourself over the edge and you're away—and in-flight drinks and snacks are available through hatches one and two."

There was a popping sound, and Casper jumped as several numbered levers burst through the walls of the basket.

"Please listen carefully to the safety briefing," Zip added.

Casper's ears pricked up. This sounded hopeful.

"In the very *likely* event of a fire, crash, or sudden tilt, please do *not* reach for hatch three, where the oxygen masks and life jackets are stored. Your chances of survival are minimal and it is extremely cumbersome trying to replace stock. Instead, feel free to cry—there are tissues in hatch four—and try your best not to look down. I hope you enjoy your flight in the SkySoar9000."

Casper felt a familiar panic rise inside him. He swallowed hard. He needed to be strong—for Arlo (who was currently facedown in the corner of the basket), for Utterly, and for a whole world at the mercy of Morg. He was too frightened to risk a peek out over the edge of the basket just yet, but through the gaps in the wicker he could see that they were racing across the heath. Zip seemed to tread a very narrow line between being efficient and breaking the speed limit—but they were hastening on toward Utterly and for that, Casper was grateful.

He raised a shaking hand and pulled the lever on hatch one, anything to distract himself from how high up in the air he was. There were a few clanking noises, then the sound of liquid being poured and something being squirted. The hatch opened and out popped a hot chocolate laden with marshmallows and something that looked a little like cream, only wispier, on a wooden tray.

Zip's voice sounded through the microphone. "One extra-large hot chocolate with marshmallows and cloud froth." She paused. "Because, let's face facts, life feels a good deal more bearable when you're armed with chocolate."

Casper and Arlo helped themselves—it was big enough to share and, as it turned out, delicious enough to settle their nerves. Casper popped the empty glass back in the hatch, then he ventured a glance over the edge of the basket.

There was a whole kingdom at his feet: rivers reduced to scribbles, a forest no bigger than a matchbox, and moor upon moor rolling into the distance. On seeing it all, Casper realized that very few people got to look at the world in the way he was now. There were airplanes back home, of course, but in them you had to look out through a window. Here there was nothing separating him from the endless skies. And though he was still scared, he could feel something new fizzing through his veins. Awe. This was a kingdom full of unpredictable things, but it was mind-spinningly beautiful too, even though its magic was fading in parts, and Casper couldn't help wondering whether his own world, which had seemed so small and glum before, might in fact be a little bigger and more interesting than he had realized. Perhaps he would have to address the amount of time spent hiding in lost and found baskets if he ever got home. . . .

He reached out a hand and let it trail in the wind. He shifted. The breeze was picking up, rattling between the burners and gusting against the balloon. Casper tried to tell himself that ballooners would experience high winds all the time up here in the sky. But there was something about *this* wind—something hot and stinging—that made Casper withdraw his hand and grip the edge of the basket. Arlo scuttled into the rucksack Bristlebeard had given them.

The wind started howling and the air seemed to crackle with heat, even though the sun, or what was left of it, was still all the way down at the horizon. Zip slowed and Casper reached for his cape of frozen lightning. The fur felt cool against his skin—*Was that the frozen lightning working its magic?* Casper wondered—and he buttoned it up around his chin because there was only one kind of wind that blew with the force of fire and came from nowhere. Shatterblast.

Casper held up an arm to shield his face from the heat. The air was blurred like a mirage now and the wind pulsed against Casper's cheeks and tried to needle inside his body. Casper held on to the basket, but the shatterblast blew harder, ramming against the balloon and sending Casper stumbling to his knees. Arlo poked his head out of the rucksack he was hiding in, his wings twitching with fear. Casper tucked him inside the pocket of his cape because if this fire-loaded, terror-filled wind was tearing through the sky around them now, it meant the Midnights must be close.

"If . . . if we stay low," Casper panted to Arlo, "we can leave the rest to Zip. She sounds pretty capable. Right?"

Arlo tried to nod, but the shatterblast slammed into the basket with fresh force and the balloon hurtled sideways. Casper screamed. Then Zip corrected their course once again and tried to carry on. But the wind was growing in strength and heat now, and though the cape seemed to protect Casper and Arlo from the worst of the heat and the numbing effects of the wind, still the shatterblast shunted against the basket from every angle.

The microphone buzzed. "This is your captain, Zip, speaking. Auto-fly dismantled due to weather conditions. Please fly manually."

Casper's stomach turned. "*Manually?*"

The shatterblast tossed the balloon back and forth, sending Casper and Arlo crashing into the sides of the basket. And then another noise rose above the wind.

The bone-juddering shrieks of the Midnights.

Casper couldn't see the griffins from where he crouched, but their screeches filled the sky and even Zip was beginning to sound flustered now: "Can the allocated driver please open hatch five—*immediately*—for goggles and a flying hat, then tell me how to fly through this wind!"

Casper's throat tightened. He was too terrified to move. And even if he summoned up the courage to grab the microphone, what on *earth* would he say? He couldn't tell Zip how to fly through shatterblast and dodge a flock of Midnights! Casper glanced down at Arlo, and though the dragon was shaking inside the pocket of the cape, he was looking up at

Casper hopefully. *Somehow* the dragon believed in him, and suddenly amid the howling gale and grating shrieks, Bristlebeard's words rang in Casper's ears—about friendship and jam and courage and thunder. He thought of Utterly and of his parents back home, then he pulled the lever on hatch five, shoved on the flying hat and goggles, and stood up.

Now he saw a cluster of black shapes zipping through the sky, but they were far below the hot air balloon. The griffins were patrolling the *moorland*, not the skies at all. *Of course!* Casper thought. *The Midnights will be expecting me to follow Utterly on foot across the heath! But here we are sneaking past them in the sky. . . .*

Then Casper noticed something else. He could see *patterns* in the sky—small red spirals that seemed to spin through the air and, very often, smash against the sides of the basket. Casper lifted his goggles up and the patterns vanished.

"Ballooners' goggles must be magical," he gasped, slotting them down over his eyes again and seeing the spirals reappear. "They show the pattern of the winds so the ballooners can navigate the skies without getting into trouble!"

The shatterblast drummed against Casper's face, but he could see a way out of it now—the sky was a maze of spirals and he needed to guide Zip through it—so he gripped the microphone and hissed, "Duck left, Zip! Then make a sharp right!"

Zip did as Casper said and the spirals of wind tore by either side of the basket and missed them completely!

Casper eyed a new line of spirals advancing toward them. "Now a quick plunge!" he cried. "Followed by a wiggle up. And then dodge, dodge, dodge!"

Thankfully, Zip was a lot better at following instructions than Utterly, and though the shatterblast raged and the griffins shrieked, the balloon shimmied and dropped, bounced and spun, and, just like that, Casper sailed it right out from under the Midnights' noses.

"You're nearly through the last of the shatterblast!" Casper cried. "One more duck and weave it looks like you're out the other side!"

Zip followed Casper's command and suddenly the air was no longer whirling with red-hot spirals but simply the moan of a wind fading. Casper breathed out as they flew on below a roof of white, puffy clouds.

"Auto-fly resumed," Zip said. And then, after a pause: "Please give yourself an almighty pat on the back for navigating so excellently and remember that if you feel like a celebratory sob, tissues are in hatch four."

Confident that there was no more shatterblast around them, Casper pushed the goggles up onto his forehead and grinned at Arlo, who had crawled out of his pocket and was now hopping up and down in the basket. "We're another step closer to finding Utterly."

Arlo squeaked with joy, then he fluttered to Casper's shoulder, where he curled up and purred. They gobbled down Brushwick's nut roast—because being brave was hungry work—and while Zip flew on and on, farther north, they took turns keeping watch at the edge of the basket.

After a few hours, the moorland built up into valleys: grass-covered slopes, glittering streams, and lakes—huge pools of water that spread out through the valleys like giant footprints—down in the hollows. Some of these lakes were surrounded by woodland, others by rocks, but only one was surrounded by watermills, and it was toward this one that Zip was flying.

"It is three in the afternoon local time in Dapplemere and, against the odds, you are about to arrive at your destination." Zip was silent for a second, then she added, "Well, *almost* at your destination. After the incident with the griffins, I fine-tuned my radar and it is sensing more dark magic nearby now. Dapplemere Lake is usually golden because the hillside caves holding the ingredients for sunlight feed down into it, but today it's an ordinary blue and the watermills the scamps use to pedal sunlight into marvels aren't moving at all. So I think we should hang back until we've got a plan."

Casper could've hugged the microphone because here, hundreds of meters up in the sky, was a magical hot air balloon fond of forward planning.

Chapter 19

Zip hovered behind a cloud just above the hills leading down into Dapplemere. Through the mist Casper could see the slopes formed a bowl around the lake, grassy banks filled with crags, waterfalls, and beautiful old trees, but from where they were floating it was hard to see more.

"Hatch five for a telescope," Zip prompted. "And you'll be pleased to know that its glass is enchanted so it'll bring everything you look at—from the caves containing ingredients for sunlight to the wishing trees on the slopes—right up to your nose."

Casper drew out the telescope and raised it to his eye. "Wow . . ."

Zip wasn't lying about the enchanted glass; he could see

everything in the valley in the sharpest detail. What Casper had thought were rocky crags at either end of the valley were in fact two enormous stone heads. They stretched the height of the hillside and waterfalls poured down from their eyes into jutting mouths—vast stone bowls as large as swimming pools. There were caves dotted about the hillside and Casper could make out the signposts before them: **GOLD FLAKES**, **HONEYFIRE**, **DAZZLETHREAD**, and **TREACLE**. *Were these the ingredients for sunlight?* Casper wondered. Ancient trees swayed in the breeze, with endless ribbons tied to their branches, and Casper imagined these could well be the wishing trees Utterly had paid a visit to on her birthday.

He slid his telescope down to the lake and through the haze of cloud Zip hung behind, Casper could see the exquisitely carved mills, with patterned shutters and verandas overlooking the water. But the mills didn't look like they were in good shape at all; the windows had been punched through, the wheels had been smashed to pieces, and some appeared to be nothing more than heaps of charcoaled wood. On the lake itself half-sunk rowing boats swayed aimlessly, and tucked into the foot of the hillside there was what looked like the remains of a village.

The shops lining the higgledy-piggledy streets claimed to sell all manner of things for ballooners and bottlers, but every single one had been ransacked: there was **HUFFINGTON BALLOONS (EST. 1325)**, whose sign was hanging by its hinges; **BRITTLEWEAVE BASKETS (10% DISCOUNT FOR FIRST-TIME BUYERS)**, whose contents were spilled out into the street; and **TWIZZLEQUICK TOOLS (PURVEYOR OF QUALITY TOOLS SINCE FOREVER)**, whose door was missing.

Down a winding alley, picnic tables lay overturned outside a pub called **THE BURPING EAGLE** and menu boards had been clawed through outside a terraced building called **NIBBLENOSH**. The place had been trashed—it looked like a ghost town—but over everything, Casper noticed, there were bird droppings. And when he looked back at the mills, he stiffened. Because as he peered closer, he saw that Dapplemere was not a ghost town at all.

"The Midnights are here," he whispered.

Arlo tiptoed along the edge of the basket to be closer to Casper.

"At first I thought all those rotten branches on the verandas of the mills were simply churned-up wood from the spokes of the wheels, but if you look carefully, you can see the tips of black wings draped over the edge. The Midnights have built their nests there—no wonder the sun scamps haven't been able to send sunlight out into the kingdom!" Casper steadied himself as he took in all the nests lining the lake, then he turned to Arlo. "Somehow we've got to find Utterly without disturbing them."

Arlo whimpered and Casper drew back from the edge of the basket for a few moments. The task ahead seemed impossible, ridiculous even. But if he did nothing, then the whole kingdom could fall and he'd never get home to see his parents again. He was no hero, when it came down to it, and yet he was the only one left to stop the Midnights!

Casper forced himself to look through the telescope again. The tails of the griffins hung lazily over the nests and though their wings were tucked in, every now and again their heads swiveled round to the far hillside sloping down into Dapplemere. Casper squinted through the telescope at the wishing trees and the caves there. Then his eyes rested on a larger cave tucked into an overhang of rock so near the top of the hillside that part of the cave was lost in the clouds. The signpost outside it was still visible, but the words on it didn't seem to have anything to do with ingredients for sunlight. They read:

WELCOME TO TOPPLECAVE RESTAURANT: 2-FOR-1 SUNFIZZ ON THURSDAYS AFTER 6 P.M. (OVER 21S ONLY). On the platform of rock before this cave, tables and chairs lay in pieces, but this was not what the Midnights were looking at.

Casper gasped. There were bars strung across this cave and behind them, only just visible in the gloom, was a girl with wild blond hair dressed in overalls!

Casper's heart thumped. He'd found Utterly—and it looked as if she was alive and awake, not slumped in an eternal sleep! The relief rushed through him, and though he wasn't quite sure how freeing her would destroy the Midnights and he knew that he didn't really have a sensible plan for Zip, he grabbed the microphone anyway. Because he knew, very firmly, that he had to rescue Utterly as soon as possible.

"Drop back from Dapplemere, Zip, then fly as quietly as you can behind the far hillside," Casper whispered. "When you get to those clouds bunched up around the top corner, stall a while. My friend is trapped inside Topplecave and—"

"Got carried away on the two-for-one sunfizzes, did she? Common story."

"She's eleven, Zip. And she's been locked in the cave by the Midnights."

"Ah, I see. Carry on, skipper."

"So, while you hover in the clouds, I'll drop down and free my friend."

"May I suggest the use of hatch six to create a distraction for the Midnights at that point?"

Casper was steadily falling more and more in love with Zip. "That would be brilliant. Thank you."

Soundlessly, Zip drew back from Dapplemere, then as she skirted behind the far hillside, Casper shook Bristlebeard's weapons out of the rucksack. The crossbow looked suddenly small compared to the flock of Midnights squatting on the mills, and even the axe looked less impressive than it had done up in the snow troll's hideaway. Casper felt sick with fear. But Zip was already round the other side of Dapplemere now, and as she inched into the clouds, the edge of Topplecave came into view just a few meters below them. The hot air balloon hovered where it was. Any farther and it might attract the attention of the Midnights.

Utterly was sitting in the corner of the cave closest to them, amid the rubble of broken tables and smashed-up chairs, with her legs pulled up to her chin. Her coat and overalls had been slashed by talons and her face was ghostly white, but Casper felt a little less afraid on seeing her than he had done before. Arlo hopped up and down on the basket edge and at that small, tapping sound, Utterly looked up.

She squinted into the clouds and then blinked in disbelief when she saw the hot air balloon and Arlo bouncing on the basket, but her mouth fell well and truly open at the sight of Casper, his sky goggles pushed up on his forehead and Bristlebeard's axe clasped firmly in his hand.

"Casper?" she breathed. "Is . . . is that *you*?"

"I did tell you," Casper whispered, "that I am never, ever late." He paused. "*Especially* when it comes to rescuing a friend."

And at those words, Utterly's eyes filled with tears.

Chapter 20

Arlo launched from the basket, slipped through the bars covering the cave and flung himself at Utterly. She held him tight and kissed his wings.

"You came for me! Both of you! And in a Sky-Soar9000! But how? Only Lofty Husks have access to those!"

Her voice was only a whisper, but it sounded different somehow—less sharp, perhaps, less cross.

"We can talk about all that later," Casper said. "Right now we need to create a diversion for the Midnights so that we can get you out of this cave and into the hot air balloon—because I think *you're* the familiar face I'm meant to find, Utterly. If I rescue you, then the Midnights will be stopped!"

Before Utterly could reply, he yanked on the lever for hatch six and several black cylindrical shapes, about the size of rolling pins, shot up into the air and soared over Dapplemere before exploding over the next-door valley in a blaze of color.

"Fireworks!" Utterly gasped.

The griffins shrieked and launched into the sky toward the commotion while Arlo blew hard at the bars across the cave.

Utterly blinked in surprise at the flames the dragon conjured. "You've learned to blow fire, Arlo!"

Arlo nodded, then blushed—he could tell Utterly was proud of him—but no matter how many flames shot out from his nostrils, he couldn't melt the bars.

Utterly bit her lip. "They must be cursed somehow! When the Midnights carried me here yesterday, it was just a battered-up restaurant, but then they scratched at the rock with their talons and bars appeared over the entrance." She turned panic-stricken eyes toward Casper. "What if . . . what if the bars are unbreakable and I'm trapped in this cave forever!"

Casper instructed Zip to move right up to the cave now that the Midnights were tearing through the next-door valley as more and more fireworks were exploding around them. Then he held up Bristlebeard's axe and looked at Utterly. "Just as well I made friends with the snow trolls, then."

He clambered over the edge of the basket, then jumped

down onto the hillside before the cave and raised the axe. It sliced through the first bar as if cutting paper, and the metal crumbled to dust. Utterly's eyes lit up and Casper set to work on the remaining bars until soon there was an opening large enough to crawl through. Utterly shot through it. But in her haste to escape, and in Casper's excitement to see her, neither of them noticed that the fireworks had stopped and an ill wind was blowing.

They looked out across the valley. The Midnights had massed together in the sky and were heading back toward Dapplemere. And now the air thundered with the sound of their cries as their eyes locked on to what was happening at Topplecave.

"I . . . I thought *you* were the familiar face," Casper stammered at Utterly. "I thought finding you would stop the Midnights!"

Utterly glanced at the swarm of griffins beating toward Dapplemere. "I don't think so. . . ."

Casper shook himself. "Quick! Grab my hand!"

But Utterly grabbed the axe from him instead. "It's not just me who needs freeing!" she blurted.

It was then Casper noticed a faint glow from farther inside

the cave. It grew brighter and brighter until two creatures—a boy and a girl who looked about Casper's age but who could only have come up to Casper's knees—limped into view. They had gold skin, tunics made of bracken, and moth-like wings.

"The only two sun scamps not imprisoned by the Midnights. *They're* the reason this kingdom still has any light at all! The Midnights have been burning whole mills full of sun marvels *and* any other marvels they've managed to steal from the drizzle hags and the snow trolls. These two sun scamps have been sneaking down to the caves at night to collect the ingredients for sunlight, but making marvels without a mill is wearing down their strength."

The griffins called out again as they poured over the far side of the valley and the air trembled with heat.

Utterly gripped the axe. "I need to free the rest of the sun scamps. Apparently they've been locked up without food or water for two days now. Then maybe I can use my ideas"—she pointed to the diagrams she'd scratched with a stone onto the cave walls: complicated sketches of cogs and wheels, pulleys and weighting systems—"to mend the mills and get the marvels up and running again!"

"*You* did all those?" Casper gasped.

Utterly clambered down the hillside with the sun scamps, one of whom was lugging a very large, impractical bag with him. "I want to be a bottler, Casper—engineering is what I do! Now get back into the balloon with Arlo and see if you can stall those Midnights! It's *you* they're really after, so if I can just get down to the Burping Eagle—the pub by the lake that the sun scamps are trapped in—then at least we're in with a chance of saving the marvels!"

Arlo clutched Casper's sleeve as he made a wild jump for Zip's basket, then as the valley darkened with outstretched wings and turned suddenly very hot indeed, Casper tightened Bristlebeard's cape around him, pulled down his goggles, and seized the microphone.

"Duck and weave time, Zip! Move like you've never moved before and don't give the Midnights any reason to dive down after Utterly!"

The hot air balloon slid away from the cave, then skirted across the hillside, skimming the tops of the wishing trees as it passed, and like moths to a flame, the Midnights and their shatterblast careered toward Casper. But Zip was a SkySoar9000 and she was faster than them, and Casper could see when the spirals of shatterblast drew close, so together they darted right, then left, then right again.

Then, just as the first of the griffins made a beeline for Zip's basket, the shatterblast pouring out from its beak, Casper yelled, "Loop the loop!"

Zip did just that, tangling the Midnight's talons in her ropes while Casper hung on for dear life. The balloon righted itself, then Casper grabbed Bristlebeard's crossbow and sent the bolt slamming into the Midnight's chest. True to the snow troll's word, the griffin crashed down the hillside, stunned by the deadly nightshade's magic.

Another Midnight drew close before Casper had time to reel the bolt back in. But Arlo was ready for the fight this time and he managed to conjure a spark of fire, which he spat into the griffin's eye. The Midnight whirled backward and slunk away but more appeared in its place, all swarming around Zip with beaks open and shatterblast swirling. Casper reloaded and, as the hot air balloon darted this way and that, he fired the crossbow again and again.

The griffins screeched together and Casper watched with dread as enormous spirals of scorching-hot wind poured into the sky, wrenching trees from the ground and sending boulders tumbling down slopes. The shatterblast beat against Casper's face and clamored in his ears, but still the cape kept him safe.

"Keep moving, Zip!" Casper screamed.

The air was too thick with feathers and talons for Casper to see how Utterly was doing, but however fast Zip moved or however quick Casper was to reload, the griffins and their shatterblast seemed to be one step ahead. And when Casper's ears snagged on the sound of a talon splitting silk, he felt his insides churn.

"Mayday! Mayday!" Zip wheezed. "Balloon torn!"

She began to sink toward the lake—at speed—and the griffins screeched with delight. Casper and Arlo huddled in the corner of the basket in the snow troll's armor, then every single griffin shrieked at once. Casper thought that the end was coming, that finally the griffins had outdone them, but there was something about this shriek that was different from the last. It was sharper, angrier.

Casper looked up as something like rope, only not quite it, slid beneath the griffins at the very moment their beaks and talons reached into the basket. It was a net of sorts—spun from glittering gold thread—and as the balloon plunged downward, the net held the flock of raging griffins exactly where they were in the sky.

Dumbfounded, Casper clung onto Arlo as the hot air balloon splashed down into the lake and then was shunted, by the last few gusts of shatterblast tearing through the valley, against the mills before the village. Casper and Arlo scrambled out of the basket to see Utterly racing round the side of the lake toward them while thousands of sun scamps held the flock of hissing griffins inside a golden net.

Casper watched, open-mouthed, as the freed sun scamps flew the net toward one of the giant heads at the bottom of the valley. Whatever this net was made of, it was not only holding the griffins captive but it was preventing them from breathing shatterblast too. Then Casper remembered the oversized bag one of the sun scamps hiding in the cave had been carrying—had the net been bundled up in there all along?

One or two sun scamps fluttered up to the enormous ear of the stone head while the rest of their kind hauled the griffins into the gaping mouth. Then the mouth snapped shut with a deafening boom and the sun scamps flew out through the gaps in the giant teeth, but the griffins—though they thrashed and screeched inside the net—couldn't escape the clamped mouth. And as if Dapplemere itself knew the threat was now contained, every single one of the caves scattered about the hillsides began to glow. A gurgling noise, which seemed to come from within the hills themselves, echoed through the valley, followed by a rushing sound that soon became a roar.

Casper watched as slowly but surely the entire lake turned gold. "The ingredients for sunlight are being released!" He gasped.

Utterly rushed round the lake until she stood, panting, before Casper and Arlo and the ruined mill the balloon was slumped against. "I was wrong," she said.

Casper wiped the sweat from his forehead. "About what?"

Utterly took a deep breath. "About you, Casper. Because never, ever being late *is* a skill. It's the same thing as being loyal. And you're the most loyal person I've ever met." There was a squeak from Casper's shoulder. "Joint with Arlo."

Casper blinked. He felt a strange tingling in his chest, and though he knew he had very little experience in these things, he wondered whether perhaps this was his heart stretching. Bristlebeard had warned him that that was par for the course with friendship.

Casper blushed. "Maybe—possibly—we could upgrade from acquaintances to friends?"

Utterly was silent for a moment, and Casper wondered whether he'd got things wrong all over again, but then she took a small step forward and, for the first time in his life, Casper was hugged by a friend.

Chapter 21

Up until arriving at Dapplemere, Casper had thought that Utterly was the fastest-moving person he'd ever encountered. Then he saw the sun scamps working. Some busied themselves in the village repairing roofs, mending windows, and righting the contents of the shops, while others poured into the mills, desperately trying to salvage the blades and rotors to get them turning again.

Despite the speed at which the sun scamps worked, it would have taken them weeks to get the ingredients for sunlight flowing into the mills and out of the chimneys as marvels, had it not been for Utterly. During her time locked up in Topplecave, she had come up with a brilliant, yet highly unorthodox, new system for the mills. Her plan involved emptying the most-loved bottling shop in the village, Blend &

Bottle, of their blending staffs to replace the spokes on the mills' wheels that the Midnights had chewed away, and then raiding Swoopers, Dapplemere's bank, for their unusually shaped comet-coins to act as cogs inside the mills. In fact, the overhaul had been so satisfactory the sun scamps decided they'd review the construction of future mills at Dapplemere in light of Utterly's findings.

Before long, more and more sunlight was drifting, glitter-bright, up through the chimneys and spreading out across the sky in a brilliant pink sunset. Casper filled Utterly in on all that had happened in Shiverbark Forest and about the Midnights patrolling the castle, but they were distracted as they spoke because neither of them knew where on earth to look for the familiar face now—or even how to fix the SkySoar9000. They pulled the hot air balloon up onto the path beside a mill, but the Midnights had torn the balloon from top to tail and no matter how many times Casper tapped the microphone and tried to speak to Zip, she didn't answer.

The sun scamps were busy fluttering about the chimneys on the mills, catching the marvels in spidersilk nets and bundling them into hampers. The sun scamps promised Utterly and Casper they'd fly to the Mixing Tower themselves, then try to slip the marvels past the Midnights before racing on to the drizzle hags to persuade them to do the same—and there was no time to lose. But on seeing that Casper, Utterly, and Arlo were having no luck with the balloon, one of the sun scamps broke away from the hampers and flew toward them. Casper recognized him from the hilltop restaurant.

"The dazzlethread we sneaked into Topplecave will hold those Midnights until sunrise tomorrow," the sun scamp said. "It's the ingredient that makes sunlight fierce, you see—there's not much that can break it." He seized a broom from a passing sun scamp and swept the steps leading up to the mill. "Once the dazzlethread's power fades, though, the Midnights will use their shatterblast to blow the roof of the giant mouth clean off and come after you. But you'll be long gone by then, I'm sure."

Casper was just about to say that there was little chance of them going anywhere and even if they did leave they had no idea where to go, when the sun scamp started speaking again while lifting a tape measure from his pocket and measuring the mill's window for a new pane of glass.

"I'm Matt, by the way—stands for 'Multitasker and Terribly Talkative'—and that's my sister you saw earlier at Topplecave." He pointed to the sun scamp reading an instruction manual entitled *Handling Marvels Over Long*

Distances on the steps of a mill. "She's called Rose—stands for 'Reading over Strenuous Exercise.'" Matt gave Zip's basket a quick polish, then he looked at the balloon and the microphone and tutted. "That'll need to be fixed." He rummaged in his pocket and drew out a roll of golden thread with a needle slotted into it. "Nothing that a good reel of dazzlethread can't sort."

Casper and Utterly watched in amazement as Matt began stitching—not only was the tear disappearing but the thread was too as it wove in and out of the fabric, so that the balloon looked brand spanking new!

"So what's your plan for destroying the Midnights?" Matt asked as he sewed.

Casper sighed. "I was told to find a familiar face—and I found my friend Utterly here in Dapplemere—only freeing her hasn't put an end to the griffins for good."

"Of course it hasn't," Matt replied. "You need to go to the source of the problem. To the place where all the griffins poured in from."

"But didn't you say up in Topplecave that you and Rose thought the Midnights had come into the kingdom from the east?" Utterly asked nervously.

Matt nodded. "From the east. Absolutely. Sun scamp wings are too frail for those parts—believe me, we tried when the Midnights started coming—but if *you* can get there and cut the griffins off at the source, you might well be in with a chance of stopping them."

Casper shifted. "And what's in the east again?"

"Volcanoes called the Smoking Chimneys . . . ," Utterly replied. "The only place in Rumblestar that is deemed Forbidden Territory, even for experienced ballooners, because the ogres produce storms there just for the fun of it. They love nothing more than a sky full of chaos."

Casper reached out a hand to Arlo for emotional support, but the little dragon had already fainted. "Bristlebeard told me that a snow troll called Pucklefist has gone to reason with the ogres there. The trolls suspect the Midnights bribed the ogres for the shatterblast, which they had been keeping in a locked trunk, so they're hoping they can persuade the ogres to call the wind back in."

"Maybe the Midnights promised the ogres a share in Morg's rule if they handed the shatterblast over," Matt said. "Whatever the reason, you should press on for the Smoking Chimneys if you want to stop the griffins flooding into the kingdom." He paused. "And by the sounds of it, it's also one of the *last* places in Rumblestar that you haven't yet looked for that familiar face. . . ."

Utterly turned to Casper. "We have the snow trolls' armor, remember? It'll help us there just like it helped you against the shatterblast earlier—and we'll have an actual snow troll on our side too. Pucklefist will help us—the trolls are meant to be *incredible* fighters!"

Casper tried to smile, but it came out as a grimace.

"And from what my dad says," Utterly went on, "the volcanoes themselves are dormant; that's why we call them the 'smoking' rather than the 'erupting' chimneys. It might not be as bad as it sounds."

Matt knotted the end of the dazzlethread, which vanished when he tugged his needle free. "One SkySoar9000 ready for departure."

Casper gasped. The tear was nowhere to be seen, and through the microphone there came a familiar voice. "Right then, skipper. Where to next?"

"Thank you, Matt!" Casper cried.

The sun scamp shook Casper's, Utterly's, and Arlo's hands. "A pleasure. I find being busy immensely satisfying. Good luck with your journey on and don't let those volcanoes put you off—you've a kingdom to save and we're all rooting for you!"

He fluttered back to help with the marvels while Casper, Utterly, and Arlo climbed into the basket. Casper nodded to Arlo, and throwing a quick glance in Utterly's direction to check that she was watching, the little dragon took a deep breath and blasted the balloon's burners with flames.

Utterly clapped, Arlo beamed, and Casper took a deep breath. "To the Smoking Chimneys, Zip."

Chapter 22

As the sun scamps cheered Casper, Utterly, and Arlo on from below, and the Midnights hissed inside the giant's mouth, Zip flew up out of Dapplemere and headed east over the dusk-filled valleys. For a while they flew silently, gazing down at the hills as they grew into mountains with ridges so high and sharp it was like looking at the spines of sleeping dragons. The sun was setting now and the sky was a fiery orange against the peaks, dashed through with golden clouds.

It was the most brilliant sunset Casper and Utterly had ever seen. And though Casper was all too aware that life, at this moment, was far from perfect—in fact, it was decidedly *wiggly-splat* if he thought about what lay ahead—he smiled. Because he had rescued his friend, Zip was fixed, and this really was an incredible sunset. And Casper concluded, as he looked up at the shining clouds, that since he planned to spend a little less time in lost and found baskets when he got home, perhaps he could spend a little more time skygazing instead. It probably wasn't going to help his homework, boost his exam results, or get Candida and Leopold off his back, but sometimes it was good just to look and think.

The sky faded to purple and the mountains turned blue, then Utterly turned to Casper. "You came for me even though I got you thrown into a dungeon." Utterly picked at the basket. "Even though I shouted at you on the Witch's Fingers and stormed off in the forest."

Casper wasn't sure whether this was an apology or a test or simply a string of facts, so he stayed quiet and tried his best to understand Utterly. Because her conversations, he was learning, were like cupboard doors—open for a while, then slammed shut. But Casper got the feeling that this time the cupboard door might stay open a little longer if it was given time and space.

"I was rude and horrid and impossibly angry and *still* you came to save me," Utterly said.

There was another pause, but now Utterly was looking

at Casper, and Casper wondered whether a small space had opened up in the conversation for him, too. He had to be careful, though—he was dealing with a stormgulper, after all—and Bristlebeard had expressly told him that he would have to be patient and kind, as well as good at listening.

"I don't think you're rude or horrid or impossibly angry," he said quietly, "whatever I might have said back in Shiverbark Forest."

"You told me I was foul-tempered and forever in a grump," Utterly mumbled. Arlo climbed up onto her shoulder and licked her cheek. "That it wasn't surprising people couldn't wait to be rid of me."

Casper winced; tempers were an ugly thing. "I'm sorry I said those things, Utterly. But I did some thinking after you left." He concentrated extremely hard on a flock of geese fanning out over the peaks below them so as not to catch Utterly's eye. "I—I think you might have swallowed a storm—and that's why sometimes you get a bit"—he fumbled for the right word—"snappy."

Utterly grabbed her throat. "I've done *what*?"

Casper tightened his grip on the basket in case Utterly decided to hurl him over the edge. "Well, not *literally* swallowed a storm," Casper explained. "But one of the snow trolls told me about how sometimes people who experience something very sad or very difficult find a little piece of the 'storm' they've gone through stuck inside them, then they carry it about with them for a while afterward. The snow troll called them stormgulpers."

Utterly looked at Casper with glassy eyes. "You . . . you can see my storm?"

Casper nodded. "I think I mistook it for something else at the beginning because I'm not very experienced at friendships, but now"—he turned to face Utterly—"I can see it."

Utterly brushed the tears from her eyes, but more fell, so Arlo yanked the lever on hatch four and pulled out the emergency tissues. He handed them to Utterly, then fluttered back to her shoulder and hugged her neck. But even he couldn't stop the tears coming. They streamed down Utterly's cheeks and squeezed her breath into sobs, but somehow the tears pushed the words, so long locked inside her, out into the open.

"Three years ago, when I was eight, I persuaded my older sister, Mannerly, to come out onto the castle roof to see a moonbow I'd spotted from my bedroom window." Utterly tried to swallow the lump in her throat, but that only drew more tears down her cheeks. "We were always watching the night sky together—sometimes from our bedroom windows, all tucked up with hot chocolates, then other times we'd creep out of the castle when everyone else was asleep and the world was ours for the taking. That night was one of the best lunar rainbows we had ever seen—a glowing arc surrounding thousands and thousands of stars. But then I told Mannerly we could get an even better view if we climbed up the spire, and when she was following me, she slipped on a loose tile and . . . and she fell. If I hadn't persuaded her to come out onto the roof, if I hadn't told her to keep climbing when she wanted to turn back, she never would've fallen. She would still be here. And *that's* why I'm not allowed to cry or even talk about any of this—because it's *all my fault.*"

Utterly slumped down into the basket, pulled her knees up to her chin, and cried even harder. There had been relief in saying the words aloud at last, but there was sorrow, too—years of it tumbling out now—because she missed her sister and all the nights they'd shared marveling at the world together.

Casper sat beside her, but he didn't say anything because if he knew one thing about tears—and he did, because thanks to Candida and Leopold, there had been nights at Little Wallops where his own had soaked right through his pillow—it was that sometimes they needed a moment to themselves.

"I was angry with everyone after that—my parents, my classmates, the Lofty Husks—but really I think I was just angry with myself," Utterly sobbed. "Because no matter how hard I tried, I could never make up for what my parents lost. I could never be as good as Mannerly. She was a brilliant bottler-in-training; she turned up on time to classes, she was awarded so many Certificates of Excellence for her exam results we ran out of wall space and so many trophies she had her own special cabinet for them, and she was easily the most popular girl in her year." Utterly paused. "But me? I'm late for everything, I win nothing because I'm always being sent out of class for bad behavior and though I *used* to find making friends easy, ever since Mannerly died, I've found it impossible to get on with my classmates because I either end up shouting at them or getting them into trouble. And that's just who I am now, on the outside anyway: the bottler-in-training who can't behave. Because at least *that* me lives up to the recklessness my parents expect of me! But you want to know the *real* reason I push everyone away?"

Casper nodded. He had a feeling it was important to let stormgulpers get everything off their chests.

"Because the thought of losing another person I love makes my heart shake. Mannerly was my best friend and I miss her. I miss the jokes we shared and the way she would tell me about the castle's secrets when I couldn't get to sleep." Utterly stroked the little dragon on her shoulder. "Arlo has been my only friend for the past three years. He showed up on my windowsill a month after Mannerly died and though I tried to encourage him to fly away, he stayed. Maybe he didn't really fit in with the rest of his kind either—not big enough to carry the marvels on to the other kingdoms and not strong enough to scatter enough moondust to make a difference."

Casper fiddled with the cuff of his coat. "I don't fit in back home either and I'd pretty much given up on ever making friends. But then I met you"—he smiled—"and Arlo and Bristlebeard. A lot can change on an adventure, you know."

Utterly nodded, then she rested her head back against the basket. "My mum hasn't been the same since Mannerly died. Before we were always laughing and having fun together, but now . . . she's closed off. Sometimes I wonder whether she wishes it had been *me* that fell that night." Arlo nuzzled into her neck. "And my dad always looks so sad and lost; most days I don't even think he notices me at all. I want so much for them to be proud of me and I thought that if I did something truly remarkable out here in the Beyond, then Mum and Dad would forget my part in what happened on the roof that night. You have to *do* things—like win certificates, bag trophies, or save kingdoms—to make people proud"—she looked down—"or even make them notice that you're there at all. That's how you end up getting loved like Mannerly was."

Casper passed Utterly another tissue. "I'm not sure it works like that, Utterly."

"Then how *does* it work?"

Casper shrugged. "I'm not entirely sure. But I don't think love has got much to do with certificates, trophies, and saving kingdoms. I think you get loved because of who you are. And you're brave and you're kind—you freed all the sun scamps when the Midnights could have killed you. Without you, Utterly Thankless, this whole kingdom would have crumbled."

"You really think so?"

Casper nodded.

"But if my parents *really* loved me, they'd have at least sent me another paper airplane. But not *one* has come." Utterly sighed. "Either they don't care or the drizzle hags didn't write to the Lofty Husks about our quest after all and everyone at the castle *still* thinks I betrayed Rumblestar!"

Casper shifted. "They know you're innocent, Utterly. Because I told them."

Utterly frowned.

"Please don't be angry with me, but I wrote back to your mum when we were in the canoe. I told her about the shatter-blast and the griffins and the fact that you weren't to blame."

For a moment Utterly looked relieved, then the hurt crowded in. "But then why haven't my parents written back? I don't think they'd care if I got lost in the Beyond forever!"

"They'd care all right, Utterly. Lots of people would. Frost-bite knew who you were—he said you had a *brilliant mind for bottling* and—"

"He said that?"

"Yes. But what I'm trying to say is that the Lofty Husks wrote back to us—they even tried to send a search party before the Midnights blocked their way out of the castle altogether—but their message never reached us because the Midnights have disrupted the kingdom's SkyFly. Now it seems to have broken completely as *no* paper airplanes are able to get over the castle walls so the reason your parents haven't written is because they *can't*." Casper paused. "But I did find this."

Utterly frowned as Casper rummaged in his pocket and dug out the scrap of newspaper he had taken from the *Unmapped Chronicle* back in the forest. He handed it to Utterly, and fresh tears welled as she read the message from her mum.

"My . . . my parents are proud of me?" she said quietly. "But . . . we haven't saved Rumblestar yet."

"Exactly," Casper replied. "Because you get loved even if kingdoms fall." He paused. "You might not be able to go back and fix what happened with Mannerly, but carrying a storm around with you isn't going to help."

Utterly was quiet for a while as she let herself accept what Casper was saying and what her mum's message in the newspaper really meant. Then she said: "I have to let my storm go, don't I?"

"I think so. I'm not sure I can face a storm ogre *and* your temper all at the same time." Casper paused. "And look at it this way: If you get rid of your storm, just think how much extra room you'll have inside you for friends and adventures and all sorts of complicated bottling ideas."

Casper stood up and surveyed the night sky, which was

deep and velvety and full of stars. "My mum once told me that if I ever have anything weighing on my mind, I should whisper it to the night. She said the sky is always changing, so if you let your problems creep out into the dark, they'll be gone when the sun comes up the next day."

Utterly pulled herself up and stood beside Casper. Then, while Arlo settled himself on her shoulder and curled his tail around her neck, she took a very deep breath. More tears rolled down her cheeks as she whispered to the stars and Casper found himself whispering too, because there was a storm inside him as well—not one built of moonbows and sisters with certificates, but it was a storm all the same and it was one that beat to a lonely drum. And as both Utterly and Casper's whispers tiptoed out into the night and were lost in the trails of stardust, Utterly turned to Casper.

"I'm ready for this now," she said. "Ready for the Smoking Chimneys and the Midnights and *everything* else that comes our way."

"No more stormgulping?"

"No more stormgulping."

Casper pulled on his cape of frozen lightning. "Then let's go save this kingdom."

Chapter 23

Casper, Utterly, and Arlo ate food from hatch two for supper—double-decker burgers with curly fries followed by a dessert of avalanche gobstoppers (which exploded upon sucking), blizzard bars (which numbed their gums upon chewing), and fogteasers (which altered the pitch of their voices upon munching). Then they slept for a while.

But when Zip's voice crackled through the microphone, they pushed back their capes and sat bolt upright. "Expect turbulence as we pass through the clouds, and possibly light vomiting."

Casper stood up and scoured the landscape beneath them. The mountains were so high now their summits were lost in the clouds, but Casper's eyes were glued to the shards of light slipping between the ridges. It was sunrise, and though there was no sign of the Midnights, the dazzlethread that bound them would crumble at any moment and it would only be a matter of time before the griffins came after them.

Zip rose higher in the sky, and Casper knew that the Smoking Chimneys must be close because the air was warmer now and hanging in its wake was the unmistakable whiff of ash. Casper and Utterly wore their fur capes buttoned up and the frozen lightning kept them cool despite the heat, just as it must have done for the snow trolls all those years ago at the Battle of the Brutes. Casper thought of Bristlebeard's friend, Pucklefist, trying to reason with the Midnights. He clearly hadn't managed to persuade them to call in the shatterblast yet, but maybe he was making inroads all the same. And Casper felt an enormous sense of relief that any moment now they'd have one of the bravest snow trolls on their side.

"In the absence of seat belts," Zip announced, "please hold on extremely tightly."

The hot air balloon surged up into the clouds, and for several minutes Casper could feel nothing but warm mist pressing against his face. Then they rose above the clouds to a perfect blue sky, and Casper and Utterly blinked at the scene ahead.

What they had thought were the bases of mountains earlier had, in fact, been the scree-strewn banks of the very volcanoes they had set out to find.

"You have arrived at your destination," Zip announced, "where the current air temperature may bring on dizzy spells and/or death."

"The Smoking Chimneys," Casper murmured.

The craters seemed to be linked to each other by a number of precarious-looking stone bridges leading up toward the biggest volcano in the middle. Great clouds of smoke and ash puffed up into the sky and the air throbbed with heat. Thankfully, though, for the time being at least, there was no sign of any ogres. But on the lip of the largest volcano, as Bristlebeard had feared, there was a very large, open trunk. The ogres, it would seem, had indeed given the shatterblast to the Midnights.

But there was a sight even more terrible than this on the banks of that volcano. A lifeless figure slumped on the scree. And from the torn silver cape strewn a little way away Casper knew exactly who it was.

"Pucklefist," he gasped. "The ogres *killed* him!"

Arlo scuttled under Utterly's hair and Utterly raised a hand to her mouth. "But he had a frozen lightning cape . . . and snow trolls are legendary fighters!"

"So are ogres," Casper replied shakily.

He hadn't realized how much faith he had placed in Pucklefist until this moment, but deep inside he had been hoping that the snow troll would take charge from here—that the final leg of saving the kingdom wouldn't really just be up to him, Utterly, and Arlo. But now it looked like it was. Poor, poor Pucklefist—the news would shake the snow trolls—and what did it mean about the ogres? Had they decided to side with Morg? And if so, what chance did Casper, Utterly, and Arlo have against them?

Casper tried his best to think logically. "Do . . . do you think we should at least *try* speaking with the ogres about the shatterblast before we go sneaking around their volcanoes?"

Utterly eyed the maze of rock and ash before them, then her gaze fell once more upon the snow troll. "That didn't help Pucklefist. And even if we were to give it a go, it wouldn't be easy. Apparently ogres can only say one word—*chomp*—so there's not a great deal of ground you can cover in a negotiation with them, even if the snow trolls thought it worth a shot to save the kingdom."

Utterly tucked Arlo, who was now sweating profusely, beneath her cape, and Casper looked out over the Smoking Chimneys. Where, in all of this, was he going to find a familiar face? Then he noticed something.

"Look," he whispered. "Over there."

There were a dozen craters bursting through the clouds, but it was the one farthest away from Zip that he was pointing at.

"All of the craters are pumping out *white* smoke, but that one over there is sprouting *silver* smoke." He paused. "The storm ogre who drank from the Witch's Fingers that you told me about . . . perhaps that's *his* volcano? You said everything he owned turned to silver."

"And the river took his sight," Utterly said slowly, "which means that if we were to start our search for a familiar face *there*, our chances of survival might be *slightly* more than in the other volcanoes because the blind ogre wouldn't see us!"

Casper nodded. "Exactly."

He tried to imagine bumping into someone he knew on the banks of the volcano or inside its crater. It was easy to picture Leopold and Candida surrounded by silver, but to picture them in a magical kingdom a million miles from home seemed so unlikely, so impossible. And yet magic was both of those things.

Casper took a deep breath, reached for the microphone, and whispered into it: "Keep a low profile, Zip. Head to the volcano spouting silver smoke, but do *not* rise above the craters at any time, because if the storm ogres are down inside them and spot us, we'll be forced into a conversation. And that won't end well. For any of us."

There was a cough from the microphone. "Stopovers in the Smoking Chimneys don't usually end well, even without passengers embarking upon chit-chat with storm ogres."

Casper reached for Bristlebeard's crossbow and slung it over his cape while Utterly slotted Sir Chopalot into the inside pocket of her own cape. They were as ready as they could be, so Zip hastened on toward the volcanoes, skulking down by the cloud line to avoid being seen.

The closer they floated, the warmer the air became. The capes kept Casper and Utterly cool, but the armor couldn't block out their fear, and when their ears fixed on the bubble and splash of lava as well as the unmistakable grunts of something large and brutish, Casper clutched Utterly's arm.

"I can't do this," he blurted. "I'm not a hero."

"Me neither," Utterly replied. "Well, not on my own anyway." She drew back her cape and Casper saw that Arlo was perched on her shoulder with his fists raised at the ready. Utterly looked at Casper. "But the three of us together? We've outwitted drizzle hags, climbed the tallest trees in Shiverbark Forest, and snared a flock of Midnights. So *you* know what, Casper? I think we can do *anything* if we put our minds to it."

And just as Casper was feeling a little bit bolder, and a little bit more optimistic, something large and mostly naked, save for the lava-stained cloth around its saggy bottom, stumbled out onto the crater of the largest volcano. The storm ogre's skin was steel-gray and his belly was so huge it looked like he'd swallowed a beanbag. But his head was small and bald.

"CHOMP!" the ogre roared.

At his call, more ogres scrambled out of the volcanoes until there was one on the edge of every crater. Casper held his breath as he took in the blind ogre beating his chest on the lip of the volcano above them.

"CHOMP! CHOMP! CHOMP!" it bellowed.

Casper clutched the microphone. "Duck in behind that crag, Zip."

The balloon hovered beneath a jutting rock on the banks

of the volcano sprouting silver, and while it waited in the shadows, Casper and Utterly peered over the basket. They couldn't see much from where they were, but they could hear a lot of stampeding and, a little while later, all the storm ogres appeared on the lip of the largest volcano.

"They're clutching spears tipped with lava and shouting into the volcano," Utterly hissed. "What are they *doing*?"

Casper craned his neck and saw the ogres banging their spears on the rocks and hollering "CHOMP!" for all they were worth. A cloud of smoke rose up from the largest volcano, but it was neither white nor silver this time. Instead it was a bruised blue-black and as it bulged across the sky, it broke apart into thousands of dark tendrils that swayed eerily above the volcanoes. Then the first rumbles of thunder began.

"They're conjuring a storm!" Casper cried.

"And those trails of black clouds spreading out into the sky must be marvels!" Utterly gasped.

There were no cauldrons, conveyor belts, or mills to organize these marvels, Casper noticed, just a sky full of chaos as the tendrils spilled out. He glanced at the volcano immediately above them, which was still puffing silver smoke. "We need to get down into this crater while we still have the chance."

Casper reached for the microphone, but at the same time the thunder growled again and more marvels pulsed out of the largest crater. They swarmed across the sky and sank between the volcanoes until the darkness was so thick it was as if the sun had set. A bolt of lightning split the sky. Bright and terrible, it burst up from the largest volcano, then zigzagged down through the clouds, missing the hot air balloon by a whisker. Once again the sky fell dark and Casper and Utterly were left blinking in the lightning's wake.

The ogres roared and the clouds kept coming, bringing with them more thunder and more lightning. Then the darkness returned and Casper gripped the microphone with shaking hands. But the command he wanted to give Zip wouldn't come—the words were trapped in his throat, along with his courage—until he felt Utterly's hand thread through the dark to clutch his.

And together, they told Zip what to do: "Fly on—into the silver volcano."

Chapter 24

The thunder shook Zip's basket and the bolts of lightning scarred the sky, but still the hot air balloon inched up through the storm clouds toward the volcano's crater. Casper could hear the ogres urging the storm on in the distance and he knew that the Midnights couldn't be far away, but they were level with the crater now, and though they couldn't see much beyond the storm and the silver smoke, he was sure that *this* was where he would find the familiar face they'd been searching for.

"You have arrived at your destination," Zip said. Then she paused. "I hope you have a memorable stay at the most undesirable holiday location in Rumblestar. Please use hatch seven for a descent ladder, and may I take this hugely unrelaxing moment to thank you for flying in the SkySoar9000. It's been a pleasure to have you on board."

"You're . . . you're *going*?!" Casper cried.

"The SkySoar9000 is yet to be fitted with a lightning-proof balloon," Zip replied. "It is, in short, a miracle that we have not burst into flames already, so I will be making a sharp exit at this point to avoid immediate death."

Utterly yanked the level on hatch seven and a rope ladder tumbled out. She threw one end over the edge of the basket and fastened the other to one of the ropes leading up to the balloon. "We need to get going, Casper! The ogres might start summoning storms from the other volcanoes—or the Midnights might arrive with their shatterblast—then we'll be done for."

Casper grabbed the microphone one last time. "Thank you for everything, Zip. You've been incredible. And if you change your mind and want one last adrenaline rush before returning to the castle, we'll probably be fleeing from a pack of ogres or a flock of griffins shortly."

Utterly slotted Arlo into her cape pocket and made her way down the ladder. Casper followed, his heart thundering against his ribcage. The silver smoke pulsed around them and lightning flashed, but still their capes kept them cool and safe. They jumped off onto the crater and Zip darted away, then Casper and Utterly looked down into the volcano.

At first all they could see was the billowing smoke, but then a gust of wind blew that sideways and the storm ogre's home was revealed. The volcano was deep, really deep, and it plunged down to a pit of belching silver lava. But it was the rocky ledges lining the cavern that held Casper's attention. They were packed full of treasures: jewels, mirrors, coins, crowns, goblets, tiaras. *This* was the storm ogre's reward for drinking from the Witch's Fingers and yet because of the price he'd paid for his riches, the ogre couldn't see any of it. Casper scanned the crater for any sign of a person—that familiar face that always seemed to be just out of his reach—but only the silver sparkled back at him, and the bubbling lava far below.

Utterly was already racing down the steps cut into the side of the volcano, which wound their way through the treasures, and when the ogres roared again and the storm clouds swelled, Casper sped after her.

They ran on and on, past glinting treasures and through clouds of silver, but when the smoke pulled back for a second time, Arlo squawked from Utterly's pocket. She stopped in her tracks and Casper bumped into her. Then they peered down into the volcano where Arlo was pointing, and to Casper's surprise he saw that there was a tree standing upright in the middle of the bubbling lava. Only this tree wasn't silver like everything else in the volcano. It was a perfectly normal tree.

"What sort of tree could grow in this heat?" Utterly muttered.

Somewhere above them the ogres bellowed as a sheet of lightning lit the sky, but Casper and Utterly were running down the steps now because both of them could feel that something about this tree was important. It wasn't particularly tall or impressive—it didn't even have leaves, just a cluster of crooked branches—but something about the way it stood there, surrounded by silver but untouched by its magic, sang of power.

They drew level with the boiling lava, and as they did so the silver smoke vanished and the lava stilled, as if the volcano itself had sensed their presence. Where the steps ended Casper could see an alcove littered with bones and upturned goblets. *Perhaps this is the storm ogre's den*, he thought. His gaze slid to the roots of the tree, which were thick enough to walk across and which spread out across the lava at all angles in a web of tangled wood. He placed a nervous foot on the nearest root.

"Careful!" Utterly whispered. "The snow trolls' capes have got us this far, but I'm not sure how we'd fare splashing around in lava."

But Casper wasn't listening, because the tree was beckoning him on. He could feel the pull of something familiar, something half-recognized rocking through his bones. Utterly followed him over the roots, with Arlo whimpering from her pocket every time she wobbled, then they were all there together before the tree in the middle of the lava.

A ripple of shock slid down Casper's spine. "This isn't just a tree," he breathed.

Utterly frowned at the trunk. A long, rectangular door had been carved into the wood. It was open and something long and silver was hanging down inside it while above the door there was a clockface. "It's a grandfather clock," she said quietly.

And it was then that Casper understood what the wind had meant when it whispered its secret to Slumbergrot. Casper stared at the grandfather clock in disbelief. "I was never meant to find a person. Not *you* or my parents or anyone from home." Casper looked at Utterly. "All along we were looking for a *clockface*."

Utterly shook her head. "I don't understand."

"This is the clock my dad was repairing back home in the Faraway!" He pointed to the pendulum, which wasn't lolling from side to side as it should have been. It was jammed, and instead of ending in a circular disc, this one was just a blunt tip. "The pendulum in the clock back home was broken, too—Dad was trying to fix it! This is the clock that brought me here. . . ."

Casper reached out a hand and touched the clock, and a yearning for home filled his chest.

"It can't be the same one," Utterly replied. "The Unmapped Kingdoms are separate from the Faraway. You can't have one object being visible in two totally different worlds!"

"But it *is* the same!" Casper cried. "Even the hands on the clock are like those on the clock back home: They're stuck on the hour." He paused. "What if that phoenix tear I found in the grandfather clock key blurs the links between the Unmapped Kingdoms and the Faraway . . . ? Somehow its magic turned the clock into a portal that can exist in Little Wallops *and* here!"

"But you arrived in the Neverlate Tree," Utterly replied. "Not here at the bottom of a volcano." She paused. "Unless . . . the Neverlate Tree's magic interfered with things. It's been known to give messages to Unmappers in the past when trouble is brewing; perhaps it sensed your coming here and knew that you and I had to meet so we could stop the Midnights *together*. It had to make sure that you were in the tree at the same time as me because if you'd stepped out here when you arrived in Rumblestar, you wouldn't have stood a chance—not without a snow troll's cape!"

"And not without you and Arlo either." Casper narrowed his eyes at the scratch marks lining the hollow where the pendulum hung. "Only a talon or a claw could make those marks."

Utterly nodded. "And look! There are feathers scattered about the clock, too. Black feathers."

From her pocket, Arlo gulped.

"I don't think this clock is just a portal from the Faraway to Rumblestar," Casper said. "I think Morg is using it to send her Midnights from Everdark to Rumblestar, too, and the Midnight pretending to be Frostbite thought *I* could help Morg because she wants to use *this portal* to join her followers here. . . . Didn't you say that Everdark is a forest located somewhere *between* the Faraway and the Unmapped Kingdoms?"

"Yes. A forest full of enchanted trees . . ." Utterly looked at the tree before them now, then she reached out a hand to the door and her eyes grew wide at the words carved into the front of it:

TO FINAL ENDINGS

"Smudge and Bartholomew stole Morg's wings in Everdark," she said slowly. "What if they locked them inside an enchanted tree they knew wouldn't open?" Utterly looked up at Casper. "They couldn't have known where the tree would lead, but this could be the *very* tree Smudge and Bartholomew locked Morg's wings inside all those years ago! Without her wings, Morg isn't strong enough to rise up out of Everdark herself, but she could have found a way to bring her feathers to life, and they've been pouring out of this clock into Rumblestar as griffins. *That's* why they're so powerful; they haven't just been conjured by Morg—they're a *part* of her!"

Casper was silent for a moment as the horror of it all sank in. Then he said: "But why did the Midnights hold you as bait in Dapplemere if *this* is the portal Morg wants me to open for her? Why not bring you here so I'd follow you?"

Utterly looked around them. "There must be a reason the Midnights can't come here."

"But if the ogres gave the griffins the shatterblast, then

surely the Midnights *would* be able to come here because they're working together?"

Utterly nodded. "Something about this doesn't add up. . . ."

The storm raged on above the volcano, but as Casper looked at the grandfather clock, all of the commotion seemed to fall away. Here, after everything, was a link to his world. What if he could climb inside this tree right now and find his way back to his mum and his dad? It was all that he had wanted ever since he set foot in Rumblestar: to go home. And as he listened to the ogres shouting and the thunder groaning and he thought about the flock of griffins speeding closer, he felt every nerve in his body strain toward the clock. Because what hope, really, was there of crushing the Midnights and stopping Morg's plans? How could *he*, Casper Tock, not brave or particularly clever or even armed with a fully formed plan, destroy every griffin in the kingdom with this battered old clock? Or had he misunderstood the wind's message—maybe it had been leading him home rather than toward a battle with Morg's followers?

Casper thought of the turret in Little Wallops and his bedroom with his perfectly made bed and his neatly folded clothes, and of how relieved his parents would be when they saw him again. Wouldn't it be best to go home now and leave the heroics to a more capable person?

"You're thinking of going home, aren't you?" Utterly said.

Casper didn't reply.

"I missed the castle like I never thought I would when I was trapped in Dapplemere," Utterly said. "So if you want to go home now, I understand. I do. Somehow me and Arlo will fix all this. We'll find a way to use the clock and make everything right again."

The thought of home ached inside Casper. With every bone in his body he wanted to climb inside the clock and hope that somehow it would take him back to Little Wallops. But then there was Utterly beside him, and Arlo. They had come so far. Could he really just leave now?

Casper stared at the clock, then he looked at Utterly. "I do want to go home," he said, "but not yet. Not while the Midnights are on the prowl and the marvels are still in danger and the lives of everyone back in the Faraway are in danger."

Utterly breathed a sigh of relief. "Good. Because Arlo's chest would've packed in completely if you'd decided to leave right now."

"But what I don't understand," Casper said, "is how this

clock can destroy all the Midnights. It's not a weapon . . . it's . . . it's furniture! How is *that* going to help us?"

But it wasn't Utterly who answered.

It was twelve furious-looking ogres who had gathered at the lip of the crater above them. And though they were hundreds of meters away, Casper and Utterly could hear the clang of spears banging on the rocks and the holler of a single word.

"CHOMP!"

Chapter 25

Utterly raised Sir Chopalot in trembling hands and Casper held up Bristlebeard's crossbow.

"We can't fight all of them at once!" Utterly cried. "Not from way down here!"

Then another sound rose through the ogres' roars: a sky-shattering shriek that sent ice rippling through Casper's veins. This was the call of the Midnights.

"We—we need to come up with a plan!" Utterly blurted.

But Casper, for what might be the first time in his life, was beyond to-do lists and agendas. He thought fast. "We need to reason with the ogres! If they don't call back the shatterblast, we're done for!"

"They'll never listen to us!" Utterly cried. "Look what happened to Pucklefist!"

Casper was also beyond weighing up risks, so he threw his voice out into the volcano. "You've *got* to listen to us, storm ogres! Whatever the Midnights promised you, it's a lie!"

His words rang through the volcano, over the shrieks of the griffins, and the ogres bashed their spears and roared again. They'd clearly heard—even if it was just the echoes of Casper's words all the way up there—and it gave Utterly the courage to shout too.

"Morg won't share her rule with you!" she shouted. "She wants *all* the Unmapped magic for herself! You killed a snow troll for trying to reason with you, but you mustn't kill us because—"

There were growls and cries from above, and then something else. Words were echoing down to them, albeit grunted ones half-stifled by "chomps," but they were words all the same and Casper and Utterly listened, open-mouthed, to what the ogres had to say while the cries of the griffins drew nearer still.

"Ogres not give wind to Midnights. CHOMP! Midnights steal. CHOMP! CHOMP! Ogres not kill snow troll. CHOMP! Midnights did. CHOMP! CHOMP! CHOMP! Ogres not like Midnights. CHHHHHHOOOOOOOMMMMMMMMMPPPPPPPP!"

Casper and Utterly couldn't believe what they were hearing. The ogres hadn't been bribed to give away the shatterblast and Pucklefist hadn't been killed by them; it had *all* been the Midnights' doing!

It was no wonder the griffins hadn't brought Utterly here as bait, Casper thought—the ogres loathed them! It was one thing to break through the clock and fly away from the volcanoes but quite another trying to hold someone captive while dodging a sky full of lightning. But Casper still didn't understand why the ogres hadn't gone after the Midnights to steal the shatterblast back. Surely they could have defeated the griffins in the end? Then he remembered Bristlebeard's words about the Victory Seal at the Battle of the Brutes—if the ogres left the volcanoes, they'd crumble to ash. . . . Maybe the only way of taking the shatterblast back would be if a great flock of Midnights came *here* for the fight. For a second, Casper felt hopeful at the scene unfolding above them, but then more words tumbled down from the crater and his hopes were dashed.

"Ogres not trust no one now. CHOMP! Ogres eat you up! CHOMP! CHOMP! CHOMP! CHOMP! CHOMP!"

The cries of the Midnights were even louder now and Casper's legs were close to crumpling. "You can't eat us!" he screamed at the ogres. "We're the *only* ones who can stop the Midnights and restore peace to Rumblestar! We know a way." He panted. "And it's right here in this volcano."

His mind spun wildly at the thought of *how* he was going to use the grandfather clock to beat the griffins, but Utterly was yelling up at the ogres now because she wasn't taking *being eaten* for an answer either.

"You listen to us RIGHT THIS SECOND!" she cried. "If you eat us, Morg and her Midnights will tear this kingdom apart. Your volcanoes will crumble and you with them. Casper is right, we're your *only* chance! The Midnights know that, which is why nearly every single one of them is flocking here now—"

"CHOMP?"

Utterly paused and looked at Casper. There was something different about that "chomp," as if, perhaps, the ogres were considering her words. . . .

"Many griffins come?" the ogres roared. "CHOMP?"

"Yes!" Casper screamed, half-crazed with panic now. "Except for the few patrolling the castle, the whole lot are after us!"

"And you *have* to help us beat them!" Utterly cried. "Call back the shatterblast if you can and play your part in saving Rumblestar!"

The cries of the griffins filled the volcano and suddenly there, strewn across the stormy sky, were the Midnights. The ogres looked down at the children, then up at the beasts, then down at the children once again.

"We're running out of time!" Casper shouted.

One by one the ogres turned away from the crater and Casper's heart plunged. Were they turning tail to flee? Had that been why they had questioned how many Midnights were coming—because they had wanted to know whether to stand their ground or run away? But only a few disappeared from sight completely. The others, to Casper's surprise, threw back their heads to the sky and began chanting.

Moments later, great forks of lightning flashed above the volcano. The Midnights darted this way and that to avoid the lightning, but it sought them out, and when it struck, it held them where they were in the sky. Then suddenly the ogres who had left reappeared, hefting a large trunk on their shoulders, and Casper and Utterly realized that something truly incredible was happening. The ogres were getting ready to call the shatterblast back!

Casper blinked. His hunch had been right after all—it *had* been impossible for the ogres to call in the deadly wind when, for the most part, the Midnights had been scattered across the kingdom—but now a great deal of shatterblast was right here in the Smoking Chimneys, which put the ball back in the ogres' court. . . .

The griffins twisted in the air as if trying to wriggle free from an invisible hold, but they couldn't stop what the ogres had started, and now that they were in the very place where the shatterblast had been conjured, Casper and Utterly found that they could see the wind clearly—a red, hot, glittering substance trailing out of the griffins' beaks and making its way back into the trunk.

The lightning vanished, the Midnights reeled in the sky, then the storm ogres snapped the trunk shut and, to Utterly and Casper's horror, hurled it down into the volcano.

"Look out!" Casper cried, grabbing Utterly and darting closer to the tree.

The trunk careered past them and landed, with an almighty splash, in the lava close by. But it didn't open, as Utterly and Casper had feared. It simply sank out of sight, lost for good, and up above the Midnights screeched.

"The ogres," Utterly gasped. "They're bent over and panting—maybe summoning the shatterblast back took all of their magic!"

Casper gripped his crossbow tighter. "But it hasn't taken all of their strength."

The ogres were struggling up again, then launching spears and rocks and what looked like lava grenades into the flock of hissing griffins. But the Midnights were too many in number for the ogres and moments later two griffins slipped past the fight and shot down toward Casper and Utterly. Casper fired the bolt from his crossbow at the first, and stunned by the blow, it clattered into the treasure-filled ledges before dropping down into the lava. Casper gaped at what he and the crossbow had done, but there was no time to think on it because now the second griffin was diving toward Utterly with outstretched wings.

Utterly swung the axe and it sliced through the Midnight's wings. The creature crumbled into a wisp of dust, and seconds later another griffin sped down, and Casper only saw it in time because Arlo squeaked in his ear. He ducked and the Midnight snatched at his back with its talons as it raced on by, and had Casper not been wearing his cape, the griffin would have clamped his talons over his spine and wrenched him upward. But the frozen lightning had a steel-like strength, exactly like armor, and it gave Casper the time he needed to reload his crossbow.

Then two Midnights rocketed down at once, and while Casper and Utterly turned to face them, neither noticed the third griffin tearing down behind them—until it spun round in front of Casper, slipped its talons through the gap in the front of his cape, and pulled hard on Casper's chest.

Casper screamed as the griffin batted his crossbow from his hands and wrenched him toward the clock. Because he knew that the Midnight wouldn't be dragging him back to the Faraway—if he went through the clock door with one of the griffins, he would be trapped inside the tree in Everdark, and Morg would stop at nothing until somehow she found a way to use Casper to transport her to Rumblestar.

Casper kicked and yelled, and Arlo shot out of Utterly's cape, risking the searing heat of the volcano to blow fire into the griffin's face, but it was only when Utterly grabbed onto the griffin's ankles that the Midnight stalled before the clock. It thrashed its wings as it tried to shake Utterly off, but Utterly wasn't letting go and so the griffin changed tack by springing into the air and shaking its wings.

"I . . . I can swing at its talons if I grab the axe inside my cape!" Utterly gasped.

"It's too dangerous!" Casper cried as the Midnight beat

upward. "If you don't hold on with two hands, you'll fall into the lava!"

Casper winced as he felt the hold on one of his legs go when Utterly seized her axe, swiped at the griffin . . . and missed. Realizing it wasn't going to shake Utterly away, though, the Midnight tightened its grip on Casper, then turned tail and thundered back down toward the clock. And this time it had momentum on its side.

Utterly swung again, with all the force she could muster, and just as the griffin tucked in its wings to shoot inside the clock, Utterly's axe cut through its talons and the creature crumbled into dust. Casper smacked down onto the roots of the tree, but when he spun round, Utterly and Arlo were nowhere to be seen.

Another griffin had sneaked past the ogres, and on seeing that Utterly's cape was twisted up round her neck after the tussle with the axe, had snatched her by the arms and was wrenching her up, up, up. And though Arlo was trying his best, he couldn't keep up *and* blow flames all at the same time.

Casper grappled for his crossbow because he could see what was happening. The griffin knew that Utterly was only causing trouble and that it was *him* Morg really needed—and now that

Casper was within the Midnights' grasp, this particular griffin wasn't thinking twice about killing Utterly. Casper fired the crossbow, but the Midnight was flying fast and the bolt fell short.

"Casper!" Utterly yelled as the Midnight yanked her higher still.

Casper tore across the roots of the tree toward the steps, but no matter how fast he climbed the volcano and no matter how many Midnights he brought down, he knew he couldn't match the speed of a griffin's wings. He watched as the Midnight carried Utterly out of the volcano and into the storm, and Arlo followed.

Then Casper felt his world slide.

The griffin had torn off Utterly's cape, then punched Arlo away, and Casper could only watch as both the girl and the dragon fell through the sky somewhere far beyond his help.

"Nooooooooo!" Casper shouted as he charged on up the volcano.

Then the air was punched from his lungs as a Midnight barged into him—sending his crossbow plummeting into the lava. Casper went to pull his cape across him, but the Midnight was too quick and it seized him by his wrist and dragged him toward the clock.

This time, though, as the hollow in the tree gaped before them and Casper's pulse pounded in his head, his thoughts whirred back to Slumbergrot's words right at the beginning of their quest: "To protect the marvels, you must destroy the Midnights, and to destroy the Midnights, you must find a familiar face." If the clock *was* the familiar face and it could *defeat* the Midnights, did that mean that somewhere inside it there was a secret weapon? His eyes locked onto the pendulum and suddenly Casper felt the smallest trickle of hope.

The griffin shuffled backward into the clock, never letting up on its grip on Casper for a second. But at the very moment it made to snatch Casper inside with it, Casper planted his feet either side of the opening and yanked hard on the pendulum. He tumbled backward with it, and the griffin flapped and screeched and clawed at Casper. But in his hands lay the pendulum, only this long piece of silver wasn't a pendulum at all. It was a blade and above the blade, tucked out of sight when it had been hanging in the clock, was a hilt studded with rubies.

The pendulum was a sword.

And the rubies were the same fiery red as the feathers of the phoenix in the painting Casper had seen in the castle—and he understood then that there was a magic stronger than the Midnights and stronger even than Morg. The magic of the phoenix, the very creature who had created the Unmapped Kingdoms and the Faraway at the dawn of time.

Casper held the sword high and the griffin shrank back before scuttling over the roots and cowering in the ogre's den. But then it narrowed its eyes and let out a throaty snarl as it heard the cries of its flock hurtling down into the volcano. They had beaten a way past the storm ogres.

Casper stiffened with fear as the volcano filled with talons and feathers. How could he possibly kill *every* Midnight before they dragged him into Everdark? And was it too late now to save Utterly and Arlo, wherever they were?

Then a breeze that smelled musky—like the way pine trees smell when the wind rushes through them—sifted down into the volcano, moving faster and surer than any of the Midnights. Casper didn't know which of the winds this was, but he knew that it was magical because it carried a whisper in its wake: "*The Midnights are a part of Morg—they are her selfishness brought to life—and so only a truly selfless act can rid Rumblestar of their presence.*"

Casper's pulse drummed, but the wind said no more. He glanced up at the griffins racing down toward him, then he looked from the sword to the clock, and suddenly Casper realized what he had to do.

"Destroy the portal," he whispered. "My way home."

For a second, Casper faltered. The cost of winning—of saving the Unmapped Kingdoms and the Faraway—was his freedom to leave. . . . The truth spun inside him, sharp and sore. Would he ever find another way to return to his own world? He thought of his parents and their cozy turret in Little Wallops and his heart trembled. Could he really give up the chance to go home? But the Midnights were swooping closer now and only a truly selfless act would stop them, so without thinking, without assessing the risks, without giving so much as an ounce of thought to a to-do list, Casper plunged the sword into the clockface.

The glass smashed to smithereens, the clock chimed—a hollow sound like a ghost calling—and as the noise rung out, the Midnights tearing toward him broke apart in the air until all that remained were hundreds of jet-black feathers tumbling down around Casper. They fell silently, eerily, as the clock continued to chime, then one by one they were swallowed by the lava and Casper was left blinking into the empty volcano.

The Midnights were gone! The familiar face had destroyed

them! And the ogres on the lip of the crater were quelling the storm. Casper blinked again in shock and relief. He'd done it! Against all the odds, he'd beaten the Midnights!

But before he could dwell on what that meant for him, the roots of the tree began to wobble beneath him. The clock shook. The walls of the volcano trembled. And Casper ran, because it felt like this Smoking Chimney was about to blow. . . . He raced up the steps two at a time as the lava sucked the mangled clock, his only way home, down into its clutches. He ran on, any joy he had felt a moment ago now spiraling into panic, but he was glad of the cape around him as the lava spat and sizzled against its fur.

Silver smoke filled the cavern, and as the walls began to judder, the ogres backed away from the crater. Rocks tumbled, treasure fell, and the whole volcano was filled with ash, but still Casper ran, wrapped in his cape and holding his sword, even though he was a long way off from the crater and the way ahead was locked in smoke.

Then, amidst the haze and the heat and the groan of a volcano about to erupt, Casper heard Utterly's voice.

For a second he was too stunned to breathe.

But there it was again.

"Casper! Over here!"

And what Casper saw, through the blur of falling rocks and smoke, made his heart soar. A rope ladder dangling down from a hot air balloon that hadn't left them after all but was risking one final journey—and leaning over its basket, a girl with wild blond hair and a miniature dragon bouncing on her shoulder. His friends had come back to save him.

Chapter 26

Casper swiped at the rope ladder, but as he did so, the step beneath him fell away and he stumbled against the side of the volcano. His cape held the worst of the heat back, but the rocks were scorching and pain seared Casper's palms. The smoke had thickened and he could no longer see the lava below him, but he could hear it gulping and belching. The eruption was coming. Casper scanned the smoke for the ladder again, and when it did slip through the ash in front of him, he saw that Utterly was standing on the very last rung, holding out a hand toward him.

"JUMP!" she yelled.

The volcano groaned.

"NOW!"

Casper glanced at the gap between him and Utterly. If he

misjudged the leap, he'd fall to his death. But Casper flung himself toward Utterly, trusting as she grabbed his hand that she wouldn't let him go, because as Bristlebeard had said, friendships were sticky things.

Utterly yanked Casper up the ladder, then while Arlo nuzzled into Casper's neck, she seized the microphone and yelled, "Let's go, Zip!"

Zip shot upward at the speed of light, and as she burst out of the crater and flew as far away as she could, the volcano finally erupted. A bulging mass of ash and rocks and lava shot out of its crater, spewing into the sky and surging down the sides of the volcano. But the most overwhelming thing was the noise—the roar of the earth's core—which shook through every bone in the children's bodies.

Zip careered on, away from the explosion, as Casper, Utterly and Arlo huddled down in the corner of her basket. Eventually, the volcano stopped roaring and a strange whistling sounded in its place. Stranger still, though, was that as this whistling rang out—deep and low like an owl's hoot—the smoke and ash cleared away until just a river of lava was left, and the sky was once more blue.

Casper, Utterly, and Arlo peeped over the edge of the hot air balloon. The ogres were standing round the crater of the largest volcano, and it seemed the whistling was coming from them.

They can conjure winds with a chant, Casper thought, *and they can blow volcanic eruptions clean away with a whistle. The Midnights have gone and their magic has returned to them.*

The ogres grew quiet and Zip's voice crackled through the microphone. "This is your captain speaking. I would like to congratulate all three of you on being the bravest individuals Rumblestar has ever known."

Casper held on to the basket to steady himself. He, Utterly, and Arlo had *truly* done it! They had rid Rumblestar of the Midnights and now the marvels would be restored, the links between kingdoms would remain and the weather in the Faraway would go back to normal! His parents would be safe! And for a moment Casper didn't think about what that meant for him.

He looked across at Utterly. There didn't seem words big enough to hold in everything they'd done. So he simply said, "We did it."

And Utterly laughed because she knew as well as Casper that there might not be certificates and trophies for this kind of thing, but there was a kingdom still standing.

"But how?" Utterly gasped. "I thought it was all over

when the griffin batted Arlo away and dropped me hundreds of meters up in the sky. But Zip broke my fall—an 'unprogrammed emotional crisis overrode her homing device,' she said. How did you stop the Midnights, Casper? I thought all was lost for you down in that volcano."

"So did I," Casper replied. Then he opened his cape and drew out the sword. Arlo fluttered onto the hilt and stroked the rubies. "The pendulum turned out to be a sword filled with phoenix magic, so I ran it into the clock and—"

"Set off a volcano, destroyed the Midnights, and blocked Morg's portal into Rumblestar!" Utterly grinned. "How's *that* for completing a to-do list, Casper?"

Casper smiled, but then he looked out over the volcanoes and sighed. Because he'd blocked another portal, too. His way home. He told Utterly what the wind had whispered to him, and as he spoke, Arlo climbed up onto his shoulder and cuddled into his ear.

"This isn't the end," Utterly said. "We'll find another way home for you. I promise."

And on hearing the certainty in Utterly's voice, Casper wondered whether she might be right. Rumblestar was full of unexpected things, after all.

The storm ogres were waving at the hot air balloon now. "Well-CHOMPING-done!" they boomed. "Well-CHOMPING-done!"

Casper waved back. "Thank *you* for your help!"

"You were incredible!" Utterly cried as Arlo did a celebratory somersault in the air.

Casper turned to Utterly and whispered: "It would've been a lot less faff if the ogres had realized the pendulum was a sword; they could've stopped the Midnights just like that."

"Storm ogres struggle to say more than one word, Casper. Understanding that a pendulum was a sword that could save a kingdom would be completely beyond them. And anyway, the Lofty Husks always say phoenix magic is unpredictable—I don't think the ogres could have used the sword like you did, as they had no connection with that clock."

Their conversation was interrupted by Zip sparking into life again. "The SkySoar9000 would like confirmation that you have no more battles planned before we begin our journey home."

Utterly looked at Casper. "I'm sure any other Midnights around Rumblestar will have disappeared along with the ones in the volcano. Which means the snow trolls, sun scamps, and even the drizzle hags should now be able to deliver their marvels, so unless you have any last-minute fights on your—what did you call it back in the canoe? Your *agenda*?—then we should get going."

Casper tilted the microphone toward himself. "No more battles," he said sternly. "Definitely no more battles." He paused. "Thank you for coming back, Zip. You risked everything to rescue us—you're the finest hot air balloon around."

Zip coughed. "On the SkySoar9000 we do try to make your experience as memorable as possible. And on that note, feel free to open hatch one for some celebratory milkshakes."

Utterly yanked the lever and drew out two glasses filled with purple liquid and a thimble full of brown goo.

"Thunderberry shakes!" she exclaimed. "My favorite! And a toffee tornado for Arlo!"

Casper took a sip, which was a refreshing burst of what tasted like blueberries, cookies, ice cream, and possibly a sprig of mint. "Please could you fly us back to the castle, Zip?" He was about to add *via the safest and quickest route possible,* but instead he found himself saying, "Via the most *interesting* route possible."

Zip stayed up above the clouds for a while and Casper blinked in delight at the hidden world the eagles and the falcons owned, then the hot air balloon sank through the clouds, and once again mountains spread out below them. Lakes sparkled, waterfalls rumbled, and when the mountains ironed out, forests appeared. And it was only when the light began to fade that Utterly, Casper, and Arlo finished talking about all that had happened since they set off down the Witch's Fingers.

They looked out over a lake surrounded by meadows that held the reflection of twilit clouds, then as dusk came and night rolled in, the lake turned silver under the moonlight. Casper held his head up to the darkness. There weren't any stars out yet, so he was surprised to see that the night air glittered. It was the sort of shimmer you might miss if you only glanced at the sky for few seconds, but Casper knew to look at the world more closely.

"Moondust," Utterly whispered to him. "The very thing that is keeping the magic here in Rumblestar turning." Then she smiled. "It's a good sign; it means the dragons are stirring. They'll be getting ready to collect the marvels from the castle and transport them to the other kingdoms. Things are finally going back to normal."

Casper stretched out his hand and let the moondust slip through his fingers. It felt soft and cool and full of magic, and it shone all the brighter when the stars blinked through the dark. He'd seen stars back home, of course, but they were nothing like this. The sky here was jaw-droppingly brilliant and there were so many stars it seemed like the night itself was having to make way for them.

The balloon sailed on through the night and then, some time later, when the night was at its deepest, two silhouettes with jagged wings, long forked tails, and spines full of ridges glided past the moon.

"The dragons are here," Utterly said quietly.

She, Casper, and Arlo watched as the sky filled with faraway silhouettes that soared and dipped and rolled through the moondust. And while Casper was thinking that the sky couldn't be any more incredible if it tried, it let the last—and best—of its secrets into the night.

A moonbow.

A beam of brilliant white light arched over the whole kingdom. Even the stars weren't as bright as the moonbow, and as Casper looked at it, he thought of Utterly's sister climbing out onto the roof.

"I would've wanted to go up onto the spire with you for this, Utterly," he said. "It's soul-smashingly magical."

Utterly's eyes shone with tears. "Some people go their whole lives without realizing how incredible our world is, but me and Mannerly, we knew it." She smiled. "Just as you do now."

"I'm glad I met you, Utterly. You *and* Arlo. And I'm glad we've seen and done all that we have—even if I'm so bruised I'm not sure I can sit down."

"It's been a cracking adventure, hasn't it?"

Casper snuggled into his frozen lightning cape. "It really has. And if I can't ever find a way home, at least I'll have you and Arlo."

Utterly smiled. "You'll always have us, Casper, wherever you go."

Zip flew on through the night while they slept, then at sunrise she announced that they were nearing the castle. Casper and Utterly squinted through the morning light to see that they were high above the Dusky Peaks now and that on their left was the Edge but straight ahead of them there were waterfalls pouring down from towering walls, and domes and spires beyond those.

"Not a Midnight in sight." Utterly beamed.

They were a mile or so away from the castle still, but to Casper it looked different from how it had the week before. It was as if something about the shape didn't quite make sense.

"What's happened to the castle?" he said slowly. "The roof is all higgledy-piggledy and the bridges seem to be moving, but I can't see Slumbergrot or any other giants thrashing around."

Utterly frowned. "You're right. It does look different. And what's that noise?"

It was a roar of sorts, and the closer they flew to the castle, the louder it became. But Zip showed no sign of slowing. As they drew closer, they could make out fire-red flags rippling from the tower tops and banners strewn down the castle walls, and then Casper and Utterly understood why the castle had looked a different shape. There were people—men, women, children, and grandparents, who definitely should have known better—huddled on the roof of the castle, bouncing up and down on the bridges, leaning out of the windows, and waving from the ramparts. And the sound—the glorious, heart-warming, thundering sound they had heard—was applause.

Rumblestar was welcoming them home.

"But . . ." Utterly turned to Casper. "We stole a canoe, stayed out after curfew, and nearly died about twelve times—"

"But we also stopped the Midnights and saved Rumblestar," interrupted Casper with a smile.

Utterly and Casper laughed in disbelief. They were the most unlikely sort of heroes, but they were heroes nonetheless.

Zip flew on toward the castle and to Casper and Utterly's surprise, a paper airplane dropped into her basket and landed at Utterly's feet. Just as Utterly was making to open it, another one dropped in at Casper's feet. Then another. And another. And another. Until the basket was suddenly filled with hundreds of paper airplanes scattered around them both. Utterly and Casper tore them open.

Keep going, Utterly and Casper! And Arlo, too!

We're thinking of you all the time!

We love you, Utterly! We miss you!

We're so proud of you and Casper. And Mannerly would be too!

The messages went on and on. Each one was different, but every single one was signed from the same two people. Utterly's mum and dad. And though it made a part of Casper sad to think his own parents were so very far away and he still didn't know how to reach them, he was happy for Utterly because this was what she needed: a hundred paper airplanes telling her she was loved.

Casper grinned. "Looks like the final curses the Midnights put on the castle walls have, at last, been broken."

Zip dropped down over the wall and Utterly and Casper climbed down the rope ladder into the throng of people, but it wasn't being hoisted up onto shoulders, high-fived by Utterly's classmates, or having their hands shaken by the Lofty Husks that Casper and Utterly remembered most that day. It was the words Utterly's mum said as she tore through the crowds to find them.

"Utterly," she said, clasping her daughter's hands. "Your dad and I have been so worried about you!"

"I wanted to make you proud," Utterly mumbled. "After everything that happened."

Her mother hung her head. "I'm sorry if your going in the first place was because we ever made you feel anything less than perfect to us. You are a wonderful, wonderful daughter—nothing that happened in the past can change that—and you are loved more than you will ever know."

Tears rolled down Utterly's cheeks and she fell into her mother's arms. She was loved and she knew it now in the deepest parts of her, the parts that before had been filled with pain.

Utterly's mum turned to Casper, too. "Both of you have been magnificent! When the last of the Midnights vanished last night, the snow trolls, sun scamps, and even the drizzle hags came to deliver their marvels, and they told us about your journey in the Beyond. But I think what makes you two *real* warriors is the strength that lies inside you. You are brave, and you are loyal, and you have learned, in only a few days, what most people take a lifetime to realize: that kingdoms are built on kindness—and that friends, when they work together, can bring evil to its knees."

And at that, Casper's heart soared. Until now, he had always assumed that the only things worth knowing were written in textbooks, but perhaps the truest, most important things in life couldn't be taught at school. Because at the end of the day, it had taken an adventure with a furious girl and an oversensitive dragon for him to learn that courage and friendship weren't things that simply happened to *other* people. *He* was brave and *he* was loyal, and those two discoveries definitely felt like things worth knowing.

Chapter 27

There was more whooping and cheering and hugging inside the castle, and though it felt good, Casper found himself thinking about home and how much he missed his parents. Even the prospect of a celebratory feast couldn't shift the longing inside him.

But just as he, Utterly, and Arlo were making their way toward the banqueting hall on the twelfth floor, Casper felt a hand on his shoulder. He turned around on the landing to see a very tall, very narrow figure wearing robes of ancient parchment. Casper blinked. It was Frostbite, and he was looking much better than he had when Casper had left him in the forest!

"You made it back to the castle!" Casper cried.

Frostbite nodded. "I owe the snow trolls my life." The Lofty Husk looked from Casper to Utterly to Arlo. "Congratulations to all three of you. What you did out in the Beyond was truly remarkable and Rumblestar will forever be in your debt. Because of you, Morg can never meddle with our kingdom again; we have had word from the ogres that the opening she forged from Everdark into the Smoking Chimneys is sealed forever."

Utterly frowned. "But what about the other kingdoms? What about Crackledawn, Jungledrop, and Silvercrag? Can Morg still reach them?"

Frostbite's face turned grave. "Yes. Morg may still be able to find a way through to the other kingdoms. And I have no doubt that she will try."

Utterly and Casper's faces fell.

"But the Lofty Husks there will be ready," Frostbite added. "They will brew stronger spells and bigger protection charms. They will not let the harpy win. Just as you did not." He smiled. "Your names will go down in legend, like Smudge and Bartholomew's did all those years ago, and on this day every year Unmappers will remember that you achieved something astonishing."

Casper blushed, Utterly beamed, and Arlo took a little bow from her shoulder.

"I want to present you all with a token of gratitude for saving the Unmapped Kingdoms and the Faraway." Frostbite looked at Utterly first, then he reached into the pockets of his robes and, rather unexpectedly, drew out a walking cane, a tambourine, and a signed edition of Digby Blethersecret's *The Castle and Its Quirks.*

"I forgot to tell you this bit about the Lofty Husks," Utterly whispered to Casper. "They have endless pockets."

Frostbite continued to rummage in his gown. "I would be most obliged if you could hold this for me, Casper. It is ever so valuable." He handed Casper a golden chandelier, then reached a little farther into his pocket and smiled. "Ah yes, *this*." He drew out a piece of silver in the shape of a star and handed it to Utterly.

"A bottler badge . . ." Utterly shook her head. "But only qualified bottlers get these!"

Frostbite nodded. "Which is precisely what you are, Utterly."

She blinked. "But I keep getting chucked out of the classes! I never win any awards—and . . . and I'm only eleven!"

"Eleven you may be," Frostbite replied, "but because of *you* the mills in Dapplemere are still working, even though the sun scamps feared the worst when the Midnights ransacked them, and the marvels there are safe." Frostbite opened his palm and there was another, smaller badge inside with the letters *RIB* inscribed on it, which he pinned onto Arlo's knitted waistcoat.

The dragon squinted up at Frostbite.

"Remarkably Intelligent Being," the Lofty Husk said. "When the drizzle hags delivered their marvels—begrudgingly, it has to be said—they kept asking if they might be able to pickle the dragon who had solved their riddles with ease if he got back to the castle in one piece. I said no, naturally, and decided to promote *you* instead. Arlo, *you* will be the Lofty Husks' first point of call for any mathematical issues and *your* role will come with a lifetime supply of toffees."

Arlo ruffled his wings in delight.

Frostbite looked at Casper, and the longing inside Casper grew. He wanted to be home with his parents again, to be back in the turret curled up next to them on the sofa, knowing the winds couldn't harm them anymore, and before the Lofty Husk could open his mouth, Casper found himself spilling out a half-formed hope.

"The portal I came through to Rumblestar has gone," he blurted, "and I know it might sound mad but if the *only* link from here to the Faraway is the dragons, maybe you and the other Lofty Husks could at least *try* and summon just one—preferably a vegetarian one—to take me home?"

Frostbite choked. "A dragon, carry a child?! Absolutely not.

They are far too wild, dangerous, and unreasonable. It would be like riding a volcano. And if you were not thrown off, you would probably be eaten or squashed. No. Riding a dragon would be a terrible idea. But there might be another way." He paused. "If a certain sun scamp is as efficient as he claims."

Casper heart shook at the possibility.

Frostbite looked at his pocket watch, which, Casper saw, bore words instead of numbers:

NOW

IN A SHORT WHILE

LATER

NEVER

Frostbite said the word "Casper" and the hands on the watch swung round to the words: "In a Short While."

Casper didn't dare ask *how* or exactly *when* he might be able to go home, because he felt any words might break the tiny glimmer of hope he still harbored that at the end of all this, he would see his parents.

Frostbite smiled at the group. "Feast," he said. "Most definitely time for a feast."

* * *

The banqueting hall blew the oak-paneled dining room back in Little Wallops out of the water. The room was incredibly tall—so tall in fact that there were birds nesting in the uppermost corners—and its walls were covered in enchanted mirrors, which Casper guessed were the message mirrors Bristlebeard had mentioned back in the forest, because when they drew near to one, it clouded up, then words appeared, as if someone had breathed on the mirror and written in the fog left on the surface.

Well done, Casper! It's your old friend Bristlebeard here. Thrilled to learn you found Utterly and you gave those Midnights the beating they deserved. How was Sir Chopalot?

The last sentence was hastily rubbed out, then the following words appeared in their place.

Brushwick sends her love. Keep up the meditation and the tofu.

"And over here!" Casper cried as another mirror nearby misted with words.

Chomp xxx.

Casper and Utterly giggled.

"Another message for you down this way!" a girl Utterly's age cried.

Casper and Utterly hurried over.

Matt from Dapplemere here. Fantastic work at the Smoking Chimneys, Utterly, Casper, and Arlo. Can't chat for long, though. Got something to do for Frostbite, a new batch of dazzlethread to collect, and plans to build an extension on my mill. Cheerio!

The words faded and then, in the mirror next to them, a few more appeared.

Hello, you filthy little ragpots.
We hope that you had a truly miserable

**trip and that you got sunburnt in
Dapplemere, trodden on by ogres in the
Smoking Chimneys, and pecked at by
griffins along the way. If any of your limbs
have fallen off or are bruised beyond
repair, let us know and we'll get pickling.
Yours in mild hatred and disgust,
H, G, and S (no kisses).**

Casper and Utterly burst out laughing, then finally they sat down at one of the long wooden tables spread with cups of tea that puffed out mist and bowls full of what looked like whipped cream.

Casper eyed the bowl in front of him. "What exactly *is* this?" he asked.

"A snow pie," Utterly replied, dunking a spoon into the middle of hers and taking an enormous mouthful. "Heaps of snow cream balanced on a tower of sun-drenched pancakes and topped with a handful of cloud berries." She paused. "It's a dessert, basically."

"Which you eat *before* the main course?" Casper asked, dipping his own spoon into the snow pie, then letting the soft sugariness dissolve on his tongue.

Utterly nodded. "Don't *you*?"

But Casper wasn't able to reply because he and Utterly were bombarded with questions from the boys and girls in Utterly's class.

"How big were the storm ogres?"

"Where *exactly* do the drizzle hags live?"

"Are the snow trolls as scary as everyone says?"

"What does dazzlethread feel like?"

"Just how often *does* it rain in England, Casper?"

Arlo found the whole ordeal so profoundly overwhelming that he curled up in a teacup and went to sleep, but Utterly and Casper chattered away to everyone and Casper noticed that Utterly was a different girl from the one who had left the castle a week before. She laughed easily, scowled less, and only shoved someone once (when they asked her if Arlo was in fact the real brains behind the whole operation).

The Lofty Husks ate at a larger, taller table at the far end of the room. Frostbite was among them, and after the food had been cleared away, it was he who stood up and addressed the banqueting hall.

"I would like to propose three cheers for Casper, Utterly, and Arlo—without whom this kingdom would not be standing."

There were cheers and whoops and stamping feet, and one or two people clapped Utterly and Casper on the back. And then the hearth behind the Lofty Husks' table—which had been empty when Casper looked before—suddenly burst into bright red flames.

"This is a sign," Frostbite said. "A sign that even though Morg still lives in Everdark, there is phoenix magic lingering there and whatever lies in store for the Unmapped Kingdoms, hope will always triumph over darkness."

There were more cheers, and Arlo fluttered into the air and let out a celebratory snort of fire.

Frostbite smiled. "The dragons will come by to collect more marvels soon—after recent events, the Lofty Husks in the other kingdoms have sent word that Crackledawn, Jungledrop, and Silvercrag need as many marvels as we can muster to make up for the ones the Midnights ruined. There is much bottling and ballooning to be done, so I shall not keep you any longer." He paused. "But because we rulers are known for our terribly amusing jokes, as well as our wisdom and long life expectancy, I will just leave you all with a little jape now."

"Give them the one about paper!" one of the other Lofty Husks remarked.

"No, no," Blustersnap tutted. "It's *tearable*."

Frostbite scowled. "I have a perfectly good joke up my sleeve, thank you very much." He drew himself up. "What did the rain cloud wear under his raincoat?"

The Unmappers winced because they knew Frostbite, of all the Lofty Husks, told the very worst jokes.

"Thunderwear," he chortled.

The rest of the Lofty Husks chortled with him until they were laughing so much tears streamed down their wrinkled cheeks, so everybody else in the banqueting hall laughed too—because that's what happens with laughing—it's even more contagious than yawning.

There was a rush of noise as everyone stood up and pushed their chairs in, but Casper didn't move. Because Frostbite was heading over toward him and he was smiling. The hall emptied until there was just Casper, Utterly, Arlo, and Frostbite left behind. Then the Lofty Husk reached into the pockets of his robe again and this time he drew out a small key set with a turquoise gem.

Casper gasped. "The key to the grandfather clock!"

Frostbite nodded. "The Midnight pretending to be me fled the castle the night Slumbergrot awoke and flew directly to his roost at Dapplemere, and after a detailed search of the valley, Matt and his friends found the key he took." Frostbite handed it to Casper.

"But there's no clock anymore," Casper said quietly. "I can't find my way home that way."

Frostbite beckoned Casper, Utterly, and Arlo out onto the landing, into the bathtub lift, then down to the hallway. It was quiet and empty, and as Frostbite drew out his pocket watch, Casper saw that the hand on it was pointing at another word: *Now*. Casper's skin tingled as the Lofty Husk cast an arm toward the doors of all shapes and sizes that lined the walls.

"Take a look," Frostbite said. "A close look."

Casper's eyes ran over the little plaques nailed above each door: **River Imps** above a door the size of a cushion whose handle was so shiny clean Casper could see his face in it; **Marsh Goblins** above a circular door covered in grime and weeds; **Sun Scamps** above a golden door the size of a cat flap; **Hippogriffs** above a door so big it took over an entire wall and was covered in bolts and chains. And then there was another door in the far corner of the hallway, one that Casper could have easily overlooked had it not been for the word on the plaque above it, which simply said: **Casper**.

Casper felt his legs sway. "I . . . I don't understand. Was this here before?"

Frostbite shook his head. "I know this castle very well, but every time I walk through it, I notice something new. It changes daily. And shortly after I used a summoning charm to retrieve the key from Dapplemere, I noticed this door. Perhaps Rumblestar wanted to thank you for sacrificing your greatest desire—your way home—for the sake of the Unmapped Kingdoms and the Faraway by opening up another door for you." Frostbite paused. "That is if the key fits the lock, of course."

Casper slipped the key into the lock. It fit perfectly and as he turned it, there was a quiet click. Casper's heart quickened. Here it was. A way home at last. And he would have thundered through this door a week ago—but now he found himself standing surprisingly still.

He glanced at Arlo, who was poking up out of Utterly's overall pocket, the way he had been when Casper first met him inside the grandfather clock, then he looked at Utterly. Her hair was still in desperate need of a brush and her overalls were smudged with ash and the remains of a snow pie, but her eyes no longer held the fury of a long-kept storm.

"Will I"—Casper looked at his boots, then up at Frostbite—"will I ever find a way back to see Utterly and Arlo again?"

"It is not for me to say whether you will or will not come back to the Unmapped Kingdoms," Frostbite replied, "but if you did happen to find another phoenix tear—there are seven in the Faraway, after all . . . I do not think you will come back through your grandfather clock. Magic rarely works the same way twice." He paused. "But friendships are a strange thing. My best friend is a cloud giant who only wakes up every hundred years, so really our time together has been rather short. And if the legends are to be believed, then Smudge and Bartholomew only started speaking to one another when the monkey realized he and the girl were *not* embarking upon a retirement cruise to play golf, as he had thought, but rather a life-threatening mission to steal Morg's wings. It would be foolish to measure a friendship by its length, though. It is the depth that counts. And your friendship with Utterly and Arlo has taken you to the tallest trees in Shiverbark Forest and to the deepest volcanoes in the Smoking Chimneys—just as Smudge and Bartholomew's took them all the way to Everdark. So when you find yourself back in the Faraway, all you really need do to find Utterly and Arlo is look up at your marvelous sky."

Casper looked at the door in front of him. "But how will it work?" he said, hardly daring to hope that it might. "When I close the door behind me, will I be back in Little Wallops right away?"

Frostbite shook his head. "As to exactly *what* you will find behind that door, I am afraid I cannot tell you. Because that is the thing about locked doors, Casper. You never quite know what is on the other side."

Chapter 28

Casper had imagined this scene many times since arriving in Rumblestar, but in all that imagining he hadn't foreseen how wobbly his legs would feel or how clogged up his throat would be when looking at the girl who had arrested him after two minutes of knowing him when he first set foot in the kingdom.

Casper turned to face Utterly, the sadness of things dawning inside him. "Whenever it rains, whenever it snows, and whenever the sun is so bright I have to squint to see through it"—Casper's voice wavered—"I'll remember our adventure."

Utterly swallowed, then she swallowed again, and Casper wondered whether she, too, was having trouble with her voice. *Friendships really do knock it out of you,* Casper thought.

Eventually Utterly managed to find the words. "You turned

out to be a brilliant criminal in the end," she said. "It's a good thing the Lofty Husks didn't feed you to a dragon."

She looked away suddenly, then brushed a sleeve across her eyes and muttered something very unconvincing about a dust allergy. But Casper knew what was really going on because he was finding it hard to see too. It seemed that their friendship had stretched them both, just as Bristlebeard had told Casper it would, and that the shape of their hearts had been changed forever.

Utterly sniffed and then smiled. "I won't forget you, Casper."

Casper smiled back through misted eyes. "Me neither. I don't suppose you ever forget your first real friend."

Utterly reached out and hugged Casper while Arlo clung to his ear and purred inside it. Casper held his friends tight for a while longer, then he took a deep breath. He'd been brave enough to save a kingdom; now he had to be brave enough to leave it.

He drew back and, in a fluttering of nerves and hope, pushed the door in front of him open and stepped inside.

He was in a passageway lit by torches. Casper closed the door behind him and walked slowly over the flagstones as the passageway led right, then left, then doubled back on itself before leading up a flight of stone steps. Casper paused on the steps. Was he back in Little Wallops already, in some overlooked passage of the school that he knew nothing about? He hastened up the steps to find another door in front of him. Spurred on by the thought of seeing his mum and his dad and their cozy little flat, he pushed it open.

And frowned.

He was standing at the top of a turret attached to the farthest corner of Rumblestar Castle, and from where he stood he could see the whole kingdom spread out around him. The sky-tumbling waterfalls glinted in the afternoon sun and the Witch's Fingers trundled on through the trees toward the Edge. Why had the door with his name on led him *here*? Casper placed his elbows on the turret wall, sank his chin into his hands, and sighed. Home wasn't any closer after all.

But as Casper looked out over the kingdom, he had the strangest feeling that he wasn't alone in this turret and an even stranger feeling that the stone beneath him was moving. Not significantly—more of a slow but steady rise and fall—like someone, or something, breathing.

Casper straightened up and placed a hand on the stone. It

felt suspiciously warm for the time of day. And it was only when he craned his neck out of the stone arch that he saw what he had been leaning on: the back of a very large gargoyle perched on a plinth of stone just beneath the top of the turret. Its wings were tucked in by its sides, and its back was ridged and covered in scales. Casper gulped. *Could this be . . . ?* He leaned as far out of the tower as he dared just to be sure—and there, hanging down beneath the gargoyle, was a forked tail and two large talons.

Casper froze. This was a dragon.

As soundlessly as he could, Casper pulled himself back into the turret and tiptoed across the flagstones toward the stairs. Because dragons were wild, dangerous, unreasonable, and—what had Frostbite said?—fond of eating and squashing. But as Casper placed a foot on the first step, he found himself thinking about magic. It was unpredictable and full of risk and often it was so very strange it left the cleverest of grown-ups stumped by its ways. So, what if the Lofty Husk had been wrong? What if this particular dragon hadn't come for the marvels but had come instead to take him home? Because it did feel very much like the creature might be waiting for someone, and Casper couldn't help feeling that that someone might just be him.

But would the dragon know where Casper lived? Or, if he even managed to climb aboard it, would it dump him somewhere horribly confusing, like London? Or somewhere hopelessly out of the way, like Wales? Casper shuddered, then he clenched his fists. If this was his *only* way home, he had to give it a try.

He tiptoed to the edge of the tower and peered over as far as he could. For a moment he wondered how he could have ever thought the gargoyle was made of stone, because now that he looked closely, he could see that it was leathery and speckled silver. Casper stayed exactly where he was for several minutes. He wasn't quite sure how you went about hitching a ride with one of the most unreasonable creatures in Rumblestar. Then the dragon, sensing Casper's hesitation, hope, and fear all bound up together, turned its scaled head toward Casper and looked at him with wide, gold eyes.

Casper swallowed but didn't move. The dragon's pupils were long and black, like openings to a cave, and as Casper held the dragon's gaze, he saw in those burning eyes the wildest kind of magic—the sort that rides on the wind and revels in moondust. The dragon dipped its head, and with his heart clamoring in his throat, Casper climbed out of the turret and put a shaking hand on the dragon's back.

It was warm but sturdy and at the touch of Casper's palm the dragon let out a rumbling breath. Casper hoisted his leg between two of the silver ridges scoring the dragon's back until he was sitting astride the dragon. And no sooner had Casper breathed out than the dragon rolled its shoulders, flexed its muscles, and then launched off into the sky.

Casper clung to the ridges on the dragon's back as the creature beat its mighty wings higher and higher into the sky, but he didn't scream or faint or start panicking about to-do lists or safety harnesses. He just let the dragon carry him and as he felt his way into the dragon's rhythm, he threw back his head and laughed. Riding in Zip had been fun (and the hatches were nothing short of genius), but riding a dragon was like letting your spirit gallop along with the wind.

Nobody saw Casper soaring over the castle that afternoon—the bottlers and the ballooners were too busy rushing about their business—nobody, that is, except the girl and the miniature dragon looking out of the bedroom window on the sixty-third floor. Casper and Utterly waved at each other until their hands ached, and even when the dragon flew out over the Neverlate Tree and off the Edge, Casper turned to see that Utterly was still waving him goodbye.

The dragon flew on and on over the Boundless Seas, and Casper lost all sense of time. He let the wind rush through him and once or twice he cupped handfuls of cloud. After a while, though, the sun began to wane and a twilight settled pink and orange on the clouds around them. Then, as the light began to change, Casper noticed that through the openings in the clouds the landscape below him was changing too. It wasn't only an ocean down there now. There were fields and farms, train tracks and villages. And rain.

Casper's heart thumped. He recognized this.

"England," he breathed. He must have crossed one of the magical links between the Unmapped Kingdoms and the Faraway!

Suddenly it wasn't twilight below the clouds. It was a drizzly afternoon and Casper was home again. He took in the familiar flattened forests and churned-up roads, but the air, despite the rain, felt calm. There was no breeze at all and the few clouds that were clumped in the sky hung lazily where they were. And when Casper looked down again, he saw that people were going about their day as carefree as they had before the terrible winds started: a couple were walking a dog over a field, a man was cleaning his car in his driveway, and a handful of children were playing tag in a park.

Casper blinked. Was this the same afternoon he had crossed into Rumblestar? Utterly had said that a day here was a month in the Unmapped Kingdoms, so if he'd been away for a week, was that just an hour or two back here? Or had time not been different back home after all? Maybe days had gone by. . . . Casper stiffened. What did that mean for his parents? Were they safe? Was the school still standing?

The dragon flew into the clouds for a while, but when it emerged and once more the landscape came into view, Casper gasped. Far, far below was an avenue of beech trees—some of which had obviously been torn down by the winds—and they led to a very large and very old stone building. Beyond that were the remains of a cricket pavilion and a copse of partly destroyed woodland backing up against a tumbled-down stone wall.

"Little Wallops!" Casper cried in relief.

And there was his parents' car parked in front of the school and the outbuilding his dad used as a workshop for his design and technology classes and there—just there!—was the turret Casper lived in. Casper peered down at the window to see his mum and dad walking around the flat! His heart surged. He had no idea what day it was, but he had come home, at last, and it looked like his parents were safe.

The dragon circled the school high in the sky. For a second, Casper thought about Candida and Leopold and their stinging words. Again and again they had told him he didn't belong here and he never would. But that was before Rumblestar. Before he had met a whole kingdom full of people and creatures who had been nothing like him but who had still treated him like one of their own. *Things would be different now,* Casper told himself. Because he was brave and he had learned that his timetables, and all the hiding in lost and found baskets that came with them, weren't the way to stamp down evil.

The dragon dipped suddenly, and Casper felt sure the groundsman dismantling the sirens on the roof of the school or the gardener clearing branches from the soccer pitch would look up and scream. But neither did. Because when you're not expecting a silver-scaled dragon to glide over your school, you don't look up and search for it.

The dragon made for the copse of woodland before the wall closing in the school grounds, but it showed no signs of slowing as the oak trees loomed closer. Casper bent low to the dragon's back and held his breath as they careered toward the branches, but just at the last minute the dragon tucked in its wings and slipped through the canopy of the trees still standing, landing seconds later with a thump on the ground.

The dragon shook its scales and Casper slid down its leathery back. As his feet touched the ground, he breathed the woodland in—it felt good to be home.

He walked round to the dragon's head. "Thank you."

The dragon dipped its head and at the movement Casper noticed something behind it that he would have missed before his adventure in Rumblestar. But now that Casper had learned to look at the world more carefully, he saw that there was a small hole in the wall, a space where the stones didn't quite meet, and it made him think about something Utterly had said about the weather scrolls: "Dragons leave them in the overlooked corners of your world—like cracks in the wall, hollows of trees, and deep inside caves." And had Casper arrived home at sunrise, he might just have seen the three wax-sealed parchment scrolls tucked into the crack there melting into thin air as the sun came up.

The dragon before him stretched out its wings to prepare for flight, then it paused and its enormous ears swiveled. Casper listened. Then he heard it too.

Twigs snapping. And voices close by.

Chapter 29

The dragon backed away behind a large oak, and Casper nipped behind a half-toppled elm beside it. And then, to Casper's surprise, his classmate Sophie came running through the trees. Her face was stained with tears, and she was clutching half a book. The other half lay in the hands of Candida, who was stalking through the trees after her, with Leopold panting at her high heels.

"There's no point running away!" Candida snarled. "You know as well as I do that you'll have to stop running when you get to the wall!"

Sophie turned to face Candida and Leopold. "You . . . you didn't have to tear my book in half," she sobbed.

Candida climbed over a fallen tree, then plucked a page

from the half of the book she was holding. She let it fall to the ground before stamping it into the soil.

"Good one," Leopold sniggered. "You totally, like, ripped her book."

Candida took a stride closer to Sophie, whose shoulders were bunched up around her ears. "All I want to know is where Casper is. Leopold just sat through an hour of detention because of him, and when I snooped around Casper's flat earlier, his wretched dad came back, so I had to scamper. But I had a good enough look round the place to know he wasn't there. Are *you* telling me he's legged it off campus now the weather service has given the all-clear and the lockdown is over?"

Casper flinched. It *was* still the same day he had left! Utterly had been right about the time differences between her world and his—only an hour or two had passed since he hid inside the grandfather clock—and somehow the weather service back here knew that the storms were over. But *how*, when before they'd struggled to predict them at all? It didn't make sense, but Casper didn't have time to think about that now, because Candida was curling her lip at Sophie.

"You know Casper as well as anyone in the class," she spat. "Where is he?"

Sophie shook her head. "I've already told you. I don't know. I just came out here to read when the headmaster announced the storms were finally over. I haven't seen Casper all afternoon."

Leopold peered at the pages of the book Sophie was still holding, then he squinted at the cover, just visible between Sophie's shaking hands.

"I know that one," he grunted. "That weirdo librarian, Mrs. Whereabouts, made me read it in detention once. *The Lion, the Witch and the* whatsitcalled—the window, windmill, wall, washing machine? Nope. Can't remember." Then his eyes lit up. "Got it! *The Lion, the Witch and the Watermelon.* Total rubbish from start to finish."

He walked up to Sophie, grabbed what was left of the book, bit it—which Casper thought was odd as well as outrageous—then hurled it into the trees.

Sophie started sobbing uncontrollably then, and Casper knew that Candida and Leopold were having so much fun they probably wouldn't notice if he darted through the trees back to his flat. But there was Sophie to think about. And the fact that Leopold had just bitten a book. And the fact that Casper had learned what it meant to stand up against wrong.

He stepped out from behind the elm. "Leave Sophie alone!"

Candida's face broke into a delighted smile and Leopold blurted out a statement so crashingly obvious even Candida winced.

"Look! It's Casper."

For a second, Casper hesitated. Was he really going to take on Candida and Leopold at the same time? Sophie gawked at him, then began hastily picking up the pages of her book and stuffing them into her school bag. But she didn't run away. She was small and shy and often overlooked by her peers and teachers, but Sophie was standing her ground in the woods. She wasn't leaving Casper alone quite yet. And nor was the dragon. It was hiding still, otherwise the others would have screamed, but Casper could feel its presence behind him like an invisible but very strong shield.

Candida took a predatory step toward Casper. "Why are you wearing overalls covered in paint?" she spat. "And how did you slip out of Little Wallops without me seeing?"

"Yeah," Leopold grunted. "Overalls. Little Wallops."

Casper bit his lip. Leopold was running out of words again and he knew what happened when his words ran out. His fists stepped up to play. . . . Casper ducked as Leopold swung a meaty one toward him and Leopold looked surprised at Casper's lightning-quick reaction. But then again, Leopold didn't know that Casper was fresh off an adventure that had involved dodging a sky full of griffins.

"Back off," Casper said as fiercely as he could. "Both of *you*."

Candida circled him. "Or *you'll* do what?"

Leopold readied his fists again. "Yeah, what?"

And now Casper didn't just feel the dragon's presence behind him. He *heard* it too. A low growl at first, which grew in sound so that the leaves on the trees around them shuddered and the ground beneath their feet shook.

Candida and Leopold backed away several steps.

"What . . . what was that?" Candida glanced at Leopold.

The growl came once more, loud and rumbling and full of fight.

Sophie's eyes widened and Candida clutched Leopold's arm. "It's . . . it's a wild boar or an angry cow!" she hissed. "Make it go away!"

Leopold reached into his pocket and drew out his most trusted weapon: a fistful of five-pound notes. He hurled them toward the tree where the noise was coming from. But the dragon was not interested in money.

There was a loud thud, and though Casper knew the sound was the dragon thumping its large, scaled tail against the ground—he'd heard the same sound when the creature landed in the grounds earlier—the others had no idea what was going on. Only that the ground was still juddering after the thud and the growling had started again. Then an enormous scaled foot ringed with claws curled round a tree and shook its trunk, and Candida started to scream.

"Run!" she yelled, flinging her ponytail back from her eyes and bolting out of the trees.

Leopold followed as fast as he could, which wasn't very fast because his pockets were filled with so many coins it meant moving at any sort of pace was problematic. But he and Candida ran nonetheless, howling as they went, back to Little Wallops. There was a rush of wind behind Casper, then a *whrum* of beating wings and then a sort of hushed silence that is often left in the wake of magic. The dragon had gone and so had Candida and Leopold, which only left Casper and Sophie, who was squinting at the tree the dragon had been hiding behind.

"The strangest thing," she said quietly. "I could've sworn I saw something enormous and gray with—with claws and wings—bursting up out of the woods."

Casper paused. There were a lot of things he could have told Sophie that afternoon—about dragons and drizzle hags, snow trolls and cloud giants—but he felt like there were other things he wanted to say first. Normal things. Like asking if Sophie wanted to hang out over the Easter holidays, which, he imagined, would be back on now the weather seemed to have returned to normal and the lockdown was no longer in place. Or whether she wanted to team up again for the science project next term. So he didn't say any more about the dragon than this: "Could've been a pigeon? A very large one. Like Leopold, only more feathery."

Sophie giggled. "You stood up for me," she said, after a while. "No one's ever done that before."

Casper picked up the last few pages of Sophie's book from the ground and handed them to her. "Well, I think it's time we started."

"But Candida and Leopold are terrifying. . . ."

"Just because we're frightened, it doesn't mean we can't be brave," Casper said. He thought of how he'd jumped into the Witch's Fingers after Arlo and the moment he had plunged the sword into the grandfather clock. "Sometimes *you've* just got to do things scared."

Sophie thought about this. "I suppose it might be easier if there are two of us standing up to them at the same time."

Casper smiled. "It won't be nearly as bad. Because with two of us, we can face almost anything."

They walked back through the woods together. Casper's mind was buzzing with questions about how on earth the weather service had known to give the all-clear, but thanks to his training with the stormgulper, he knew that firing questions at someone early on in a friendship wasn't the best way to start. Instead he said: "Isn't it amazing that the storms have finally gone?"

Sophie nodded. "When the teachers started cheering and calling us into any room that had a television, I knew something exciting was happening—but actually *seeing* the hurricanes in Europe stop mid-spin and the tornados in America unravel in front of us was incredible. Everyone is saying that we can't be *sure* that the terrible weather has gone for good, but for now it seems like it's returned to normal."

Casper listened, spellbound. It was hard to believe that he, Utterly, and Arlo had been the ones to save the world. And yet they had.

So happy was Casper in that moment that he didn't give a

second thought to the dangers still lurking in the Unmapped Kingdoms or to the harpy who was, at that very moment, crawling through the depths of a dark and knotted forest. . . .

Because while the battle to save Rumblestar may have been won when Casper plunged the sword into the clockface—destroying the door to final endings and making the tree in Everdark vanish, taking Morg's trapped wings with it—there would be more courage, hope, and faith needed in the future to rid the Unmapped Kingdoms of evil for good. For harpies are not just known for being greedy; they're known for being cunning, too, and Morg had already begun to plot and plan. Her wings were gone, but all she needed was to find a way to conjure up *new* wings, which may not prove as powerful as her own but would allow her to fly up out of Everdark all the same. It might take years, decades, centuries even, but the harpy *would* escape. And, when she did, her sights were set on the kingdom of Jungledrop and the Forever Fern that grew there—a mythical plant that could grant immortality and restore her power. The inhabitants of Jungledrop were, of course, unware of Morg's plan, because dark magic rarely comes knocking in advance, but soon they would need to be ready. . . .

For now, though, Rumblestar was safe, as were the other

Unmapped Kingdoms, and Casper was right to be proud of the role he had played in making that happen, so he listened with a smile as Sophie chattered on.

"When the headmaster announced the lockdown was over, I cried I was so happy!" She paused. "Come to think of it, I don't think I saw you in the hall during the announcement?"

Casper suspected that launching into an explanation of his ordeal in the Smoking Chimneys might not be the best response, so he settled for: "I was right at the back—behind some really tall high schoolers."

Casper and Sophie chatted all the way back to Little Wallops and Casper realized what an awful lot he had been missing out on by sticking so rigidly to his lists and timetables. Sophie was clever (she could recite the entire periodic table), interesting (she knew seventeen facts about monkeys' bottoms, which they laughed about but which, really, Casper thought was deeply cool), and she had a cracking sense of humor (she did such a brilliant imitation of Leopold speaking, Casper's cheeks ached from grinning). Casper decided, there and then, that since he'd made room for one friend already, two if he counted Arlo, it was, perhaps, time to make room for another.

In fact, Casper had such a pleasant walk back to Little

Wallops that he only half noticed the golf balls scattered here and there on the woodland floor. For a second, he wondered about them—about something he had heard Frostbite say in Rumblestar—but then he turned his attention back to Sophie and he forgot all about it as he carried on walking.

They parted ways in the library. Sophie went back to her dormitory to pack her suitcase for the Easter holidays that were, apparently, starting the next morning—and Casper back to his turret. But as he crossed the library, Mrs. Whereabouts looked up from her desk.

"Well done," she said quietly in that singsong voice of hers.

Casper looked behind him, but there was no one else in the library. Just him and Mrs. Whereabouts. So it did seem that she was congratulating *him*.

"What for?" Casper asked.

Mrs. Whereabouts cocked her head and Casper caught a glimpse of something on the old lady's neck—not scars *exactly* but what looked like little ridges under her skin—and Casper wondered whether perhaps the reason Mrs. Whereabouts wore a turtleneck every single day of the year (even in spring and summer) was because she was trying to hide these marks. But then there was the nose ring and the spiky silver hair. It was all a bit peculiar for an old librarian in a boarding school in the middle of the English countryside.

"Well done for dealing with Candida and Leopold," she said eventually. "They tore through the school earlier saying you and Sophie had put a curse on the woods." She paused and then, in a softer voice, she added: "But well done for all the other stuff, too."

Casper stiffened. She couldn't mean . . . Could she? He looked at Mrs. Whereabouts, and she looked innocently back at him, and then—just for a second—Casper noticed the old lady's lips twitch. It wasn't much of a movement, and afterward Casper wondered whether it had happened at all, but Mrs. Whereabouts' eyes were twinkling, and as Casper walked toward his turret, he got the feeling that perhaps there was more to the librarian than what everybody else saw.

He hastened up the steps—his pulse racing with excitement at the thought of seeing his parents again—then he burst into the flat.

"Mum! Dad!" he cried. "I'm home!"

His mum was curled up on the sofa, watching a beaming weather reporter declare "Blue skies and balmy temperatures for England for the next few weeks—even sunshine in

Scotland tomorrow!" while his dad, dressed in the overalls he'd been wearing that morning, stood before the grandfather clock, brandishing a screwdriver. At the sight of them both Casper's heart filled with joy.

"Fixed it!" his father declared. "Pendulum's swinging, hands are turning—good as new!" He turned to Casper. "We tried to find you when the news started flooding in that the storms seem to be over—isn't it *wonderful*?"

Casper rushed over and flung his arms around his dad. Ernie laughed in surprise. But before he could say anything, Casper pulled back, leapt over the sofa, and snuggled into his mum's warm, familiar arms.

Ariella held Casper close, as if perhaps she had been waiting for this moment for a long, long time, then she smiled. "You look different." She brushed Casper's hair back from his face. "Very different."

"And you're wearing overalls!" Ernie chuckled. "Where on earth did you find them?"

Casper thought about it. "Lost and found basket."

The grandfather clock chimed six times. "You're back later than usual too." Ernie paused, then he poked Casper in the ribs and grinned. "Not sure your timetable would like that."

Casper laughed. "No, I don't suppose it would. But I've been doing a bit of thinking lately."

Ariella looked at Ernie with hopeful eyes, then she turned back to Casper. "Oh, yes?"

"And I won't be needing my timetables or my lists anymore."

Casper's parents said nothing for a moment. They were too stunned to speak. Then Ariella scooped Casper into her arms again and Ernie ruffled his hair. Because Casper's declaration was about more than timekeeping and organization and everyone in the turret knew it.

Ernie sat down beside Casper on the sofa. "If you won't be needing your timetables and your lists." He clasped Casper's hands. "Is there anything else you might like instead?"

Casper thought about this for a while, and his parents did that thing that parents do when they ask a question and pretend to be terribly relaxed about the answer. But Casper knew that hopes and dreams were pinned on this, that his parents wanted nothing more than for him to be happy and surrounded by friends.

He took a deep breath. "Walking boots, a sleeping bag, and maybe a flashlight, too."

Ernie's eyes grew large and Ariella choked on her tea.

"What marvelous suggestions," Ariella said when she had collected herself. She paused. "But might we just ask *why* you need all that?"

Casper smiled. "Because Sophie and I thought we'd go camping over the holidays."

"Oh, Casper," Ariella cried, her eyes shining. "I think that's a brilliant idea."

"You'll need a stove and a firelighter and a map to find the best forests," Ernie said excitedly. "I think we've got our work cut out for the weekend."

Casper nodded and then, as casually as he could, he said: "We might need to get another school blazer, too. And a shirt and some shoes."

Ariella frowned. "What happened to yours?"

Casper considered his answer. "I have absolutely no idea." Then he added: "Belongings are a bit harder to keep track of once you've ditched the lists."

Ariella smiled. "Tell me about it. I have no idea where I put my reading glasses this morning."

Ernie put a hand on her arm. "They're in the fridge, darling."

They laughed and laughed and after a long dinner—a feast of samaki and rice, one of Ariella's mouth-wateringly tasty fish specialties from Tanzania—Casper pulled on his pajamas and went to close his bedroom curtains. He looked out over the grounds of Little Wallops. The moonlight had turned the playing fields silver, the sky was pinched with stars, and any windows Casper could see from where he stood had curtains drawn across them. Except for the one belonging to the turret next door where Mrs. Whereabouts lived. That was lit up and in its frame there was a silhouette. On first glance it looked to Casper like the silhouette of a cat. But then Casper pressed his face up to the glass and looked closer.

This wasn't a cat at all. And, in fact, when Casper really thought about it, he couldn't recall ever having seen one—only a glimpse of something black and furry behind Mrs. Whereabouts when he knocked on her door the day they moved to the school. Casper blinked in surprise. It was a monkey! And it was holding something long and thin with a rounded tip. Casper frowned. Was that *a golf club*? Then he remembered the golf balls he'd seen strewn through the woods earlier and the truth of things tiptoed closer.

Mrs. Whereabouts didn't own a cat at all. She owned a

monkey. And she didn't wear turtlenecks to hide the scar-like markings on her neck. She wore them to hide her *gills*. Because this strange old lady was from the Unmapped Kingdoms! Unbeknownst to Casper these past few years, he had been living next door to the only two people from Utterly's world who had found a way through to Everdark: Smudge and Bartholomew, the golf-loving monkey. Smudge would have been over two thousand years old had she stayed in the Unmapped Kingdoms, but she hadn't. She and Bartholomew must have found another door in Everdark that led to the Faraway, where time passed much more slowly.

"But that's the thing about locked doors," Casper whispered to himself as the monkey tugged open the window, steadied itself on the ledge, then drew back his golf club and thwacked a ball out over the grounds. "You never quite know what's on the other side. . . ."

Acknowledgments

One last to-do list from Casper Tock:

1. Thank the amazing team at Simon & Schuster for being so excited about my story from the very start (even though I was bricking it): Sarah McCabe, Mara Anastas, Eve Wersocki-Morris, Sarah Macmillan, Laura Hough, Sam Habib, Jenny Davies, Stephanie Purcell, and finally, Jane Griffiths—who knows me as well as Abi (without her my story would never have been told)
2. Thank Heather Palisi for making me look extremely brave and even a little bit dashing on the front cover
3. Thank literary agent Hannah Sheppard for her delightfully quick replies to Abi's emails during the writing of my story (Hannah's up there with Zip for efficiency) and her unfailing support of the whole Unmapped world
4. Thank all the brilliant teachers and librarians for placing my, Utterly, and Arlo's adventure into the hands of kids all over the globe

5. Thank Abi's family and friends (especially the wonder-woman that is Zofia Sagan) because, let's face it, family and friends are what keep you going when you're down on one knee in a forest full of Midnights
6. Thank Abi's husband, Edo, because without his love and support I reckon Abi would be a total lunatic
7. Thank Little Elph—he showed Abi how to wonder at the world all over again and that paved the way for my story
8. Keep eyes peeled for weather scrolls at sunrise on camping trip with Sophie
9. Restructure meals in light of Rumblestar adventure: eat dessert before main course
10. Look up at the sky at least once every day and remember that it's full to the brim with magic

Turn the page for a peek at an exciting new adventure in the Unmapped Kingdoms!

Fox Petty-Squabble flopped onto the sofa in the penthouse suite of the Neverwrinkle Hotel. It was the summer holidays—or at least it was supposed to be—but rather than heading to the seaside, or relaxing with a barbecue in their garden, the Petty-Squabble family had descended upon the sleepy village of Mizzlegurg in the Bavarian countryside for a business trip.

Although originally from England, Gertrude and Bernard Petty-Squabble had moved their family to Germany shortly after Fox and her twin brother, Fibber, had been born. Bernard had a very wealthy German ancestor, a duke called Great-Uncle Rudolph, and when he passed away, the Petty-Squabbles found themselves inheriting his enormous mansion in Munich because they were his only living relatives. Bickery Towers was one of the biggest and grandest houses in all of Europe, which was just as well because being bigger and grander than everyone else mattered enormously to Mr. and Mrs. Petty-Squabble. So much so that they filled every summer holiday (and indeed every Christmas and Easter holiday too) with business meetings, because making heaps of cash was, to them, the only way to ensure they remained more important than everybody else.

And so, as today marked the start of the twins' summer holiday, the Petty-Squabbles had all set off from Bickery Towers that morning, complete with matching luggage, matching business suits, and matching scowls, before bullying their way through the day—as was their custom. The family motto, etched in gold across the trunk of their car, was:

DO NOT BE AFRAID

Then, in smaller letters below this:

TO STAMP ALL OVER OTHER PEOPLE'S FEELINGS.

Gertrude Petty and Bernard Squabble had been living by this code for as long as they could remember, and it had made them very rich indeed. Even before the move to Bickery Towers eleven years ago, Gertrude was running one of the world's leading antiaging skincare lines, Petty Pampering, and Bernard was the founder of Squabble Sauces, a global corporation that claimed to make cooking sauces that did all sorts of improbable things like reduce tiredness and increase intelligence. In reality, neither the skincare products nor the sauces actually fulfilled any of their bold promises. The Petty-Squabble empire was built on lies. But bullies and liars often go from strength to strength until someone is brave enough to take them down.

Needless to say, no one was brave enough to take the Petty-Squabbles down the day they left for Mizzlegurg, for they were very much in a stamping sort of mood. The family's long-suffering driver, Hans Underboot, took the brunt of it first. Mrs. Petty took it upon herself to dock his pay every time he obeyed the speed limit or got stuck in traffic, because she had an appointment at the Neverwrinkle Hotel that she really didn't want to miss. Then, upon arrival at the hotel, Mr. Squabble clouted the porter round the head when he asked if the family had had an enjoyable journey because that was *clearly* none of his business. And Fox sneered at every single person who crossed her path—the receptionist who smiled too much, the waiter who asked too many questions at lunch, and the pool attendant whose mustache was "stupid"—purely because that was how she had been raised to behave. To be kind was to be weak and to be weak was to be stamped on by everyone, which, admittedly, did not sound ideal to Fox.

Only Fibber had held back on the stamping. In fact, Fox had noticed that her brother had been unusually quiet since the end of term a few weeks ago. Suspiciously quiet, she thought.

Fox and Fibber were twins, not that you would have known it to look at them. Fibber was tall with sleek dark hair, like their mother, while Fox was short with a tumble of red hair, which had come from their father. But, though they might not have looked alike, they had one thing in common: a sharp tongue. And the only thing the twins liked more than insulting strangers was being horrid to one another, especially if it meant that they could show their sibling up in front of their mother and father.

This interfamily competitiveness had been handed down to the twins from their parents. For, while Gertrude and Bernard ultimately wanted to amass one giant Petty-Squabble fortune, they valued rivalry over romance. Working *against* family members, rather than *with* them, added a competitive edge to moneymaking schemes and got you richer quicker, as far as Gerturde and Bernard were concerned. And so they were constantly seeking sly ways to get one up on each other, and this rivalry overshadowed every aspect of Fox and Fibber's relationship too.

Moments after the twins' birth, Fox had given Fibber a black eye for being born three minutes sooner than her, and that was to set the tone for the rivalry to come. When they were barely a year old, Fibber knocked over Fox's crib back in Bickery Towers when his parents weren't looking. Fox then retaliated by biting the head off Fibber's favorite teddy, and Fibber had fought back by flicking the brake off Fox's baby carriage the next day, which very nearly sent his sister hurtling under a truck racing down their street.

The Petty-Squabble parents delighted in these feuds and even named their children in such a way as to heighten the sense of conflict: Fibber because they hoped he'd turn out to be a brilliant liar (which he did), and Fox because they hoped she'd turn out to be as sly as the animal itself (which she didn't, because being impulsive makes it near impossible to be sly). Even outside their home—in the local neighborhood and at school—Fox and Fibber's arguments had earned them the title "the Bickery Twins." So this sibling rivalry, fueled by their parents and widely accepted by everyone else, went on—through early childhood, preschool, and school—reaching a peak a few months ago when Fibber tricked Fox into flushing her homework down the toilet, causing Fox to dangle her brother by his ankles from a fifth-floor window in Bickery Towers (to the cheers of their parents down below).

But Fox was uneasy. Since the dangling incident, Fibber hadn't tricked or cheated or—his favorite—lied to his parents to get his sister into trouble. For months, she had waited for her brother to fight back, but instead Fibber had remained uncharacteristically quiet and thoughtful. So now, as they sat together in the hotel suite booked by their parents, Fox watched him with narrowed eyes. He was sitting in an armchair opposite her, his briefcase parked by his feet and a pad of paper open on his lap. Fox craned her neck to see what he was up to, but he inched his pad higher to shield the page from her.

Fox plucked at her braid. "What are you scribbling about?"

Fibber didn't look up. He didn't stop writing either. Fox was used to her brother's calm, collected manner when he was stamping all over other people's feelings, but she had always found it easy to bait Fibber into bickering with her when it was just the two of them alone together. These newfound silences were starting to unnerve her, because Petty-Squabbles who were silent were usually plotting something.

Like the aforementioned Great-Uncle Rudolph, who apparently hadn't said a word for forty-three years, then announced he was digging a tunnel from Munich to London so that he could kidnap the queen and hold her hostage for an unreasonable sum of money. Great-Uncle Rudolph had gotten as far as Poland before realizing he had been digging in the wrong direction; he was then silent for another forty-three years, for different reasons.

Fox tried to conjure up some mutinous moneymaking thoughts of her own, but she couldn't help feeling that kidnappings, robberies, and large-scale revolutions might be more effective when performed with other people. And Fox was very much a solo act, both at school (where avoiding being stamped on meant insulting classmates and teachers on a daily basis) and at home (where conversations were limited to business, smiling was frowned upon, and hugging was completely out of the question).

Fox pulled off her tie, wedged it down the side of the sofa, then looked across at her brother again. "You're working on the Petty Pampering business plan, aren't you?"

There was an edge to her voice now because she knew that if Fibber was putting in the hours attempting to rebrand the

Petty Pampering products, it meant she should be doing the same for Squabble Sauces. The twins knew that both companies were based on lies, but there was too much at stake to start messing around with the truth. Customers had slowly but surely been starting to realize they'd been duped, and now profits were falling and contracts were being dropped, which was why the twins spent every holiday traipsing round luxury hotels while their parents tried to persuade the spas and restaurants to stock their products.

But Fox and Fibber weren't brought along on these trips because Gertrude and Bernard couldn't bear to be parted from their children. Oh no. They were here to work. Their parents had cornered them at the end of first grade and informed the twins that only one of them would inherit the Petty-Squabble empire; if Fox came up with a way to save Squabble Sauces, it would be her, but if Fibber swept in and rescued Petty Pampering first, it would be him. So, just like that, the rivalry between the siblings deepened.

And Gertrude and Bernard didn't stop there. To spur Fox on to recover the family fortune as quickly as possible, her parents frequently told her that Fibber's cunning lies would, eventually, be the key to his success. While at the same time (unbeknownst to Fox) her parents goaded Fibber into believing that Fox really was sly enough to rebuild the Petty-Squabble empire without him even noticing and would push him out in the process. This meant that the twins were always jealous of each other and constantly convinced that their parents loved one more than the other. So they had grown up in the firm and somewhat terrifying knowledge that they were rivals, not siblings.

In truth, Gertrude and Bernard didn't care which child saved the family fortune. The only reason they had had children in the first place was in the hope that one of them might eventually make them lots of cash. Indeed, when Fox had asked her father what would happen to the child who didn't inherit the Petty-Squabble empire, his response—"They will be packaged up, mailed somewhere very far away, like Antarctica, and politely wished all the very best"—had not been altogether reassuring.

Fox reached inside her blazer pocket for her phone and began tapping away in the notes section.

"Just opening my list of secret, and utterly brilliant, ways to save Squabble Sauces," she muttered, loudly enough for her brother to hear.

Fibber looked up briefly, then carried on writing.

Fox tapped away with a smirk. "Just adding in a few more winning thoughts to clinch the deal."

Which was entirely untrue. There was no list of breathtaking ideas that would save the dwindling Petty-Squabble empire. Fox knew all the right words to bluff her way through the weekly family business meetings—"expenditure," "capital," "profit margin," "asset"—but she had no idea what any of these terms actually meant. And she was absolutely hopeless at strategic thinking.

For a moment, Fox felt the weight of something dark and unlovely shifting inside her. Fibber was a businessman-in-the-making. He was clever and smooth-talking—he could fool even the most intelligent grown-ups with his silky lies—and although at school he was far too arrogant to feel the need to make friends, he had, this term, endeared himself to a teacher, Mrs. Scribble, with whom he now took extra lessons during lunch break because she sensed in him some "*hidden potential.*"

The darkness inside Fox flinched. No one had ever thought that she was special. That she had "potential." What was she good at? Too much of a solo act to be picked for the sports teams, not bright enough to achieve top grades, and not nearly popular enough to be picked for Head of School in sixth grade next term. Everyone in her class seemed to be good at *something*, even the really quiet ones who (much to Fox's annoyance) looked perfectly ordinary, but ended up being fabulous at spelling, feverishly fast on ice skates, or shockingly good at the clarinet.

Fox had concluded some years ago that her obvious lack of talent was what made her unlovable to her parents. Stamping on other people's feelings every day was all very well—after all, Fox didn't fancy being kind, because being weak, as well as talentless, would only add to her misery—but the heart is a fragile thing, and sometimes people assume that the best way to keep theirs safe is to build a wall round it. And that was just what Fox had done. Hers was a very high wall that had grown up over the years without her truly realizing because it made dealing with being unlovable ever so slightly easier.

She stole a look at Fibber. Was he quieter than usual because he had, finally—and perhaps predictably—come up with a way to save the family fortune? Maybe he was just moments away from announcing his triumph. Fox contemplated her options. She could pin Fibber down, snatch his business plan, then—she thought fast—*eat it*? Or was it time to do a Great-Uncle Rudolph (without the tunnel drama): grab the plan and hold it hostage until Fibber agreed to say that he and Fox had come up with all the ideas together?

Before Fox could do either, the door to the penthouse suite opened. In stormed Gertrude Petty, wearing a white bathrobe, white slippers, and a white towel twisted up over her hair. She was wearing so much white she looked uncannily like a meringue, while behind her, red-haired and red-faced, was Bernard Petty resembling a volcano rammed into a business suit.

Bernard flung the door shut. Then he and his wife eyed their children with the kind of look that is usually only reserved for traffic wardens and large spiders. Fox gulped. She knew all too well that when her parents barged into a room like this, it was never good news. . . .

About the Author

ABI ELPHINSTONE grew up in Scotland, where she spent most of her childhood running wild across the moors, hiding in tree houses, and building dens in the woods. After being coaxed out of her tree houses, she studied English at Bristol University and then worked as an English teacher in Tanzania before returning to the United Kingdom to teach there. When she's not writing, Abi volunteers for the Coram Beanstalk charity, speaks in schools, and travels the world looking for her next story. Her latest adventures include living with the Kazakh eagle hunters in Mongolia and dogsledding across the Arctic.

EXPLORE NEW WORLDS.
EXPERIENCE NEW ADVENTURES.
New York Times and USA Today Bestselling Series
KEEPER OF THE LOST CITIES
SHANNON MESSENGER
New York Times Bestseller
STORY THIEVES
JAMES RILEY
FABLEHAVEN
Brandon Mull
"THE HUNGER GAMES MEETS HARRY POTTER."
THE UNWANTEDS
LISA McMANN
NEW YORK TIMES BESTSELLING SERIES
Pegasus
THE FLAME OF OLYMPUS
KATE O'HEARN
ALADDIN
SIMONANDSCHUSTER.COM/KIDS